The Miracle Maker and the Misfits by Dixie Koch is at once powerful and frightening, engaging, as it offers safety and salvation. Miracles and misfits will linger in your heart and mind long after the final page. It is a book of opposites that lead you in one direction: Damnation vs. salvation, fear vs. safety, terror vs hope, abandonment vs. rescue, surrender vs. despair, with the real message being to rejoice in love, faith and hope. A recommended read that is sure to become a favorite and a best seller.

Billie A Williams
Award-Winning Mystery Author

The Miracle Maker and the Misfits is a very engaging book about new beginnings and God's healing love. Dixie has an incredible gift of using descriptive language that easily paints the picture in your mind.

Karen Wolner,
Educator

Dixie Koch's *The Miracle Maker and the Misfits* is a work of art that will grab you from the very first word and won't let you go until the very last. Her descriptive writing method paints a picture for you that will draw you in and make you ache for more. It is a novel of apocalyptic proportions which will leave you with the lingering feeling that you may not know everything there is to know. Sure to be a best seller and...my prediction is...it will definitely become a motion picture.

Gwen Lewis RN/PHN,
Public Health Supervisor

D1067160

The Miracle Maker and the Misfits is a tale of murder, intrigue, and the supernatural, all tied into one thought provoking novel. This must-read mystery comes with a kingdom message to boot.

Rozanne Rector,
Vice President, PHRI

The Miracle Maker and the Misfits is a very timely message about hope for the hopeless and healing for the brokenhearted.

Deb Samuelson,
Crime victim advocate

The Miracle Maker

and The Misfits

DIXIE KOCH

The Mark *of*
God Series

The Miracle Maker
and The misfits

TATE PUBLISHING
AND ENTERPRISES, LLC

Published by Tate Publishing & Enterprises, LLC
127 E. Trade Center Terrace | Mustang, Oklahoma 73064 USA
1.888.361.9473 | www.tatepublishing.com

Tate Publishing is committed to excellence in the publishing industry. The company reflects the philosophy established by the founders, based on Psalm 68:11,
"The Lord gave the word and great was the company of those who published it."

Book design copyright © 2012 by Tate Publishing, LLC. All rights reserved.
Cover and Interior design by Jomel Pepito
Artwork by Andrea Anderson

Published in the United States of America

ISBN: 978-1-62147-793-8
1. Fiction / Christian / Suspense
2. Fiction / Suspense
12.11.13

Dedication

I dedicate these pages to my grandchildren: Zach, Andrea, Levi, Josiah, Lydia, Hannah, Moriah, and Asa.

Each of you are a precious, loved, and cherished gift from God. Thereby, I have been promoted to praying from a gramma's heart. Daily I see your faces as I whisper your names in prayer. I pray that you will be a part of a new generation of young people who will believe in the Miracle Maker, a group of kids who will defy a lukewarm Christianity and rise like a firestorm to redefine what it means to walk and to love with the heart of Jesus.

In memory of my sister, Mary Lou, and my brother, Bud. I miss you both so much!

Your lives were marked by the love of God! You were truly carriers of His love everywhere you went. I look forward to spending eternity with you, where forever we will celebrate His love.

And to my sister, Janet, and my sister-in-law, Arlene. I cherish every moment we share together down here.

Acknowledgments

How grateful I am for family! Thanks to each of you, my stories will always be richer because I have been blessed to be a daughter, a sister, a wife, a mother, and a grandmother! Thanks for the selfless understanding that the writing of this book would involve lots of time. Losing Mary Lou and Bud during these months have been especially difficult, and you all were there for me. It is with love and appreciation that I say thanks to my husband, Jim; my children Barry (April), Angie (Larry), and Sandie; my grandchildren; my sister, Janet; my sister-in-law, Arlene; and my extended family members.

A special thanks to my very talented granddaughter, Andrea, for the beautiful cover artwork! And, to my son, Barry, I can't thank you enough for all your patience and computer expertise. I couldn't have managed without you.

Thanks to my supervisor, Gwen Lewis (Public Health), for reading my manuscript, endorsing it, and for cheering me on to get it published. Thanks to my daughter, Sandie, and to my friends Rosie, Karen, Bev, and Deb, for reading, editing, and endorsing this book.

A special thanks to award-winning author, Billie Williams, for all your help, advice, and for endorsing this book.

Thanks to all my friends (too numerous to mention) for all their support and prayers.

Pastor Cory, thank you. I am so grateful God brought me to your ministry. I came hungry, and you fed me some powerful truth. I came in an emotional prison and experienced His healing and deliverance to be real and for today. I felt like a misfit. You taught that God qualifies me. You just wouldn't let me forget who I am in Christ! Many of the treasures I have coined while under your ministry are woven in this novel. Thank you, Pastor, for all your encouragement and wise counsel.

Thanks to the staff at Tate Publishing for providing me with this awesome opportunity to become published. Each person I have spoken with has been professional, kind, and helpful.

Above all, I want to thank Jesus Christ. He gave me this story to write, and He has been my source of inspiration. I write knowing there is not a heart too broken, but He would heal it, and there isn't a sinner too messed up, but He waits and longs to forgive.

Introduction

There is none so deaf as he who listens to the wrong voices.

There is none so bound as he who is chained to lies.

His home was a graveyard. No person could tame or restrain him, for he was very strong. He could pull the outward shackles in pieces with his own bare hands. But the chains that held him to his thoughts, he could not bend.

His is a true story (from Mark 5). He lived where dead people were buried. Day and night he was tormented and cried out in anguish. He bruised and cut himself with stones.

Then a great miracle happened. Someone bigger than the voices of lies stepped into his life. Those chaining him to such emotional misery and shame were commanded to leave by the greatest voice of authority, truth, and power. The demons behind the lying voices were rushed into a herd of swine, causing the pigs to run violently into the sea and drown.

He wasn't the same after that. His mind was healed, and he was free. His address changed. He walked out of that graveyard of darkness and death and into the kingdom of truth and light.

And I wondered why the people asked Jesus to leave the region. Why weren't they happy that this man could now be in the land of the living, healed and free? What would be the reaction if such a miracle happened today? And I heard these words, "Write about it."

So I write because today there are so many hurting people. Haunting voices from abuse, abandonment, and rejections have chased many to a graveyard of despair. Deep inside, where eyes cannot see, people are chained by invisible hands to emotional wounds and to their pasts. I write because it is my prayer that these people would direct their cry for help to the Miracle Maker.

In such brokenness, people are ripe for a miracle. But they must turn to the powerful voice of truth. "And you shall know the truth, and the truth shall make you free" (John 8:32).

Chapter One

*P*ut me in that casket too! Put me in there with my sister! Let me die there.

The wind howled and slapped a cold hand at Abby's face, chilling her tears to sleet. She felt numb on the outside and raw on the inside.

"We now commit Julie's body back to the dust," the reverend droned on.

His words ignited a mental bomb, which exploded in Abby's mind. *Like everyone else, you thought Julie was a misfit, a hopeless kid. All she needed was a place to fit. Now she fits in a pine box!*

A handful of people from the church, like a football team in a huddle, stood braving the weather. But Abby stood alone like a young sapling unbending in the wind.

"Amen."

She hadn't heard the prayer.

Church was just a place Abby occasionally attended. As tiny children, she and Julie had been happy to be a part of Sunday school here at the God's Love Fellowship Church. An elderly neighbor couple had faithfully picked them up and brought them Sunday after Sunday.

They had been little girls looking for love. They had hoped God might be in the church somewhere. Maybe there He could give someone special eyes to see, special ears to hear, or special arms to hold them. So they came, listened, and watched, and waited. They looked into so many eyes, like the store windows in a busy plaza, but the eyes did not seem to see them back.

Abby pulled her hood's drawstring snugger to her face. Her steps were quick in the cold. As she opened the church door, childhood pain, like dirty bug smears on a windshield, still stained her soul. She no longer had a listening ear. Abby didn't want to hear cotton-candy words inflated with air, such as, "I'm so sorry for your loss. Such a tragedy." Nor did she care to hear something dreadful like, "It must be God's will." Was it God's will that she and Julie were physically and sexually abused as little girls? Why didn't God cause them to be born into a home where there was love instead of violence? Why did He let Julie tragically die now? *Of all times, why now? We could have had a chance together now. We could have had the chance life never gave us as children.*

Abby yanked off her wet cap and slipped out of her jacket. She wasn't hungry and walked past the sandwiches and chips. All she wanted was something hot to touch and to drink. Her fingers laced around a warm Styrofoam cup like a child latching onto candy. Abby didn't look around her. She didn't care to be acknowledged or to acknowledge anyone. She moved to the way back table and sunk into the chair still holding tight to the coffee cup.

Tears were waiting. Until today, tears had been a stranger to Abby. She had built a cement wall somewhere inside of herself. She had become tougher than tears. Still, at this very moment, she realized that Julie was all the love she had known. Julie had been her sister-parent. Julie was finally coming home. This was to be a birth of love and hope. Instead it was stillborn.

Abby sat up straighter and took a sip of her coffee. More tears were not welcome.

"Abby?" a warm voice asked.

"Yes?" Abby looked up into the large and moist eyes of a familiar face.

"Maybe you don't remember me, honey. I'm Mable. I was your foster mom a long time ago." The rounded, cheeky-faced lady relaxed as an understanding smile pushed wrinkles to each side. "Oh, it was when you were just eight years old."

"I do remember now." Abby's heavy eye lids raised slowly. "Yes. You were very kind to me, and I didn't want to leave you."

Mable pulled a Kleenex from her handbag and dabbed her eyes with it. "It broke my heart when they put you and Julie back with your folks." She took a sip of coffee, and her eyes searched into Abby's.

"Yes, and just several months after that, we were removed permanently from our home. I was nine. Julie was fifteen."

"I was in the process of moving to Chicago at that time, or I would have begged to have you girls again.

My mom was very ill, and I thought I needed to be there for her. I had asked if I could adopt both of you, but I didn't hear back from the county."

"It was our loss, Mable." Abby's hands clasped more tightly around the cup.

"Were the new foster parents good to you?" Mable whispered.

"Julie was eight months pregnant when we arrived in the next home. She was very angry and hurt."

"I see." Mable reached across the table to squeeze Abby's fingers. "I can understand. It's hard to trust strangers when those you should be able to trust hurt you."

"You're right, Mable. I think my truster is broken." Abby's words were fading.

"Anyway, Abby, I have just moved back to this area. My mom passed on, and it was getting lonely in Chicago. I have family here. So it seemed right to come back. And then I picked up the paper and read about your sister's tragic accident. I'm so sorry." Mable's voice was genuine.

"She was on her way back. I hadn't seen her for so long. Julie had begun to call me more. She sounded changed." Abby looked up into Mable's eyes for courage to say more. "She said she had found joy and peace. She said she had found a reason to live. She was on her way home to me. We were going to be a family again and this time find happiness." Abby choked on her words. "She had not planned to come home for her funeral. It is like a bad dream, a cruel joke."

"What about you, Abby?" Mable asked. "Is there something I can do to help?"

"I don't think so. I need to be by myself. I've just got so much to think through."

Mable dug into her purse and pulled out a pen and paper. "Let me write down my number. Know you are welcome to call anytime. If you need a place to get away, my door will always be open to you."

Mable's hands were a little shaky. Abby guessed Mable to be in her early eighties.

"What happened to Julie's baby?" Mable asked as she handed the paper to Abby.

"That's a story in itself. Charley was taken away from Julie when he was born." Abby smashed the Styrofoam cup between her hands. "He lived in three different foster homes until he was placed in a juvenile boy's home. From there he was sent to various group homes that housed emotionally disturbed and mentally ill youth."

Mable shifted uncomfortably in her chair.

"Finally"—Abby winced—"about three years ago, he was placed at the Wilderness Group Home out in Perjure County. Charley is there because he rips off his clothes and runs wild. He doesn't talk. Still, no amount of therapy has been able to tame him."

Mable's eyes widened in unbelief. "Oh, my dear." The silver-haired woman stood. Before she left, she placed a kiss on Abby's cheek. "I care, Abby. Please do me a favor and come visit me soon. Would you do that for me, honey?"

Abby stared back, her eyes wide. *Warm. You make me feel warm. I've been so cold and scared.*

"Abby?" Mable's hand cupped Abby's chin. "Please come and see me."

"I will, Mable."

"Good." Mable's sweet, droopy cheeks entertained ripples of wrinkles with one tender smile.

Abby watched Mable walk slowly out the door. Then her eyes scanned the room. Several folk were collecting their plates and napkins and returning them to the kitchen. Some turned to nod or smile at Abby as she stood to leave. Before she made it to the exit, Reverend Staunch moved his lanky, tall form forward to shake her hand and bid her well.

"It is a pity about your sister, Abby. Please accept my sympathy."

"Yes, thank you, Reverend."

"I don't suppose Charley would understand. Well," Reverend Staunch stammered, "Julie never kept in contact with him anyway, so it probably doesn't change anything. I guess I was wondering if you would be telling him about his mother's passing."

"First of all, Reverend, Julie didn't give Charley up." Abby's eyes flashed with fury. "He was taken from her. I know she cared for him. She would have been a good mother. And don't you worry. I will go and tell him. I'll tell him that his mom was coming home to be with him again. I'll tell him that Julie loved him and never wanted to give him up."

Abby didn't mind that the reverend's eyes were flinging burning darts back to her. She turned and with a click of her heels left the church.

————

In the corner of her small apartment sat the pile of whatever had been valuable enough for Julie to want to bring home. Just three nights ago the police brought it to her doorstep along with the unwanted news. She would never forget the two officers standing there that night. The younger one handed her the luggage. The older one had said, "I'm sorry, Abby, but there has been a terrible accident. Your sister, Julie Frank, was killed." All Abby had learned was that the roads were very slippery. It had appeared as though Julie had dodged another vehicle and had crashed into a tree, dying instantly. Someone, possibly the driver of the other car, had called 911.

Abby had not been able to open the bags and suitcases containing Julie's belongings. Now with the funeral over and the need for some kind of closure, she needed at least to look. *I am unbelievably lonely for you, Julie. Our recent phone calls brought you back. It has made you alive in my heart. I can't believe that hope has ended. I had begun to hope again.*

The large suitcase was too heavy for clothes. When she opened it, Abby was surprised to find dozens of notebooks. As she paged through them, she was not surprised any longer. *You and I were always alike this way, Julie. Our lives have been a story that we could not tell others. We had only hoped people would read us kindly.* Abby pulled a notebook close to her heart. *I am so thankful for these. You have left me all that you felt and all that you hoped for. I will read them, and I will cherish them. I will keep them for you. I can't let you not live on in my heart. These notes will help. I love you, Julie!*

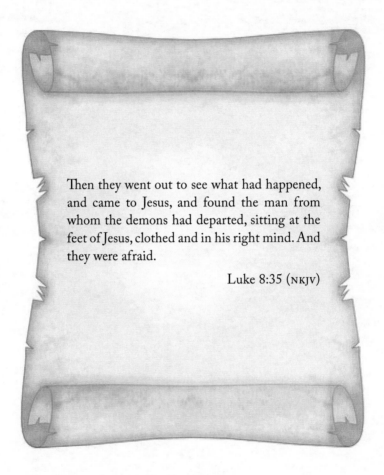

Then they went out to see what had happened, and came to Jesus, and found the man from whom the demons had departed, sitting at the feet of Jesus, clothed and in his right mind. And they were afraid.

Luke 8:35 (NKJV)

Chapter Two

Abby tucked the comforter around her body, sinking into it as though it were someone with tender arms coming to rescue her at last.

The lonely quiet was like a heavy fog settling in over her. The stillness was as black as it was thick. She gagged on it. Then there were movements, like dark fish below the water surface, happening in the midnight of her room. Her heart began thundering beats of fear. The bolts shot through her, stinging into every extremity. Each ripple caused her toes and fingers to prickle.

They're back. The unwanted visitors, familiar entities were back. Like corrupt landlords greedy to collect, they stalked where there was no light of escape. They cried out, "We own you." Since childhood, they had threatened and harassed. Abby's body trembled remembering how she had clung to Julie, so terrified by the invaders. These mysterious forms…these voices… had brought fear of every imaginable kind. Abby would bury her face in Julie's chest. She would listen to her sister's heart thrashing inside of a body stiffened by fear.

Abby had never dared to tell anyone. Now they came again. Abby felt them. Sinister fingers were tightening around her throat and constricting until she fell into a lifeless trance. Her thoughts once again began to reel. She was spinning out of control on black ice.

So where is this God Julie sought? He isn't here, is He? His games are cruel. He leaves you alone and hopeless. There is no hope, Abby. Why do you struggle to find hope? He has taken everything away from you. He took your sister. He took your hope. The only family you have now, Abby, is a crazy nephew. You are crazy, too. How long can you pretend you are normal? You are a fool, pretending to belong somewhere. You should join Julie. You have nothing to live for.

―――――――――

Abby was exhausted when her eyes opened again. She sprung from her bed and shivered as her feet hit the cold floor. Abby glanced out the window as she grabbed for a sweater and slipped her feet into the slippers by her bed. "Blasted winter again! Flying snow! It's supposed to be April first today. Well, happy April Fool's Day."

Once downstairs Abby flicked the "on" switch of her coffee maker and waited to hear the first sound of percolating. *Julie will never come home.* Coffee was spitting into the pot. Abby's hand reached for a cup.

A shrill ring from her cell phone, and the cup twirled toward the floor, where it shattered in several sharp, plastic pieces.

"Who could be calling this early in the morning?" She found her phone under yesterday's newspaper.

"Hi, Ab."

"Phillip, what's going on? It's Saturday. I don't work today."

"You're going to want to work today, Ab. I've got an urgent front-page story for you. There's no time for dilly-dallying around. You better bust your butt getting over to Mr. Shafers's farm now!"

"This better be good, Phillip. It's snowing and blowing and cold out there. And"—grief, like a festering sore, found its way to her tongue—"they just buried my sister."

"I'm sorry about that, Ab. I really am. But this is the chance of your lifetime. Get this story and your career as a journalist is set!"

Abby shivered as she tracked through the new spread of snow. The crust under it grated and snapped with each plunk of her boots. Under it all was still the cold brown earth not yet brave enough to think of sending out shoots of green. March had gone out like a lion, and April was still her frozen cub.

Abby could picture Phillip's jaw jutting out and his gray eyes growing into steel. He had been fired from the police force a couple years ago. She believed his story. The drunken attorney was guilty of manslaughter. Phillip had been honest and bold enough to say so. But it had cost him his job.

In Abby's opinion, Phillip was a good and decent man. She liked that about him. After he bought out the *Edge Water Times*, he had hired her to write for the paper. All she had to show him were a few pieces of prose she had written in her journal. He had said, "These are incredible. Yes, you have a job with me for as long as you desire." That day the sun muscled its way into Abby's dismal and none-too-promising world. She was very grateful to Phillip and had worked hard ever since not to disappoint her boss. Today would not be an exception.

———⁓᷾᷾᷾᷾᷾———

Abby dreaded the drive to Jasper Schafer's place. Guilt clawed at her soul. It was the road to the Wilderness Group Home, where Charley lived, which bordered Jasper's farm.

Abby hadn't been out to see Charley for months. She had been too busy trying to pursue a career in writing. Phillip believed in her, thought she could write, and that provided a sliver of self-esteem, a prayer that someday she could make it as an accomplished journalist. Now Phillip sounded very excited. Was her career as a journalist about to become big? She could make it a point to stop and see Charley later. He didn't seem to know her anyway. But was she letting Julie down? Julie had loved Charley and had asked Abby to take care of him. Could Charley possibly understand love or the lack of it? Was he as miserable as she was? Could one so mentally handicapped as Charley even understand that Julie loved him or that Julie was tragically killed? Was Charley able to be offended that for these past many months his aunt Abby had abandoned him in chase of something to live for?

Young, willowy poplar trees bent spitefully toward the glare of headlights reflecting off the snow as Abby drove down the long stretch of back roads. No thanks to the nasty weather and messy driving conditions, the drive was more distressing.

She wasn't relieved to see the jagged etches of light from the group home shooting across the depressed-looking, snow-covered grounds. In the early fog of dawn, they looked like eerie fingers pointing into her soul.

"What the—?" Abby blurted out. In the short distance away, flashing lights from everywhere fractured the craggy attempts of daybreak. Fire trucks, an ambulance or two, and it looked like the whole highway department surrounded and filled the Schafer residence. Large equipment made it nearly impossible for her to squeeze her car close to the troubled farm site. "Maybe Phillip is right. Maybe this will be the cover story I need. This looks big. Really big."

Bodies were rushing everywhere, skirting through the lifting darkness. Abby grabbed her camera and hurried to join the interested parties. Heavy gray clouds were spewing out a fine icy mist, and people, dismal under the cloudy curse, were yelling, shouting orders, scurrying so. The whole place was in a state of panic.

Abby blew out a confused and frosty breath of her own, pulled her parka tight, and with a curl of her lip moved toward the mess. She guessed most of the action was headed toward the river.

Ropes were attached to heavy equipment. Cranes stretched their strong iron necks over and down to the problem area, and from her view, it appeared as though they were removing large-bodied things. "Did a whole part of the country fall in the river, or what?" Abby tried to ignore the intense spasm threatening to shut off her airway.

"Those are cows!" Phillip's answer was like a paddle filled with electric shock attempting to jolt her senses to some form of normal.

"Cows?" She turned to him, her eyes wide with confusion and fright.

"Yes, cows," he said, a half smile cocked victoriously on his face. He reached for her hand and dragged her through the mob of people to a place where she could get a better view.

"Cows?" Abby's tongue felt thick. "They are all bloated and so still. Are they dead?"

"Yep, drowned pregnant cows," Phillip said, shifting his weight to the opposite leg. "And lots of them."

"They are pregnant?" Abby's legs suddenly felt rubbery. "But why? What could possibly possess a herd of heavy, pregnant cows to rush to their deaths in a river covered with thin ice?"

"I am not sure at this moment, but be very sure, I will find out."

"Oh, I know, Phillip. You will figure it out. I know you will."

"Hey, girl. You are going to get the story before the big papers pick up on it." He smiled back at her. "I'm sure that stack of bloated heifers would be a perfect snapshot to validate the facts. It's bound to hit the front page for you."

Abby's eyes were like bulbs pushing from their orbits. She walked through the piles of bovine devastation. "Unbelievable!" She began snapping pictures and trying to control the retching feeling that was pulling at her gut.

Equipment operators were pulling out fewer beef now, and many of the waders were stepping out of the river straddled with ice chunks. Abby snapped a picture of a rescuer stepping out of his wet suit as someone wrapped a warm blanket around the man.

Abby recognized Jasper Schafer waving his arms and shouting to a group of uniformed officers. She moved in for a scoop on the event.

"I'm telling you," the distraught Jasper bawled out, "I saw him out in the fields just the other day, naked and streaking as usual. Then about two this morning the dogs were barking, and I got up. That's when I saw it with my own eyes. There was nothing I could do to stop the cattle. They were mad, crazy, running and plunging through the ice. That's when I called for help. I drove down my driveway to see what might have caused such a ruckus, and then I saw him again. There he was lifting up his hands and dancing. There was some older man standing next to him. I couldn't tell in the dark who it was. But the kid was definitely Charley. It was him all right."

"Charley!" Abby gasped. "He wouldn't have any reason to harm your cows. He's just simple."

All heads turned toward her.

"You sticking up for him?" Jasper's voice threatened. "Hey," he continued, taking a step toward her and pointing an accusing finger into her chest, "aren't you related to that kid?"

"Look," she answered, her heart pounding against her chest, "I'm sure there is a logical explanation to all of this."

Phillip stepped up, hulking over the angry, red-faced Jasper and asked, "You said the kid was dancing in the middle of the night, not streaking?"

"That's correct," Jasper snarled back. "No doubt he was celebrating his evil accomplishment."

"Doesn't this kid ever sleep? Have you ever seen him dance in the night before?" Phillip questioned.

"I'm not his babysitter! I don't stay up all hours of the night watching his crazy stunts. But I see him streaking about in the daylight hours. Don't matter if it's cold or hot, he runs naked in all kinds of weather."

"Was he naked and streaking last night when you saw him?"

"No! I told you, Charley was dancing. He was lifting his arms in the air and waving them about wildly."

"And was he naked?" Phillip repeated the question.

Jasper scratched through a growth of red whiskers. "No, come to think of it. He was dressed. Even had a coat on. But what's that got to do with anything?"

"Has Charley ever been a threat to your herd of beef in the past?" Phillip squared his shoulders and continued to drill for answers.

"He's probably been planning this for years," the older man shot back, pressing his lips thin.

Abby caught the menacing squint of Jasper's weaseled eyes.

"You saying he has the capability to plan something this sophisticated?" Phillip's back stiffened. "It seems hard to believe that one person, especially someone like Charley, could be such a strategist. It would be quite a remarkable accomplishment for a posse of rustlers to get a herd of pregnant beef to leave their hay and shelter in the sort of weather we had last night. This was something big, Jasper."

"You calling me a liar? That kid is behind it. I don't know how, but mark my words, he had something to do with it. And," Jasper rasped, "you better find out the how and why of it all. Because of Charley, I've lost everything. Those cattle were my livelihood."

"I'm sorry for your loss, Jasper. I will find out all the details. You can count on that. But for now, I'm just doing my job, asking questions."

Abby was amazed at the investigative abilities Phillip possessed. He was the owner and editor of a newspaper. That was his job. But he would take this a few steps further. He would present facts and evidence, no matter how long it took to get the job done.

"I'll keep you to your word," Jasper exclaimed with a harrumph.

"For now I'm going to have a look around the barn. I'll need a sample of the hay. We can't rule out toxins of some kind."

Bizarre, crazy old man! Abby watched as Jasper stomped off in a huff of energy. She walked off to snap a few more pictures. *Charley! I've got to get there first!*

Guilt snapped her like a green bean between its fingers. She should have been there for Charley all along. He didn't even know his mother was dead. How would she handle all of this at one time?

Dazed, Abby tried to shake off the hounding guilt and regain some composure. The situation was grave, and she needed to be in charge for now.

"Okay, you can do this," she breathed out a promise to herself. "This is going to be hard." Abby groaned as she stopped to knead the back of her neck. "He can't process anything. He doesn't talk. He isn't going to have a clue of what is going on, much less care about a herd of bloated, drowned cattle. All I know is I need to get the missing puzzle piece first and get it in black and white before someone else makes a real mess out of things." She blew out a determined breath as her eyes focused on Phillip, who was poking around in a hay pile. Abby knew he was good at what he did. He could find a needle in a haystack. This gave her some comfort for now.

A few threads of sun were pushing through the gray and announcing that it was indeed morning now. Jasper's rooster was crowing as though it was just another day. But a lot of people, including herself, knew there was nothing usual about today. It was like a bad dream. Her car tires spun in the slush beneath them as Abby backed her car and then attempted to drive out of Jasper's long driveway. She was both tired and hungry, but all of that would wait. Abby was on a mission. She needed to protect Charley from all this unwanted publicity.

The group home was busy with morning activity. A kitchen worker was pushing a cart loaded with breakfast trays. At first the food smelled heavenly to Abby; then she eyed it as it rolled by. *What is that? What kind of slop do they feed these people?*

People sat humped over in their chairs with blank stares on their faces; others were talking to themselves. She watched as one unshaven man spooned his runny eggs and directed them toward his mouth. More of the yellow contents slimed down his bushy face than what was swallowed. Abby made her way to the information desk. A gray-haired woman with rim glasses hanging loosely on her nose looked above them at Abby.

"Could you direct me to where Charley Frank might be?"

The woman raised her eyebrows as an amused expression tightened the wrinkles under her eyes. "Have you checked his room? He's probably in there praying."

"Praying? Charley doesn't pray. I said Charley Frank. Where would he be?" Abby's voice shot back at the woman still wearing a mask of surprise.

"Oh, I see. You haven't heard the news yet."

"Haven't heard what?" Abby squeaked in exasperation.

"Go see for yourself. He's not the same person he used to be. It's a miracle straight from God because there's no other explanation." The woman narrowed her eyes and zeroed in for a closer look at Abby. "You a relative? I've seen you around here before."

"Yes, and thank you," Abby sheared any explanation and turned to go.

Even the help here is crazy. Go figure.

Charley's room would have to be on the third floor, Abby thought as she inched her weary body up another flight of stairs. Her camera dangled about her neck, but would she dare snap a picture of him? At this point, anything could be used as evidence against Charley. *Or against me.* She had to be careful. Really careful.

Charley's door was open. Abby stepped in unprepared for what she saw. A young man, who somewhat resembled the Charley she knew, stepped toward her. His face was radiant, and his smile big. He stood before her now, normal. "Charley?"

"Good to see you, Aunt Abby!" he answered articulately.

"Charley! You're talking?" Abby's heart was drumming.

"Yes, I am." He reached for Abby and pulled her into his arms. "Yes, I am," he repeated.

Charley wasn't the young kid any longer who had been torn from his mom as a babe, tossed about from one home to another like a spoiled hot potato, and finally marked as totally insane and shipped to a haunted looking, three-story building filled with castaways. Nor was he any longer a sixteen-year-old wild man who wouldn't keep his clothes on. Staff had been unable to keep him dressed. Though generally cooperative, when Charley had decided to tear off his clothes, even a group of workers could not prevent it. He was too strong. Abby had been informed that Charley at times possessed unexplainable strength. Even if they had been able to restrain Charley, which they had not been able to do, new laws made it tough to use any drastic measures on him, unless he was a danger to himself or to others. But Charley had never been violent, just crazy. Doctors had ordered many forms of psychotropic medications, but nothing seemed to stop Charley from ripping off his clothing and zipping out of the building. That's why he was moved to this country group home. That's why she had hated to visit. It had been most embarrassing.

But Charley wasn't so vulnerable and embarrassing now. His clothes were on, and he seemed perfectly happy about that. *Is this real?*

Charley released her from his embrace. "You look great! Your hair has really gotten long. I like it that way, long and wavy red."

"Wait a minute." Abby gulped. "You remember? I mean you didn't even seem to know me the last time I visited, and you haven't talked since you were very tiny." Abby's mouth hinged open.

Charley smiled. "I've been healed. I've been totally set free."

"But, I had no idea they had discovered such a wonder drug. Or is there some new shock therapy?"

"No, Abby, there is no miracle drug or therapy that could have changed me. It was Him."

"Him?" She felt her heart galloping up into her throat.

"It was Jesus who set me free." Charley was smiling again, and his smile was warm. His eyes sparkled. His light rust-colored hair was combed soft and his face shaved clean. He just looked fine, almost like he came from a place untouched by anything but beauty.

"Let me tell you all about it." His voice reached into her heart.

"I think I need to sit down first," Abby said, wiping beads of perspiration from her forehead. "This is just so unbelievable. I'm wondering if I'm dreaming after all."

"No, it's true." Charley's eyes glanced upward. "Praise the Lord. Where do I begin?" A few tears gathered in the deep of his eyes. "Very late last night I had a visitor. He called himself John. He said he was a prophet."

"A prophet? What in the world is a prophet?" Abby asked, exasperated.

"Well, I'm not quite sure." Charley's ivy-green eyes shimmered. "All I know is he was a man from God."

"Oh, Charley, how can you say that? There are all sorts of strange people proclaiming to know God. Some even say they are God." Abby tossed her head in frustration. "I don't go out of my way to believe someone just because he says he's a Christian or brags about knowing God. I haven't found any to be reliable."

"If Jesus is filling them and they're listening to Him"—Charley looked heavenward as his words rolled sweetly off his tongue—"then what they do is packed with truth and power."

Abby felt like her mouth was packed with sawdust. "Charley. You have never met Jesus. How can you talk like this?"

"Well, Aunt Abby"—Charley took a step toward her, squatted down in front of her, and looked into her eyes—"all I can say is last night I was shackled to a body filled with great fear and unexplainable torment, and today I'm not. I had no control over what I did. Now I know what possessed me was not from God. It caused me to rip off my clothes and run in fear. I was always running from it, but I could never run fast enough. It had me, until Jesus set me free."

"For Pete's sake, Charley, what had you?" Abby stood and began pacing.

"Demons. Only I didn't know it at the time. My psychiatrist called me schizophrenic and said I had multiple personalities. He did not understand that those personalities were demons possessing me. But John knew because God told him."

"But how could this John man change everything for you? None of this is adding up to an ounce of sense."

"I'm trying to explain it to you, Aunt Abby. John came late last night. God sent him."

"Who is this John anyway?" Abby's back stiffened. "Were you hallucinating, Charley? Is this John some kind of mysterious being like an angel from afar who just happens to show up by your side?"

Charley threw his head back and began to laugh. "No. Not at all, Abby. He is real; just like you and me. He is touchable. He is flesh and blood," Charley answered, pinching the skin on his arm. "But he is different than most folks in that he can see things many people refuse to believe in."

"And how is it he was able to get into this building at such a late hour in the night?" Abby demanded.

"He didn't." Charley's face blushed. "The voices in my head had been screaming, and I was driven to run from them. When I returned, John was standing right outside of this building waiting for me. I have to admit, at first I was frightened. I had no idea who he was. Then he spoke my name. He said, 'Charley, do you want to be healed and free from all those voices that are tormenting you?'"

Tears sparkled in Charley's eyes. "I said yes. The voices in my head were screaming 'No!' But I was saying yes. And then he told me about Jesus. He explained that Jesus loved me so much, enough to die for me. He told me that Jesus was the Son of God and that if I would believe, Jesus would deliver me from those voices, which were demons."

Abby stared at Charley with a critical eye. "And you expect me to believe this?"

"It may be hard for you to understand, Abby, but what I had known prior to that moment was a hurricane of loud noises and voices. Every voice played the part of a crazy personality, and they all created the wind and storm inside my mind. Then John demanded in the name of the Lord Jesus Christ for every unclean, unloving, and tormenting spirit to leave me. He named some of them as he commanded them to leave. One of them was rejection, and there was abandonment, rebellion, fear, and deception. There was something he called generational. There were many. John saw them leave, Abby. All I know is I'm sitting here in my right mind, and I am tormented no longer."

Abby rolled her eyes up and back. She felt her gut rolling into a tight ball at the same time. "That's crazy, Charley! You've been lied to. I've never heard such talk before. How can these demons, these things you have never seen before, be the personalities inside of you?"

"Well"—Charley gently put a hand to her shoulder—"I think they are the same things I used to see in my bedroom all the time when I was a little boy. They just took over somehow. Anyway, I didn't know what demons were. I didn't know who Jesus was. John said Jesus came to set the captive free. Come to church with me next Sunday, and you can talk to John himself if you don't believe me." He smiled. "I haven't been in church for so long, Abby. I can hardly believe I'm going to sit in church and learn about the One who has set me free. Oh, I so want to know Him." He turned his smile toward her. "Abby, come with me."

Abby stared away, dazed.

"Abby." Charley waved his hand in front of her frozen eyes. "Abby, please come to church with me Sunday."

"No. No, Charley, that would not be a good idea. And I don't think you should go either. I mean, we've got to be careful here." Abby began pacing around Charley's small bedroom. "Do you realize that you are being blamed for a whole herd of pregnant cattle rushing into an icy river and drowning? This whole thing could get very messy. No"—Abby blew out a troubled breath—"you need to stay put. Just pretend or something. Maybe you could say you banged your head on a tree and when you woke up you had come to your senses. I don't know. There's got to be something we can say. I will write it in the newspaper, and then everything will be okay again."

"I must only tell the truth, and that is that I have been set free."

Abby ran both hands through her hair. "What am I going to do?" Her dark eyes widened in alarm. "I can't write that kind of stuff. Look, will you do me one favor?" she begged. "Would you just not say anything? I mean, nobody knows you are able to talk now. So, please, for me, don't say anything until we can get you cleared from all charges."

"Abby, I didn't do anything to those cattle. But John heard those demons hit that herd with force. It was the evil spirits that sent those cows into the river."

"Stop! Don't let me ever hear you tell that to any person. Do you understand me?" Abby grabbed at her head as a hand of horror smacked it. "I mean it, Charley Frank! I'm ordering you not to say one word to anybody." She felt as if she has flames shooting from each curl of her red hair. Abby's legs felt like well-chewed gum—thin and giving out. She sat down. "Please, Charley. Don't say anything to anyone." Abby felt her heart sliding. "There's something I need to tell you, Charley." Abby wiped her wet and clammy hands on her slacks. "There's something more you need to know. Please believe me that your mom loved you very much." She looked up tenderly, seeking his eyes. "Charley, your mom was on her way home to be with you and me. She almost made it, but she was killed in a terrible car accident. The roads were so icy and all."

"Abby." She felt his hand gently touching her shoulder. "Mom was murdered."

"Charley!" Abby screamed, shooting off her chair. "Charley, what are you saying?" Her lips were spread thin in panic.

"Abby, I can tell you no more now, except that my father is a very dangerous man. For now we could all be in danger."

"Your father? I don't even know who your father is! You certainly don't!" Abby felt sinking inside, sort of like a half-baked cake—all gooey in the middle. She latched on to Charley's arm. "Charley, listen to me. Julie, your mom, never told anyone who your father was. She said she didn't know." Abby's breaths were rapid between words. "You are being spooky. Way too mysterious. It's like I don't know you."

Abby turned away from him and pounded her small fists on the wall. "Do you have any idea how hard you are making this on me? Do you know you are going to be on the front page of the *Edge Water Times*?" She whirled around, her eyes glaring at him. "Don't you realize I am the one writing this story about you? And about pregnant drowned cows! And, about the man who lost the cows!" She began to pace. "Maybe I should have you write this story instead, huh? How about that? This is just insane!"

"Abby, I would only write the truth," Charley said without wincing a facial muscle.

"Well, you see, that's the thing. What is the truth? I sure in blazes don't know! And you, how do I know you're telling the truth? Nothing you say sounds realistic. And Jasper is blaming you. He isn't going to care about your story. This demon stuff will just be a bunch of guff to everyone!"

"Demon stuff?" Phillip's deep voice was like a jack between the hard earth and heavy iron.

"Oh, Phillip. I'm so glad you're here! I'm doomed. We are all doomed," Abby cried. She stood there wringing her hands. Her red, curly bangs drooped like wet, wrinkly curtains on both sides of her. "How am I to write something about this mess?"

Phillip towered over her like a mountain. The gray of his eyes matched the streaks of graying in his hair. Abby felt relieved to dump her frustrations on his sturdy and weathered person.

Charley extended his hand to Phillip. "I'm Charley. I'm so pleased to meet you, Phillip."

"You're Charley?" Phillip's baffled expression turned to Abby.

"Yes, Phillip. I'd like to introduce you to the new Charley Frank, who now stands before you talking, fully dressed, and possibly in his right mind. However, nothing he says makes any sense to me," Abby added with a puff of her breath.

Phillip's expression turned to one of amusement. He smiled. "Great. I like a great story. However did this happen, Charley?"

"Here goes. You asked for it, Phillip." Abby's head sunk into her hands.

"As I told Abby, Jesus set me free from all the demons which controlled my mind and my body for so many years."

"Is there some way I could talk with this Jesus?" Phillip was still smiling.

"Please, Phillip. Can't you see this is no time for joking," Abby scolded. "And there's more yet. Charley is insisting those demons rushed all those cows into the river! This whole thing feels like something punching at my gut. Can you imagine what Jasper will have to say about this?"

Phillip's head went back. A deep, throat-felt laugh filled the room. "This is good." He continued to chuckle. "I can't wait to hear what old Jasper has to say."

"Phillip, you can't be serious?" Abby's eyes shot him her desperate look. "And all of this is but the tip of the iceberg, of which I have no desire to crash into. You need to know also, Mr. Investigator, Charley is saying that his mother, my sister Julie, was murdered. He said his father—I don't even know who he is—is very dangerous and we may all be targeted. If anything he is saying is true, we must be careful. It could cost us."

Phillip's features tightened. There was no more smile. "Whoa," he said, after exhaling a mouthful of troubled air. "Who is your father, son?"

"I can't tell you that right now. My new friend, John, he wants me to stay very quiet about this. It is that dangerous, Phillip."

"Okay. But I need to talk with this John. Who is John?"

"He is the prophet who came and introduced me to Jesus. He is the man who, in the name of Jesus, commanded the evil spirits to leave me."

"It sounds like Bible days or Bible talk or something." Phillip scratched his head in amazement. "Nevertheless," he added, "I need to talk with this man. It will be on the side for now. I would be very careful with such information. How long before this John plans to take it to the police?"

"I have no idea how to contact John," Charley answered, "other than to tell you he will be at the New Vision Church this Sunday. You could come. He should be able to answer your questions."

"I'll check with my wife. She's been nagging me to take her to church. Will you be coming, too, Charley?"

Charley's face brightened. "Yes. John has arranged a ride for me."

"And what about you, Miss Frank?" Phillip jested.

"No, I think I will pass this time. But I tell you what. I am going to attend my own church. I can do another story on how a church reacts to a Bible-day event," Abby said with a not-so-convincing dimpled smile.

Phillip laughed again. "Good idea. See that you do just that."

"Of course not! I'm just kidding!"

"No." Phillip badgered her remaining sanity. "It has now become an assignment."

Abby was speechless. *Did I hear him right?*

Abby winded slowly down the three flights of stairs. She didn't have a clue how she could write up this front-page breaking news. "This story will never be kept to a few pages in a local paper. It's about to shock the community. I think even the whole world. It will unravel my life. It will be my ruin!"

———————

Meanwhile, as the evening's shadows lengthened beneath a troubled sky, the Reverend Richard Staunch, chairman of the local ministerial, locked his fingers together to keep them from fidgeting all over the place. Like a harried college student typing away at an almost late essay, the man's thumbs tapped restlessly together. He hoped the rest of him was hidden well enough behind the podium. Never before had he been such a nervous wreck.

He cleared his throat and squared his undersized shoulders. "I'm sure we all know why this meeting was called today. Bedlam is quickly spreading from one community to the next, and as clergy, it is up to us to rein in our congregations from misinterpreting the recent happening. Some are even saying this is all about a huge miracle, like in Bible days. Certainly we know that these kinds of things don't happen today."

"What gossip would that be?"

Each man and woman of the cloth turned to stare at the young stranger standing in the back corner near the door. He was a tall kid with coarse blond hair, a perfect stranger to all who regularly gathered in this fashion.

"I'm sorry, young man." Staunch used his best reprimanding voice. His words were miffed and clicked like a frog's tongue snapping after a tempting insect.

"This meeting today is exclusive to only clergy from Mirage County and its three neighbor counties, Dour, Perjure, and Blames."

The stranger walked forward. "I am a minister of the gospel of Jesus Christ. I have recently accepted a pastorate at the New Vision Church in Perjure County. I heard about this meeting and felt I should attend." He stood before the group, not caring that his blue jeans were tattered or that he was much younger than the cluster of longstanding members who were now examining every inch of his being. "I'm very interested to learn what gossip is causing our communities to be in such chaos." The corners of his lips creased upward.

Mr. Staunch harrumphed. "Come now. If you are indeed a preacher from this area, you would have heard of the news regarding the young man who has suffered with severe psychosis since his childhood and was mute as well. The whole central part of our state is in an uproar since this kid claims to have been delivered from a legion of demons. To make matters worse, these demons supposedly rushed into a herd of beef cattle, causing them death by drowning. You can imagine how this is being compared to the story of Jesus healing the crazed demon-possessed man who lived among the tombs. The story there is that those demons rushed into a group of pigs." The reverend blew out a forceful and agitated breath. "Some people are calling it a miracle. We have a real mess on our hands."

"Maybe it is a miracle," the young stranger said, slipping each thumb around a blue jean pocket. He stepped to the front and looked directly into the chairman's baffled eyes. "What if this is a manifestation of God's power? If it is, it only seems right that the devil doesn't want any of you to believe it. If you and your congregations believe and turn to the Lord, the devil knows he could lose his grip on entire towns and counties."

Reverend Staunch bent his long and knotted fingers into fists. When his knuckles turned white, he whacked them on the wood pulpit. "Who are you?" he demanded.

"Name's Pastor Paul Marvel," he answered, extending his hand toward the Reverend Staunch, who declined the handshake.

"I wouldn't advise bucking us on this one, young man," the elder minister sternly warned.

———

Abby leaned back against the headrest of her recliner. Her thoughts were spinning around in a mental blender thinned by worry and confusion. She was backed into a corner like a fox surrounded by hounds. Her next move, even her next words, would be followed by teeth or the blare of a gun.

She reached for one of Julie's notebooks. On the outside it was written 1992. The first entry was marked July 9. *Sweet Julie. You were just fifteen years old.* Abby's heart yearned to see Julie again. "Oh, God. Why did You take her from me? All I have now are her words."

> So sick today. It is very hot. It is very hard to be pregnant in this heat. Yesterday a county nurse visited with me. She asked me if I have

been drinking alcohol while pregnant. I didn't dare tell her that I have been drinking. I hope I haven't hurt my baby. I would never want to hurt my baby.

Abby turned to the next entry date, July 12.

Oh, my God! Dad was in a rage today. He blamed Abby and I because the cows got out. We had to chase after them. I am so afraid of that bull. I had Abby stay back cuz it's too hard to worry about her and that mean thing. I brought Chester with. He's a good dog, and he kept the cows heading home. Then when I got home I found Abby crying in her room. She had been beaten with a strap. She was red with welts and some of them bleeding. It was all my fault. I should have taken her with me. Dad is worse than that bull. I just don't know what to do anymore.

Abby's fingers began jerking, and her hands and arms began to tremble. Her face went numb; so did her mind. She didn't notice the tears slipping down and off onto Julie's notebook. Her head sank deeper into the cushion of her chair. Her eyes closed, but the tears continued to break loose beneath her lashes.

The sun was splashing bright light through the gray sky. The light reached her eyes and caused them to open to another day. Yet even with so much light, there was no light to guide her.

Chapter Three

A bby had barely met Tuesday's deadline. Phillip had hounded her for the report. She had despaired of what to write. In the end, she had concluded: *You have to stick with the facts. No matter how bizarre they are. Stick with the facts, Abby!*

Now two days later Abby sat at her kitchen table, sipping on coffee, listening to raindrops pelting against the window, and wishing just for once a dream could come true in her life. *I ran after a chance to make it big in journalism. Now I think I've failed at that, too. I was a fool thinking I could succeed at something.* Abby groaned. *Like a bird shot from the sky again. Shouldn't have tried flying in the first place.*

The blade of depression took a well-aimed stab at Abby's heart. No memory was her friend. She was a history book of failed dreams and of painful or broken relationships. At one time, she had even considered marriage. Chad had seemed different than the other male relationships Abby had known. *Until I realized that I was just his emotional little lap puppy. He thought he could drag me around leashed to him. If I cried, he could laugh at me. If I talked back, he could slap me. Why does love require a chain? Why can't I get that chain off my neck?*

Abby glanced at the paper lying before her. She dreaded reading what she had written. Was her dream of becoming a successful writer about to leave her? Who was this surgeon operating in her life? Who was responsible for removing the dreams and hopes from her life? What kind of powerful suction had he turned on as to suck away her very breath of hope?

Abby's face sunk to the table. "I have nothing. There is no person who could understand. I'm the misfit I've tried not to be."

After allowing hope to be gutted from her, Abby stood, and her feet led her toward the freezer. She pulled out the half-gallon container of rocky road ice cream. *I don't care anymore. I quit trying. I can never be more than what I am. Who is God anyway? How could I follow someone who has allowed so much hurt to be in my life?*

Abby heaped the ice cream high in her bowl. A caged, pacing lion inside of her soul crouched down like a kitty begging for milk. She stared at the creamy chocolate piled in her bowl, and then like a shovel scooping up its assignment, Abby pushed her tablespoon deep inside the luscious mound set before her. It hurried to her mouth. Each scoop excited her taste buds and then yelled, "You'll need more!" Tastes good for such a short second! *If only this could last longer! Where did it go so fast?* The sweet, begging kitty fled, and the lion got out of its cage. Now it stood before her. It smirked. It mocked. It condemned. *You always blow it! That's why you are fat and ugly!*

Abby hated an empty bowl more than ever. Yet empty bowls were what she always ended up with. She looked hard into the bowl, but all that remained was a chocolate ghost clinging to the plastic lining.

Abby threw the bowl into the sink.

Yuck. I feel fat. I'll never get those twenty pounds I gained off. The Fs of life. Fat! Failure! Fool! Why did I eat all of that ice cream? Why did I think it would help me feel better?

"Aaaw!" Abby complained aloud. "Phillip will be calling me. I'm sure he can't be happy by now. Why did he allow this to be printed anyway?" Abby's trembling hand touched the newspaper. It was too late to delete any mistake from the headlines. And her article was on the front page. It was the breaking news. The big story. Reluctantly she picked it up. Right there on the front page were numerous pictures showing rescue workers, cranes, other equipment, crowds of people, and a river with chunks of icy debris and mounds of dead, bloated cattle piled along its banks. "Oh God," Abby whimpered. She couldn't see the big cat stirring within her. She could only feel its big paws pressing, its claws, digging. "Oh God!" she cried again. "What have I done? Have I put everyone in danger's way now? If you are there, God, if this really is some kind of miracle, You are going to need to keep Charley safe. I told only what I witnessed and heard. I hope that's what you wanted."

The quake inside of her sent tremors throughout her body. The paper shook in her hands.

The title loomed in large, bold letters.

One Man's Freedom Versus Another Man's Loss

Abby rubbed her hands together. She glanced toward the sky from her kitchen window. *Why can't it ever quit raining?* Streaks of its heavy gray reached their talons right through the glass and hooked unto Abby's frightened soul.

Her cell phone was ringing. "Phillip!" Abby cried into it. Her jumbled thoughts became like words hitting a fan's rotary blade. "Phillip, I am so worried. I can imagine the article I wrote has the whole country buzzing by now. I shouldn't have written it."

"Ah, Ab, stop fretting. People will all come to their own conclusions on this story. You just presented the facts."

"Phillip! I'm worried about Charley. If what he says is true, what about this murder thing he is insisting on? What if Julie really was murdered? What if the killer is his father? And what if he is reading this paper?"

There was silence on the other end of the phone.

"Phillip?"

"Yeah, yeah. Gimme a minute to think." Silence again.

"Phillip. You believe him, don't you?" She could feel her blood freezing up. "This is a circle of evil becoming wider and wider, isn't it? And you and I and Charley are right in the middle. We are in the eye of the storm."

"It's messy, all right."

"What are we going to do?"

"We are going to find some answers. Don't rule anything out, Abby. Make note of everything."

"Make note of everything," she repeated.

"You can do it. It's going to be okay, Abby."

Abby stared out the window again and she hung up the phone. The rain was hiding in the black, rolling clouds like a predator hunkering in the shadows.

"Phillip has too much confidence in himself and in me," Abby fretted. "This is one scary puzzle we are hoping to put together. Problem is, the biggest pieces are missing."

Julie, I don't know what to do. If only you were here. Abby sat still. Her heart pounded madly against her chest. *The journals!*

Sadness wormed its way through the deep soil that had collected in her heart. Abby pushed the journal against her chest and held it there, waiting for that resolute moment, that rebound second, for courage to say, "I will avenge your death, Julie!"

The entry read August 25.

Julie had written across the top of the page, "God help me. I think I'm going crazy." Abby read on.

> My life is kept secret. My father is drunk again. When he found out I was pregnant, he pushed his pistol into my stomach. He said, "I oughta pull this trigger." That would have been good. I wish he had done it. I almost begged him to. He kicked me instead. I wonder if he hurt the baby. I can't protect it. I can't protect Abby or myself either. I just go through the motions. The baby's

father wants it dead. Maybe he wants me dead, too. I only know I fear him. He has warned me to listen to him.

Later, and I need to add more. The county nurse came out earlier this afternoon. I would like to tell her how bad it is here, but I think she knows. Just now child protection came out again. I wanted to cry out, "Take Abby out of here! It isn't safe for her. It isn't safe for me, either." But Dad was standing there. Mom was right by him. They deny everything. I wish Mom would help us.

Abby squirmed. Her stomach began to roll into a knot. She felt nauseous. *God, I can't take this. I feel terribly sick. Where are You anyway? How could You have let this happen to us? We were just kids!*

Abby jumped up and ran to the bathroom. She knelt down and stared into the toilet bowl as the bile rose in her chest.

A 1998 dark-green Buick rolled to the front of the Wilderness Group Home's main entrance. Charley was waiting under the canopy.

"Good to see you, John," Charley greeted as he hopped in the front seat.

"Glad you agreed to come, Charley. Hope they didn't ask many questions?" the older man asked. His face was covered with a silvery blue beard, like the appearance of a gentle cloud drawing strength from the sun above it. Slate-colored hair draped down to his shoulders. Through it all, even through the smile, Charley could read the concern on John's face.

"No problem. I just said I was going to spend a few days with a friend. Told them I would call and check in with them later." Charley fastened his seat belt. "Actually no one is saying much to me, John. They just stare at me as though I'm an alien of sorts."

"You are, son," John answered affectionately. "Did you read the paper?" John glanced Charley's way. The windshield wipers were scraping some. John turned them a notch lower.

"Not yet. I figured the article had come out just by the glares I got from all the staff." He looked at John. "It was very difficult for Abby to write. I know that. How did she do?"

"She did well." John smiled as he reached for a crumpled up piece of paper. "Listen to this! 'One hundred and twenty-six of his prize registered and pregnant black Angus heifers plunged themselves into the iced Wilderness River bordering his property. Amidst cold winds and sleet, these animals left their shelter and food and seemed driven without any apparent reason to a watery death. Every rescue effort in Perjure County was utilized along with the help of Mirage County, but only a handful of cattle were rescued.'" John's smile spread across his face, sending ripples across his beard. "It's bound to make people think. In our country, filled with churches, it seems normal to believe that the Bible days and today cannot co-exist. It's just been too easy to push God out of our culture. God is in this, Charley, trying to show people He still does exist."

John stepped on the gas and headed away from the tall, haunted-looking group home. "Here," John said, tossing the paper to Charley. "Read it for yourself." John winked. "When God delivered you, Charley, He gave you a powerful crash course in reading, too. Now you can read like an honor student!"

Charley whistled as he glanced at the article. "There's stuff in here I don't even remember." He began reading, "'Charley has lived at the Wilderness Group Home for three years because he could not be restrained by any means. Rodger Leaders, CEO of the Giant Oak's Juvenile Boys' Home, reported that Charley was sent to the Wilderness Group Home because he was too strong for restraint devices. He could break free from several male staff workers holding him back. None could keep him clothed. He would tear off his clothes and run nude, thereby becoming a nuisance in public settings.'"

"Like Abby wrote, I have been perfectly restored!" Charley stopped and dabbed at a tear in the corner of his eye before he continued. "'He was what he was: mute since childhood, greatly misunderstood, wild, and untamable." Charley looked up at John. "It really was a miracle. I'm not that kid any longer."

John was still smiling. "Not only can you read, but you can hear His voice now. You are plugged into Him. I pray you will never forget what great things the Lord is doing for you."

Charley grinned like a boy receiving the student-of-the-month award. "I am so grateful. No more voices and personalities driving me, making me wild." He leaned back against the headrest and continued to read. "'Then suddenly everything changed. Charley Frank now sits dressed and in his right mind. He talks. He claims to be perfectly restored.'" Charley took in a deep relaxed breath. "John, you are right. Bible days are suppose to be happening today. What happened to me is proof of that!"

"Yep! Jesus is the Word of God. God's Word came down to earth in the flesh. Jesus is the living Word of God. He made the Word more than just dotted *i's* and crossed *t's*." John's smile beamed from ear to ear. "There's no life in the letters of the Word. But, there is everlasting and life-changing life in Jesus. That's what happened to you, Charley. Jesus came! He sent away the darkness to bring you the light of His life."

Charley shook his head in amazement. "And get this," he read on, "'Today there are two men with mysterious stories. The one man, Charley Frank says he has found the answer. It is Jesus Christ. On the other hand, Jasper continues to blame Charley Frank. Jasper sits and moves and breathes curses to Jesus Christ, whom he says doesn't exist anyway.'" Charley folded the paper up. "Poor Jasper. If only he could believe that Jesus is alive. If he only knew that Jesus is for today."

John glanced Charley's way. "You're right, kid. If only. Jasper doesn't even realize that he is driven by voices too." John sucked in a deep breath. "The Bible days, and today, also include the devil. Without believing in Jesus, Jasper will never understand what really happened to his beef cattle, nor will he realize that he is being driven by the same forces that sent his cows to the river that day."

"John," Charley said with a twist of his head, "what about my father? No doubt he is following this. It's sad that he doesn't understand what is driving him, either."

"You're right, Charley. He is listening to wrong voices. Those voices are receiving their orders from the father of murder."

Charley could see a shiny tear drop and then soak into John's beard. "I failed your mom, Charley. She insisted on leaving to be with you and Abby. The time wasn't right for her to go. I knew that. I tried to tell her. Had she left at night, she would have gotten here during daylight hours. Such a murderous plan would have been more difficult to pull off."

"John," Charley interrupted, "will we be back for church Sunday? I promised the newspaper man, Phillip, that he could talk with you at church."

"I think it might be too risky, son. Your father has no intention of letting the truth be discovered." John's eyes met Charley's. "Maybe I can call Paul. He can help Phillip."

Phillip parked his blue super cab in front of the Kitchen Spread Cafe. He jumped out and quickly moved to the passenger side, opening the door. "Ready for lunch, my lady?"

"You can be so sweet, Phillip Acumen!" Sherry's eyes took on an ocean-blue spray as the sun met them. She reached for her husband's extended hand. "I actually am ready for lunch. Didn't have time for breakfast."

Phillip didn't feel hungry, but he wasn't about to tell his wife. She would drill him for answers. How would he explain the gnawing feeling inside of his gut anyway?

"Ah, good thing we came early. Looks like you can choose your table."

"Okay. Honey," she answered, "how about right there, close to the buffet?"

"Perfect. Instead of our legs doing the walking, our hands can."

"Yeah. I could use a break." Sherry sighed.

"Another busy day?" Phillip asked as he pulled out the chair for her.

"I could swear the CEO has been out to frustrate me lately." Sherry's eyebrows raised in wonder.

A waitress came with menus. "I think the lady and I are doing the buffet?" Phillip directed the question to his wife.

"Yes. That would be fine." Sherry smiled.

"Can I get you anything to drink?"

"Would you care for a soda or something?" Phillip asked.

"No. I think I will just have coffee. Could I have creamer, too?" Sherry asked, turning over the coffee mug.

"Sure," the waitress answered, carrying away the menus.

"Isn't it the preacher's son who is the CEO of Edge Water's Sheltering Oaks Nursing Home?" Phillip asked as the two of them stood to get their plates. "You know. Isn't your boss the son of that preacher at Abby's church? Oh, I can't remember his name or the name of the church."

"That's because you don't want to have anything to do with church, Phillip!" Sherry spouted in a half-tease, half-serious tone of voice. "And, yes. The CEO's name is Kevin Staunch. His father, Reverend Richard Staunch, pastors the God's Love Fellowship Church right here in town." Sherry put another cucumber on her salad and then looked up at Phillip. "Is that all you are having?" She wrinkled her face in surprise.

"Not too hungry today," he said, taking his place at the table. She sat down next to him. He could see the question marks floating in her eyes. He needed to say something to avoid those questions. "So why would this CEO have any reason to cause someone so beautiful and dedicated to her job as you are any harm or frustration?"

Sherry's expression changed to a more worrisome look. "I can't understand it, Phillip. He used to treat me well. I have never crossed him. I've just worked hard for him." She speared a cherry tomato with her fork. "Now he just glares at me and snaps out orders. I don't know. It's rumored that the nursing home is losing money. Who knows? Maybe he is just stressed out from that." Her voice trailed off.

"You don't sound too convinced," Phillip added.

"Yeah, well, I asked a couple other employee friends of mine, and none of them seem to even notice Kevin's personality changing." Sherry reached for her coffee, taking a long sip. "Phillip, it's like the world is changing right before my eyes. I feel lost inside for answers." She looked up at him with that same inquisitive look. "And look at you. There you are trying to hide from me again."

"Hide?" Phillip asked. "I'm sitting right here talking to you."

"Yeah. Talking to me but not being totally honest with me. I can see through you, Mr. Investigator. Something big is bothering you. But I would be the last to find out." She blew out a frustrated breath. "But I will find out. You know I always do."

Phillip, needing to change the subject before she asked too many questions, reached over and took her hand. "Honey, I know you have asked a couple times if maybe we could try church. Well, I am wondering if you would come with me Sunday to a church I've never heard of before in Perjure County."

Sherry's eyes became like the large blue sky freed from all clouds. "Whoa! Something must be terribly wrong if you want to go to church!"

"Well"—Phillip choked on a bite of potato salad—"you know the story I'm working on. I need to meet a couple people at this church and ask them some questions."

"Phillip! Do you mean to tell me that you might be inclined to believe this Charley kid?"

"Well, my dear"—he tapped his fingers on the table—"neither Charley's story or Jasper's story make much sense. But," Phillip added, clearing his throat with a little cough, "Charley is not the same guy he used to be. He is by far more rational and credible than Jasper."

Sherry smiled. "Phillip, I'm beginning to think there really is a God. There must be someone in charge out there who is bigger than you and me." She clasped her hands around Phillip's bigger hands. "Phillip, I need to know this God." A tear strolled slowly down her cheek. "I'm desperate for answers, and well, I have started reading the Bible we had tucked away in the library. I'm reading in the very first book."

"Genesis?"

"Yes. Noah believed in God. It's a good thing, too. His whole family was saved from destruction."

"So you're concluding that Noah is a religious hero, and your husband is not religious, which makes me what? Incompetent to save my family?"

Sherry wrinkled up her napkin as she blew out a troubled breath. "It's not that way. You are twisting."

"I don't understand what's gotten into you." Phillip threw up his hands in the middle of her sentence. "You've been content with our marriage for almost seventeen years. Religion wasn't mentioned. I was enough until lately, when you've been getting in my face about this stuff!" His eyes formed into slits. "And now you're gonna start some sob story about needing God?"

"Yes I am! Our family needs answers! It seems all we have been doing is playing house." Her eyes grew closer together as she stretched her upper torso across the table to look more squarely at him. "I don't want our marriage to be like papa bear, mama bear, and the baby bears. I am sick of pretending that all we need is food to eat, comfortable chairs and beds, and lots of money in the bank! Phillip, I know there must be more important things than these."

Phillip's body became rigid, livid with anger. His neck rotated in every direction so his eyes could see if any person might be eavesdropping. "Well, Cinderella, aren't you grateful now for your glass slippers?" He cursed under his breath. "You got more than all those things you mentioned as not important. I took you out of the rags of abuse and gave you everything I thought you deserved. And you're not happy with that?"

Sherry's head bowed as shame chalked itself darker under her eyes. "Sorry, Phillip. I didn't mean it that way. Honestly I didn't. I am very grateful for you, your love, and everything you have done for me. It just seems that we have gotten so caught up in making a living, that we could be missing some things. Look at Jamie. She's changing, and I fear for the worst."

Phillip shuffled his weight in the chair. "She couldn't have found a bigger dope to hang out with than Jack."

"My point is we are both so busy trying to make a living and build a home for our children, yet we have been so blind as not to see that we are losing them!"

"Hold on, sugar." Phillip felt the blood rush up his neck and cover his face. "You are talking as though religion can put everything back in order."

"I don't know what I am saying, but I need to find out if there's hope in God. I need to know if this Jesus is the miracle maker who changed an untamed castaway into a normal and happy young man. If He is, then you and I and our kids need to meet Him!"

Oh, I hate this place! Abby hurried up the dark and musty-smelling stairway in search of Charley. It had dawned on her that he did not even have her cell phone number. What if he needed her? For all she knew, Charley could be in great danger at this very moment.

Breathing harder from the jaunt to third floor, Abby stopped to suck in a mouthful of air and to rake strands of bangs from her eyes.

Why is everything painted a drab gray? Charley must feel like a prisoner behind bars in here. She knocked. No answer. "Charley?" she asked as she opened the door and peeked in. "Oh, where in the world did you go?"

Abby's eyes, akin to a spy's camera, scanned the third floor surroundings. She turned to go.

"Excuse me, young man." Abby tapped the young janitor on his shoulder. "I'm looking for Charley Frank."

"Charley signed out for a few days. Said he was visiting a friend and would check back with us later," the straggly haired young man answered without even looking up to meet Abby's gaze.

"They let Charley sign out without asking any questions like, 'Where are you going? What number can you be reached at? Who are you going with?'" Abby's voice flared as her hands poised on her hips.

"Look!" He pushed his narrow face into Abby's space. His eyes raised under bushy brows. "I am not in charge here, so don't tell me your problems!"

Abby's hands fell limp to her side. Then she recoiled quicker than a snake hemmed in a corner. "Well, I'm grateful that you are not in charge." Abby walked away as steam fizzed through her parted lips. *This place needs to be reported. It should be investigated! The staff are all mentally ill. Bunch of idiots parading around as caregivers and therapists and nurses and whatever else they claim to be.*

The same gray-headed woman Abby had met a few days ago sat straight backed behind the desk. Abby felt a nasty impulse to reach down and push the wire-rimmed glasses up over the hook of the woman's nose. Instead, she took a deep breath and tried to recompose herself. In the process, she tugged on her blouse to straighten out any possible wrinkle and attempted to paste a smile on her face.

"Hi. I don't suppose you could tell me where my nephew, Charley Frank, might be?"

"Why, just the night before last he signed himself out. Said he was going to spend a few days with a friend," the woman obliged with a blink and a smile.

"Well, where did he go and with whom?"

"He didn't say."

Abby's hands were balling into fists. "You do have policies and procedures, I assume, regulating the signing in and out of these mentally ill clients?"

"Yes, dear, of course we do. But have you forgotten that Charley is no longer mentally ill?"

Abby bent over the desk, glaring into the woman's eyes. "Has his diagnosis been changed by his psychiatrist?"

The woman continued to smile like she was a plugged-in light bulb. "Dr. Soothers has not released his medical opinion yet, but he has removed all institutional restrictions from Charley's care plan."

The woman's head rotated in all directions as though she wanted to be sure no person was within hearing distance. "Between you and me, Miss, I believe Charley. It was God, and it was a miracle! Charley is not insane any longer."

"It doesn't matter what you or Dr. Soother think about Charley. How could you just let him go when he has no place to go?" Abby's muddled thoughts pushed her words through a grinder, leaving them chopped and chewed wrong.

"He'll be okay. Hey, did you read the paper?" A couple blue-penciled veins popped out on the woman's face. "If you haven't, you ought to! Jesus is the only one who could have that kind of power. Those demons ran scared! Charley is a new man."

Abby stood stunned with big, brown deer eyes. "I wish I could believe that. If it is true, why haven't we seen more miracles? I mean, look! This place is filled with miserable and confused people. In fact," she spewed with added tenacity, "we're all like turtles looking for a shell of hope in this crazy world. You'd think He would care. You'd think He would rescue little kids from the bullies that want to hurt them. I don't see anything He has done to make this world a better place."

"Sure you do, Miss. But there you stand trying to talk away a miracle. What happened to Charley is a miracle." The woman looked up, smitten by what she believed. "It appears Jesus is the Miracle Maker, just like what was written up in the paper. I think it's written in the Bible, too. Maybe we all need to believe and then we'll see some more miracles."

Abby walked away. A tourniquet had been put around her believer a long time ago, and, throughout the years, something was tightening it. It was dangerously tight now to the point of snuffing out all hope of life.

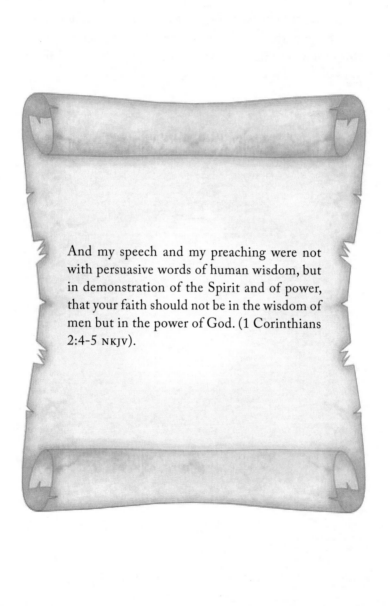

And my speech and my preaching were not with persuasive words of human wisdom, but in demonstration of the Spirit and of power, that your faith should not be in the wisdom of men but in the power of God. (1 Corinthians 2:4-5 NKJV).

Chapter Four

It was Sunday morning, and Abby did not wish to sit through a church service. She would get just as much pleasure sitting for an hour in her freezer box.

She stood outside her door for a few moments, amazed that spring had finally come. The sun beat warmly down on her. "I only need my sweater." She straightened out her blue denim skirt and felt rejuvenated to enjoy the balmy walk to church.

"I don't need to wear a tie! I don't care if we are going to church!" Phillip stood before his wife like a steed refusing a harness, eying the black-with-blue swirls tie she held in her hand.

"I know, honey, but it would go so nice with that navy shirt you are wearing." Sherry reached out and touched his arm. "And I am so proud to be able to accompany my husband to church this morning."

"Flattery is my downfall," Phillip mourned as he reached for the tie. "Are those kids about ready to go?"

"I had to bribe Jamie. Hope you're not upset, but I gave in to her and said Jack could tag along."

"You did what?" His voice raised. "You know that boy and I don't get along. Like the song goes, when it comes to brains, he has the short end of the stick."

Sherry smiled. "Yeah, there's more to that song. Remember my daddy said the same thing about you." She laughed.

"Not funny. What about Blake? You know how he pokes along. We need to be leaving in ten minutes. It's a good half-hour drive from here."

"He is staying in his room far too much. I don't understand that." The dance in Sherry's blue eyes disappeared. "He used to be a happy, busy boy. He's only fifteen, and he's not interested in anything but the dark interior of his room anymore." She sighed. "I'll check on him and hurry him along."

The outside of the church loomed stiff and unfriendly before Abby. Once inside, Abby tried to remain as inconspicuous as a porcupine blending in with a bush.

The organ was softly playing. People were streaming in. *Like watching a style show. Who will win the pious look of the day? The most alluring outfit? Hairstyles? Everyone dressed up for some special occasion? I came from the wrong side of town to enter such a contest. Misfits are just lucky to find a church chair.*

Out of the corner of her eye, Abby recognized the reverend's son, Kevin, moving ahead to take a seat. Her pulse skittered about uncomfortably. As he passed by, Abby took a bold look. Kevin's arm was linked around his wife, Lexi's, left arm, sort of pulling her forward. He looked like an important, bulky engine, pulling his cargo behind him. While Abby had always loathed Kevin for his arrogant and intimidating attitude, she had been equally repelled by his snub-nosed wife. However, something seemed different today. Lexi's nose was down. Her long blonde hair hung loose, now falling about the sides of her face as her eyes followed the ground.

Soon the organ was pumping out a joyful sound. The song leader, short and stocky, took his place in front of the congregation. Abby could see his white teeth flashing between his smiles even from one of the back rows. "Turn with me to page three hundred twenty-eight in your hymnals as we sing together on this beautiful Easter morning."

Easter? That's what the fuss is about!

"Let's stand as we sing!" The taller folks were blocking her view now. She could only occasionally see a shimmer from the song leader's balding head and the wave of his hand orchestrating. But the words of the song were refurbishing Abby's soul: "Up from the grave He arose! With a mighty triumph o'er His foes."

Abby couldn't help but wonder just how powerful this Jesus really was. *Could this Jesus have miraculously changed Charley?* She felt a deep sadness creep into her soul. When she had been a little girl she hoped to find God big and powerful. She had asked her Sunday school teacher. She had asked the preacher. She had asked so many people, "Is God really big?" In a way, here she was asking again, wondering the same thing.

Reverend Staunch's skinniness looked a little stuffy in his white collar and deep red robe. He stood behind the podium, looking over his wire-rimmed glasses. "Happy Easter to each and every one of you. You may be seated."

A rustle of skirts happened. Heads lowered. Abby scooted a little to the right on the deep-green padded pew. Between the bodies in front of her, she could see the minister poised and confident behind his pulpit. His straight-lipped smile stamped itself with pride across his narrow face. Abby glanced away.

"I read to you this morning from the gospel of John twenty and verses twenty-nine through thirty-one. This is written shortly after the resurrection of Jesus: 'Jesus said to him, "Thomas, because you have seen Me, you have believed. Blessed are those who have not seen and yet have believed." And truly Jesus did many other signs in the presence of His disciples, which are not written in this book; but these are written that you may believe that Jesus is the Christ, the Son of God, and that believing you may have life in His name.'"

The reverend looked down and over his glasses, accentuating his protruding and pointed ears. "Thomas doubted," the minister began with a grating basement voice. "He doubted even the resurrection of Jesus. He had been with Jesus and seen many wonderful miracles.

Shouldn't all of those miracles have been enough to keep Thomas excited in the faith?"

Reverend Staunch thumbed through his Bible again, saying, "Right before His death, Jesus said, 'It is finished.' The works and miracles He had performed while walking this world were finished.

"What does faith today mean?" His bullfrog eyes bulged. "It means God wants you to believe in what He did. Faith isn't expecting more big miracles." He postured himself like an important political tycoon ready to bring his point home. "Faith is believing that it is finished!" A grin stretched his lips. "Don't get lost in looking for something to believe for. There are those who believe that every day they must tell a mountain to move. They proclaim that we are supposed to be laying hands on sick or crippled people and believing that they should all be healed, like what happened when Jesus walked this earth. In other words, they think they need to make something big happen so they have something to write home about." The Reverend's face puckered like he had the inside of a lemon in his mouth. "No, it is time to believe that He did it all. People, it is time we believe what has already been done. Would you add more than what is already written? When Jesus left here, He expected men to begin using their brains. Look around you and see how modern technology has exploded. He doesn't need to do any more to prove anything to you. All that is expected of you now is to do your best down here. Use your brain. Contribute to the welfare of others. And spiritually believe that through and beyond what we can accomplish, He is in control of everything that happens. It is simply submitting to God's will."

The reverend slapped his Bible against the podium. "Jesus now resides in heaven. He did not come down to earth again and walk over to Charley and tell demons to chase a bunch of cows into that river. He said, 'it is finished.' All that He did down here is finished! He gave men brains to rule the earth. He gave doctors. Many wonderful and exciting scientific breakthroughs are happening."

Abby wrote, "He just doesn't do that kind of stuff today."

So that's why miracles are not happening today. Jesus is not walking down here any longer. If Jesus is here, then He must be walking around like an invisible ghost. Even if what happened to Charley is a miracle, I would need Jesus to come right here and tell me in person that He made Charley well again.

The thin-faced minister slumped himself over the pulpit, sighing like air being released from a tire. "Are you looking for more signs today? Can you believe without seeing a miracle?" With an accomplished smirk reaching to his pronounced cheek bones, the preacher asked, "So what about Jasper's cows? What about Charley? Was he filled with demons? Did some prophet happen by and command those demons to drive those cows madly into the icy river?" With a harrumph, he added, "No. This was not a sign. It was not a miracle. Jesus himself said in Matthew twelve, thirty-nine, 'An evil and adulterous generation seeks after a sign, and no sign will be given to it except the sign of the prophet Jonah.'"

Reverend Staunch shot a toothy grin. "There was a time when Jesus did miracles. There was a time when people needed prophets. It was back then when people needed signs. But people, these things are not happening today. Jesus gives us the Holy Spirit now to teach us all about what has already happened."

Abby jotted down the verse. *Wow, I think deep down inside, I really wanted to believe that miracles happen today. I mean, if I were to believe in God, I would want a God who was capable of doing miracles. Too bad He left. It's rather unfair to those of us still stuck down here. If this Jesus had still been here and had really freed Charley from all of his misery and hopelessness, I think I may even have found a reason to hope again, too.*

"We may not understand why God willed for Charley to be mentally handicapped, poor, and despised by all around him, but who are we to question God the Creator? God chose the way things would be way back before the world was created." The robed leader shook his head like a dazed man who had just walked into a tree. "Who are we to think Charley was worthy to bother God for a miracle? God doesn't need to prove anything to his unworthy creatures. But maybe a modern intervention has come to Charley's rescue. Wouldn't that be wonderful?"

Anger sent its troops to infiltrate Abby's emotions. She seethed at the minister's words. *Who are you to say who is a poor, despised, and unworthy misfit? You treated Julie that way too! If the God who created everyone invites only a few into His palace and confines the rest into a forsaken orphanage, then I want nothing to do with Him!*

—————

The little old schoolhouse was cradled in the dark shadows of the tall pine trees around it. Sherry's eyes grew big with disappointment. "Oh. It doesn't look at all like a church. It's so little."

"It's an old schoolhouse," Phillip interjected. He turned to see the do-we-have-to-go-in look on Jamie's and Jack's faces.

Blake stepped out of the car. His baggy, black pant legs drug on the gravel.

"If you must dress in black all the time, could you please find a pair of britches that aren't falling off?" Phillip snapped at his son. "The least we could do is try to look presentable for church."

"But it's not much of a church setting," Sherry answered in one deflating breath. "And there are only four cars besides ours here in the parking lot."

The door creaked with age as Phillip opened it for his family to enter. Inside a handful of people were kneeling before a rickety pew.

"Do we have to?" Blake grumbled.

"Yes," Phillip huffed back.

"What are they doing?" Jamie asked, wrinkling her nose.

"Well, my guess is they are praying," Phillip said as he slipped his hand into the pocket of his trousers. His fingers jingled the coins.

A young man, with sky-blue eyes, a fair complexion, and bristly blonde hair stood. He smiled as he approached them. Phillip reasoned the young man to be in his early twenties.

"I'm Paul," the stranger said, extending his hand. "I'm the pastor here at New Vision Church. Please come in."

Phillip felt like a rooster out of his familiar coop. He cleared his throat and met Paul's extended hand with his own. "Thank you. I'm Phillip. I'm a newspaper reporter and," he continued, "this is my wife, Sherry; my daughter, Jamie; Jamie's boyfriend, Jack; and my son, Blake."

"Yes. John told me you might be here." Paul answered as he greeted each of them with a gentle smile. "There are only a few of us," Paul said unashamedly, "but our special guest is delighted to have you join us today."

"John? I mean, is he your special guest? I will need to talk with him."

"No," the young man answered with a smile. "Our special guest is Jesus." With a click of the heels of his cowboy boots, Paul turned and gestured Phillip to follow him. "You simply must meet my wife."

A slender young woman with stunning features smiled at Paul as he approached. She reached for Sherry's hand and cupped it between her own hands.

Sherry stood paralyzed in what seemed like moments of awe. The hands holding her hand seemed so warm. How welcome she instantly felt as though some unseen, even divine, presence was wrapping about her.

"This is my wife, Victoria," Paul beamed.

"Please know you are very welcome here. We are just a few, but the One we worship here will be glorified and lifted up."

Tears were welling up in Sherry's eyes. "I'm sorry." She sniffed, wiping away the tears one by one. "I don't know why I am crying. It's good to meet you, Victoria."

Phillip felt a need to harness his antsy feelings. He wondered why the display of foolish emotions from his wife. He felt the gnaw of embarrassment. Awkwardly he patted Sherry on the back and then pulled back his hand as though she were a prickly cactus.

"Tears are okay here." Victoria smiled. "I'm afraid the pews aren't much, but we are new here. Just be careful not to snag your nylons." Her voice was like soft music.

"Yes, our lovely pews." Paul gestured with his hand to an empty and rickety piece of wood with legs.

With closed mouth and ragged breathing, Phillip took the cue and directed his family to sit.

Paul and Victoria picked up guitars, and another young man with a long, dark ponytail, dressed in blue jeans and a biker's jacket, took his place behind the drums. An older, silver-haired woman sat by the piano.

"Interesting choir," Phillip whispered in Sherry's ear. He felt a little peeved at his wife, who appeared moon-stricken, staring straight ahead as though she hadn't even heard him.

The small congregation of about eight other people stood. Phillip struggled to pull his large frame off the bench without accepting a splinter in his rear on the way up.

"This is one of my favorites by Dallas Holm." Paul's face was shining. "Jesus Christ rose again. No matter what people are saying about Jesus. He is the powerful risen Christ today. He wants to live powerfully in each of our lives. But the choice is ours." He signaled to the others about to lead praise and worship with a nod of his head.

Words in bold black appeared on the screen behind the music team under the title "Rise Again."

The strumming and drumming rhythm was amplified and riveting. The small assembly joined in, singing along. The words melded into a glorious harmony. Phillip felt his heart bucking like a wild colt as the words penetrated his mind. Beautiful words were falling all around him like soft rain. He was mesmerized, listening: "Go ahead; drive the nails in my hands. Laugh at Me where you stand."

Phillip felt a strange presence. He could see it on all the faces around him. Sherry was sobbing uncontrollably. Blake's eyes were wide and fixed. Jack leaned forward so far on the edge of his seat, he could be in danger of falling off from an air puff. Jamie sat firm and uncompromising against her seat. Her unyielding eyes were slanted to the side of her seat. The people on the other benches were lifting their hands, and celebration seemed to be etched in their faces.

"Go ahead," the singers continued. "Say I'm dead and gone. But you will see that you were wrong."

A quiet hush filled the small room. The stillness felt almost unbearable to Phillip. All the strangers about him had bowed heads.

After asking the assembly to turn to Mark 16, Paul's voice came bold and clear. "'Now when He rose early on the first day of the week, He appeared first to Mary Magdalene, out of whom He had cast seven demons. She went and told those who had been with Him, as they mourned and wept. And when they heard that He was alive and had been seen by her, they did not believe. After that, He appeared in another form to two of them as they walked and went into the country. And they went and told it to the rest, but they did not believe them either. Later He appeared to the eleven as they sat at the table; and He rebuked their unbelief and hardness of heart, because they did not believe those who had seen Him after He had risen. And He said to them, "Go into all the world and preach the gospel to every creature. He who believes and is baptized will be saved; but he who does not believe will be condemned. And these signs will follow those who believe: In My name they will cast out demons; they will speak with new tongues; they will take up serpents; and if they drink anything deadly, it will by no means hurt them; they will lay hands on the sick, and they will recover." So then, after the Lord had spoken to them, He was received up into heaven, and sat down at the right hand of God. And they went out and preached everywhere, the Lord working with them and confirming the word through the accompanying signs.'"

Phillip's mouth hinged open briefly, taken back in surprise. *How can one who seems so meek and laid back speak so valiantly, so sure of what he is saying?*

Sherry bent over to whisper in Phillip's ear. "Oh. I knew this Jesus was so powerful. It says it in the Bible. And I can tell this pastor and his wife have been with this Jesus. He is written all over them. I just know that. They seem so plain, yet they are bold and excited and full of the kind of life I want. They have what I want!"

Phillip rolled his eyes. "Please refrain from such quick conclusions. This is just one man's opinion."

"But that man is Jesus who said it." Sherry's voiced raised slightly above a whisper.

Embarrassed, Phillip looked up and met Paul's eyes.

"What I have just read are the very words of God." Paul smiled and laid his Bible on the shaky pulpit. "As you might guess, we are celebrating a risen Jesus. Jesus did many miracles while walking here as a man. He came as man, yet He was God, walking in flesh. He was called Emmanuel, meaning 'God with us.' The Apostle Paul said, 'That I might know Him and the power of His resurrection.' You may ask today why there are not as many miracles as happened in the days when Jesus walked as God in the flesh down here. The Bible tells us that there were times when He wanted to do miracles but was not able to do them because of unbelief. One time He came to His own hometown, and He wanted to show them His power. But they didn't believe Him. It's like that today. Many do not believe in a God of miracles.

"Isn't it interesting," Paul continued, "from the Scripture we read about a woman named Mary Magdalene who encountered the resurrected Lord. She believed Him to be God. She believed He had risen from the dead. This Jesus had delivered her from seven demons. Is it any wonder she was the first person to rise up early and seek Him? This woman was hungry for His life-changing presence."

Paul walked and stood between the pews. "I'm so excited. This week a young man experienced a miraculous deliverance from demons and mental illness. I have personally spoken with him. He is now dressed and in his right mind. Praise God! He is hungry to have the Word of God poured into Him. Why? Because He believes. He has experienced the resurrection power of Christ."

Phillip was busy jotting down words.

Paul paused and then seemed to struggle to pull a good amount of air into his lungs. "From our Scripture we read that Jesus had to rebuke His own disciples for their unbelief and hardness of heart. After He had spoken to them and they understood, He commissioned them to go into to all the world preaching the gospel. His resurrection power was to be in them, and they were to do great exploits in His name.

"What about today? Shouldn't His resurrection power still operate in the lives of those who call themselves Christians?" Paul's voice grew serious. "Or are we the generation of Christians who have grown lukewarm? Is God about to vomit out people whose belief in Him is dying and lukewarm?"

Phillip cringed. He couldn't picture a God vomiting people out of His mouth.

"I'm concerned," Paul continued. "Jesus Christ did a miracle. A young man, hurting and abused from when he was just a baby, was set free from horrible bondage. It was the miraculous resurrection power of Jesus Christ those demons encountered. They couldn't stay. They fled. Jesus Christ is the King of kings. He has the authority to set the captive free. He does what He sees His Father doing. He bears the mark of God, which is unsurpassed and what is unconditional love. He hasn't changed just because people think He no longer performs miracles. I have heard many people, and sadly many who say they believe in Jesus explain what happened to Charley was not because demons were commanded to leave in Jesus name. I tell you, it was in the name of Jesus Christ that demons were commanded to leave. It was by the name of Jesus Christ that Charley is set free today. Jesus is the captive's Redeemer."

The gathering of people stood and began praising the name of Jesus. Sherry stood. She began clapping her hands wildly. Phillip squirmed. *This thing is getting out of hand now.* He felt like sinking under the splintery bench. *It ain't big enough to hide me. I'm too big to get under it anyway.* So Phillip stood, keeping his head lowered.

"Before we close," Paul was speaking again, "I want to open the altar for prayer. If you need physical healing or emotional healing, come. If you are crying out to know Jesus as your own personal Savior and friend, or if you just want more of Jesus in your life, come and I will pray with you."

Tears were washing Sherry's face as though a pan of warm water had been dumped over her face. She moved quickly to the front of the building, dabbing her nose with a Kleenex.

Phillip stood up, his arms uncoiled, and his jaw dropped. *Why does she need to become so emotionally involved now? This is supposed to be a business trip to church. She's going to get us too deeply involved.*

Music played softly in the background. Sherry was up front weeping. Phillip, bowled over unexpectedly, felt his legs weaken. *How embarrassing. Why is she making such a fuss and over what?* Phillip noticed the pastor was standing by Sherry.

"I just know I need this Jesus, Pastor. I need to experience the miraculous things Jesus can do in my life. And I need to know He will forgive me for all the wrong I've done and caused in my life. I need help with my kids, too. I just need help. Deep inside I am a mess."

Phillip began to pace. He could hear bits and pieces of the pastor's prayer, and Sherry asking Jesus to be Lord of her life. Her sobs continued in between the words. Though he had no mental explanation, his emotional wife sunk to her knees on the floor.

As soon as the prayer altar subsided and people began streaming for the door, Phillip inquired of Paul how he might get in contact with the eyewitness man, John.

"Give me your number, Phillip, and I will have John contact you. And I will gladly give you my number as well." Paul took Phillip's hand again. "I want you to know we enjoyed having you and your family in our church today."

"You gave me a lot to think about. I thank you for that. But in my business, I need to gather all the facts," Phillip answered with an imposing posture.

Phillip felt like he had ants crawling all over his body. He needed to get Sherry out of this place before she fell to pieces again.

Phillip noticed the kids had made a beeline for the car. He turned to find Sherry. She was standing next to the pastor's wife. Sherry was listening intently. While she was still crying, there was laughing, too. Phillip's heart thumped angrily at his wife.

Then he heard Sherry say, "Yes, I will be coming back. I am so excited to learn more. God brought me here today. I know that. He has answered my prayer at last."

This is a story gone wrong.

Chapter Five

"No! I said no, Phillip!" Abby lashed out and fluttered about like an unwinding wind-up toy. "Phillip, you know how nervous I would be? They'll all be lions ready to shred what little sanity I have left!"

"Now, Ab, all you'll be asked to do is defend the facts," Phillip said calmly, towering over her like a gentle giant. "Just calm down now. Get a good night's sleep, and you'll feel better about it tomorrow."

"Calm down?" Abby asked. "Be reasonable, Phillip! Have you forgotten that Charley's miracle has captured national attention? This sort of thing isn't supposed to happen and darn it, Phillip, people are going to be glued to their televisions to listen to the debate—to find out why it did happen!"

Sherry came into the room, bringing cookies and iced tea. "This is your chance, Abby." Sherry's words glided sweetly across the room. "Hundreds of people will be watching from their own living rooms. Some of them may be just like Charley. Abby, many who listen will be broken inside. They need to know that Jesus can fix them, too. You can tell them that!"

"What happened to you?" Abby gasped. "Am I missing something here?"

Sherry's hands crossed her heart. "Well, I touched Him!"

"Touched who?" Abby's voice peaked with exasperation.

"Here we go again." Phillip grabbed onto his head.

"I touched Jesus," Sherry exclaimed. "I found out how much He loves me. It is so incredible! I was so wanting to meet Him. So I reached out and touched Him!"

"But that's not possible," Abby crossed-examined. "Jesus isn't here any longer. He left us and went to heaven."

"Just the same, I touched Him," Sherry insisted.

"What did He look like then?" Abby's eyes snapped back at Sherry in defiance.

"I didn't see Him, Abby. He was there just the same. My heart was reaching for Him somehow. He let me touch Him that way. I can't explain it really. Still it was real." Sherry's eyes became tear collectors.

"Okay." Phillip stood. "We are getting off course here," he announced while snapping his fingers.

"Sherry, what Abby needs to do now is understand the facts and stick with them," Phillip continued as he attempted to steady himself by leaning into the wall. "She doesn't need any other muddle in her head right now!"

"Tell me again, Phillip," Abby interjected, "who all is going to be on this panel? And why weren't you selected to be a spokesperson for the paper? You are the editor, for goodness' sake!"

"Well, because you wrote the article. And maybe," Phillip said with emphasis, "maybe it is because you are the closest known living relative of Charley's." Phillip glanced away and tried in vain to rub away the stress from his forehead.

"So," Abby repeated, "who else will be on this panel?"

"They can't find Charley. He has mysteriously disappeared. Otherwise he would be there. I'm sure Jasper will want to say a few things. Reverend Staunch will probably be there, and I can imagine they will ask Dr. Soothers, Charley's psychiatrist, to participate. I really don't know who all will be participating. I'm not sure why this matters to you."

"Cuz, I want to know who will be there for me!" Abby's eyes widened and froze in place. "That preacher knows me as a worthless orphan girl, tossed from home to home. Just because you picked me up off the street and gave me a job isn't going to cut it with the reverend. He's out to prove Charley's theory wrong. He's out to nail my story as well. After all, he can prove through the media that a misfit doesn't have a voice to stand on."

"Here, Abby, have a cookie." Sherry smiled as she stuck a plate of moist oatmeal cookies in front of Abby's nose. "See, Phillip doesn't trust the uppity sort of people, either. He's been knocked down by them a few times himself, haven't you, dear?"

"Liars! That's what most of 'em are. They offer a lot of bull and then send the taker home with mere bones." Phillip's words smoked.

"That's why," Sherry continued, "Phillip is such a caregiver of those taken advantage of by the bullies." Sherry's arm wrapped around Abby. "He sees honesty and determination in you, Abby. He's a good judge of character." She smiled warmly. "Anyway, I know what it's like to look down on myself. I was told all my life I was a nobody by my parents, schoolteachers, everybody. My first husband beat me silly many times with his hands and his words. I believed it to be my fault and that I deserved to be hated and abused. I thought I was a misfit too. But"—her smile sparkled—"Phillip showed me that not all people are so hateful."

"I'm so sorry to hear someone hurt you so." Abby felt an old whirlwind whipping through the history book in her mind. "It's never right."

"What's more"—Sherry's excitement soared like a kite too high to be pulled down—"I found out that Jesus loves me more than I could ever love myself. More than any person, even Phillip, could love me."

Phillip unwrapped his arms from around the chair he had straddled and reached for another cookie. "Like I said, Ab, all you need to do is stick with the facts."

"Oh, Phillip"—Sherry lit up brightly—"wouldn't it be wonderful if Pastor Paul could be there? That would certainly ease Abby's mind."

"Sherry," Phillip said, gagging on the last cookie crumb, "that young man talks too bold for his age or his experience. What Abby needs is confidence in her own mind to stick with the facts. Nothing more and nothing less!"

Abby stood and grabbed her sweater. "Well, it would be nice to have someone there to support me." She hugged Sherry. "Thanks for letting me drop by to air my fears. It's getting so late already. Past my bedtime."

"By the way," Phillip took on his boss voice, "tomorrow's the deadline. Got your assignment done? Hope you got something good out of Sunday's service!"

Abby heaved a breath. "Yeah, but it's short. And I'm thinking of cutting it down to one line. Simply stated, that preacher said Jesus isn't here to do those things anymore." Abby looked down at the floor. "I get the sense that his incorrigible message was aimed at Charley. He thinks Charley wouldn't be worth a miracle, even if Jesus was around to do it." Abby reached into a jean pocket and pulled out a crumbled sheet of paper. "Is this good enough? It's short, but to the point. And it is only the facts."

"Good," Phillip said with a yawn. "But the New Vision Church has a different story. They say what happened to Charley is a miracle indeed! So I'll just add a paragraph to spice your report up a little."

"I know it was a miracle," Sherry piped in.

"We all need some sleep now," Phillip answered, choosing to ignore Sherry's comment. "And, Ab, stop worrying. You have a couple days to jot notes and ideas down. Just make them brief facts." Phillip walked Abby to the door. "Remember only the facts and that's all. It's not about what you feel. It's about what you observed. Charley was dressed, in his right mind, and he says it all. You need say no more."

"Right," she said with a droopy head shake. "It's going to be just a piece of cake."

———⁓⁓⌒⌒⌒⌒⌒⁓⁓———

Abby breathed deeply of the scent of growing grass mingled with fresh country air. She wondered what it would be like to be loved and married and have a nice home in the country like Phillip and Sherry. The sky had changed into a dark set of pajamas by the time Abby drove into the little town of Edge Water. Everything seemed so still. There was very little traffic. There was no bright moon or singing stars to accompany Abby to her apartment door. *Eerie when it's like this.* She could feel her heart beating drums with each quick step she made.

Click. Click. Abby took her clogs off. She could walk faster without them; less noise too. Her fist was clenched tight about her cell phone. Only a few more steps to her apartment door. Too quiet now. She could hear herself struggling to breathe. The straps of her purse were tight about her neck. And she needed the keys from that purse. She reached up to pull the strap away from her neck. Her fingers were like slick ice and the cell phone slipped from them. Abby jumped. The phone hit the cement and rolled into the planted undergrowth. As she grabbed blindly for it, her finger snagged on the thorn of a rosebush stem. "Ouch!" Abby cried, putting a torn and bloody finger to her lips.

She saw a quick movement. Her heart beat weakened. "It's time to come with me."

The voice chilled to her bones. A large, gloved hand pushed her throbbing, bleeding finger tight against her face. She was unable to scream.

Oh God, is this the man who killed my sister? Is this Charley's father?

Abby was feeling light-headed. She needed air, but the hand remained strong against her airway. She struggled some, but a dark fog took over and she felt like she was spinning. Her body swayed along with it. Just as the darkness was growing black, the man released his hand, and from under the flicker of her porch light, Abby caught a glint of a large signet ring dangling from the man's neck. Something like an ill-shaped goat head was imprinted on it. Then she saw the shiny surface of something under the dimness of the hiding moon. *A knife!* The moment stood still. Silence. Deadly silence. She waited in horror.

The knife flashed before Abby's face. "This is just a friendly warning. You say nothing, and nobody will get hurt. You need to disappear for a while. It's best that way."

Under the nearly moonless night and behind closed doors, some of the guys met, breathing in smoke and blowing it out. The stuff billowed around them like ghosts playing in a sauna.

"You better have had this planned well." The wide-shouldered man said, looking like a powerhouse tycoon, as he pushed his cigarette into the ashtray, grinding the thing to cold powder. "He better not kill her."

"No, boss. We know this is too important to mess up."

"How do I know that?" the voice boomed from somewhere within the man's ox-shaped head. "There've been mistakes already." His fingers were twisting and then curling into fists. "I've heard reports that he is still alive. You could have missed something, not seen something. I need proof. You say you did him in. I need proof now."

"It's the truth!" said a confident voice, as the smoother faced, mustached man stood from behind his desk. "I'm telling you, Oscar, John is dead. When he turned the ignition on, he blew up with the car. He's gone! I saw what was left of that car. Nothing, that's what. It's covered up well. Nothing to worry about."

"Then who is that mysterious man who just happened to be there when Charley got a new brain?" He cursed under his breath. "I don't give a damn if you swear that twenty-five years ago you blew this man up. There's only one man I know who could accomplish something like this. Everything about what happened to Charley reminds me of him. What happened near Jasper's smells of John."

Phillip did not feel rested. He thought it might have been his last huge toss in bed when the idea came to him. He needed to find Charley, and it couldn't wait. He had already called Paul. Paul would take him there.

"Think Abby would like to go with?" Sherry asked.

"No. She is already worked up about this thing." Phillip looked up over his cup of coffee at Sherry. "So you understand that you must not involve her in this. Just let her rest today. The kid is exhausted with worry."

"Okay. I'm planning to take Jamie out to lunch today anyway. I think we need some mother-daughter time."

The sausage patty was sputtering in its own grease, and Sherry turned down the burner. She placed a small plate with buttered toast and scrambled eggs on the table before Phillip. "Want your coffee warmed?"

"No, thanks. I've got to hurry. Need to get back to the office as quickly as possible to make sure the paper will be ready to roll tomorrow."

"Are you going to try to get Charley to the media debate tomorrow?" she questioned. "What could they say to refute his testimony?"

"Not sure," he replied, "but I suspect they are up to something."

Sherry put the sausage patty next to his eggs. Her hand reached out and rested on Phillip's shoulder. "You are worried about this, aren't you, Phillip?"

His head hung a bit. "I just have a bad sense about it all, and I'm not sure where this is all headed."

"Please, Phillip, ask Pastor Paul to pray with you about all of this. This may be out of your hands altogether. It may need to be put entirely in God's hands now."

Paul's directions were good. Phillip found Paul's house without any trouble. It was surrounded by a lovely grove of birch. Phillip stepped out of the car, and his gloom vanished. He felt the arms of the soft cloud above him reach down and pull him into its serenity. A woodpecker was busy pecking on the bird feeder. A couple little sparrows darted about, wishing the noisy woodpecker would leave.

Paul opened the door and waved for Phillip to come inside his screened-in porch.

Charley met Phillip at the door with a vigorous handshake. "I'd be honored to be on the panel. In fact, it has already been arranged." Charley turned and wrapped a lanky arm around the long, silver-haired, and bearded man standing alongside him. "And this is John."

"Oh." Phillip sounded as though he were gargling. He reached for John's hand.

"I am pleased to meet you, Phillip." John's hand felt hot in Phillip's grasp.

"You have no idea how thankful I am to have both of you here this morning," Phillip added, while noting the unusual quietness about this John guy.

"Charley," Phillip continued, "your aunt Abby is worried sick." He was shaking his head. "She gets so flustered sometimes that I fear she could make a mess of things in front of those bloodhounds."

Paul's wife, Victoria, brought a pitcher of cold pink lemonade, which sparkled as she poured it into glasses. Paul began distributing the drinks out.

Confidence echoed in Charley's voice. "She did a great job with the newspaper article. Still, I would want to be there to support her."

Phillip's eye was still on John. *Let me guess. You're a man of few words. Mysterious too.*

Phillip harrumphed. "So, John, thank you for meeting with me. As you know, I am a newspaper reporter, and I am at loss of words about all that has happened. Charley's aunt Abby works for me, and as a result she is in the middle of it all. Charley said we could all be in danger. I was hoping you could fill in the puzzle pieces for me."

The man sat down and folded his hands, his elbows rested on the patio table. "Phillip, you are a very important link in this puzzle. God desires to use you to print the truth. It isn't going to be as easy as you think."

"Why's that?"

"Do you believe in God, Phillip?" John asked as a breeze as calm as the man himself fingered through his silvery beard.

"I haven't answered that question myself yet," Phillip admitted.

John chuckled. "Yes, I see that."

"It isn't a decision to take lightly I'm thinking." Phillip smiled back.

"That question is going to be put to the test." John's words were like a chilly net wrapping about Phillip. "The bloodhounds are following an evil scent. Their ears are acutely aware of voices you and I are unable to hear. Printing the truth will not make them happy. What they hear is not the truth, for they do not know the truth." John stood and walked closer to Phillip. "To know God is to learn only of the truth, Phillip. Be aware the battle is against the truth. I would bring to your attention many religious leaders today will only accept parts of the truth. The remaining lies, however, control their minds. Therefore, great becomes their deception."

Phillip shivered. He had already made sacrifices for the truth. He had stood up and been shot down. He had lost his job because he hadn't backed down. Could he lose more for the truth? John's hand was heavy on Phillip's arm. "You will be tempted to believe a few lies in the days ahead. That will be one of the greatest dangers you will face. I am praying you will know the truth, which will set you free."

<hr/>

"Wake up, Phillip. It's already seven o'clock."

He sat up in bed, stretching his upper torso. "Is it raining out?"

"Pouring. I had to shut all the windows. You've really been out of it, honey. I heard lots of mumbling, sometimes louder than the thunder." Sherry's eyes were glued on his. "You said things like 'You better tell the truth,' several times." She moved closer to him, touching his nose with hers. "And you said, 'If it isn't the truth, it is dangerous.'"

"Oh dear. Has Abby called?"

"Not yet, Phillip."

He jumped out of bed. "Can't believe she hasn't called yet. She has to be beside herself by now."

"I'll get the phone," Sherry offered. "And breakfast is ready."

"Uh, great. Thanks. I think I need Advil, too. This headache's a bugger."

Sherry was quick to bring the phone. Her eyebrow's arched in question. "You are really worried about something? There's more to this story than Charley versus Jasper, isn't there? What's going on?"

He shrugged his shoulders. "I don't even know."

She handed him the Advil and a glass of water. Her eyes were as fixed as cement on him. "But there is more, and you aren't telling me. Why?"

"She's not answering her cell. She always has that thing with her. What a time not to answer!" Phillip's voice shot an octave higher.

"Maybe her cell isn't working. You know how cell phones are." Sherry blew out a frustrated breath. "Why don't you eat? You can try again later. And over breakfast you can tell me what's going on."

Phillip was chugging down his coffee, skipping sips. His right fingers were tapping the table in a frantic rhythm, like drumsticks gone mad.

"Okay. Yes, there may be danger, but I'm not getting a straight answer from anybody. Charley told Abby that his mom was murdered. He said his father was a dangerous man and we could be in danger. Honest to God, that is all I know."

"That is why Abby feels threatened to put her answers on the line?"

Phillip tried calling Abby again. "Still no answer."

"Phillip. We need to start praying together."

Phillip took a couple more bites of cereal. "I'm not hungry this morning."

"Please, Phillip, we need to learn how to pray together. I wanted to talk to you about Jamie, too. I've told you before that I'm worried about our kids."

Phillip looked up and met Sherry's eyes. He could see shadows, like dark curtains, hanging below his wife's eyes.

"Jamie is into something. I think it's some kind of devil stuff. I told her about Jesus, and she wants nothing to do with Him. It's as though she doesn't own her own mind anymore." Sherry wiped away a tear from her pleading eyes. "I heard her explaining something to Jack. She said she couldn't wait for him to come with her. And there was something about a goddess and a god and divinity dwelling in her inner self."

"Oh, I wouldn't worry, Sherry. Kids are always interested in the far-out things. First, they are afraid of monsters. Then they want to catch the monsters. I'm sure it's harmless," he said, picking up the phone again.

"Phillip! Like you said in your dreams last night, 'If it isn't the truth, it's dangerous.'" Sherry's words swooped down upon him as an eagle grabbing its prey.

"Yeah, yeah. But what is the truth, and what isn't the truth? That's the question." He half-growled while pushing the redial. "Darn. She is still not answering the phone. Sherry, I've got to check on her. Something isn't sitting right in my stomach."

"It's the investigator in you. You have your fingers in too far now to pull them out."

He stopped to hold her hand. "But believe me, Sherry, I haven't wanted to put anyone in danger."

Phillip pushed the apartment's buzzer down again. He was shifting his weight back and forth from one leg to another. Abby wasn't answering. He felt like a helpless critter sinking in quicksand. Where was he to look? What was he to do? "This isn't like Abby." He reached for his cell.

"Paul, this is Phillip. Listen I'm worried about Abby. She's not answering her phone or her door. I haven't a clue where to find her. So I was wondering if you have a number where I could reach John. Far as I know, he is the only one who might be able to provide me a place to start looking for Abby."

"John's right here. I'll hand the phone over to him."

"John?"

"Yes. What's wrong, Phillip?"

"I can't find Abby. I'm worried. If her sister was murdered, I think I have a reason to be concerned should Abby disappear. It is not like her not to answer her cell phone. She isn't home, either. I just checked."

"I suspect you have a reason to be concerned. I'm guessing they have her where they want her for now."

"They?" Philip could feel the blood rushing up his face. "They who?" he demanded.

"Phillip, there is usually more than one rat in a garbage dump, especially one piled up this high," John answered while stroking his beard. "These guys don't want to be found hiding in this stinking refuse they've created. They fear Charley's recovery. He didn't pose a threat to them before, but he does now. Furthermore, he could have talked to Abby. That makes her a danger to their survival too."

Phillip lifted a hand to rub his temples. "She is in grave danger then."

"They do not want her talking at the debate today. They do not yet know Charley will be on the panel. We have been careful about that. They are curious about Charley's disappearance and have been attempting to uncover his whereabouts. These are serious matters of prayer. What do you want to do, Phillip?"

"I want to find Abby. John, we've got to find her before they kill her."

"Got any ideas on where to begin looking for her? On where to go from here?" John's question hung like wet air.

"She hasn't been gone long enough for a missing person's report to become active." Phillip gave a short cough to clear his throat. "I have a friend, Caleb Mettle, who is an FBI investigator. I'm going to run this all by him. After that, I don't know what to do. I don't think God would listen to me, even if I did know how to pray."

Then they said to him again, "What did He do to you? How did He open your eyes?"

He answered them, "I told you already, and you did not listen. Why do you want to hear it again? Do you also want to become His disciples?"

Then they reviled him and said, "You are His disciple, but we are Moses' disciples. We know that God spoke to Moses: as for this fellow, we do not know where He is from."

The man answered and said to them, "Why, this is a marvelous thing, that you do not know where He is from; yet He has opened my eyes! Now we know that God does not hear sinners; but if anyone is a worshiper of God and does His will, He hears him. Since the world began it has been unheard of that anyone opened the eyes of one who was born blind. If this Man were not from God, He could do nothing."

They answered and said to him, "You were completely born in sins, and are you teaching us?" And they cast him out. (John 9:26-34 NKJV).

Chapter Six

Abby stirred and struggled to open her eyes. Her face was on a hard surface. She was lying on her side, and one arm was under her. *Have I been drugged?* She managed to wiggle the fingers of her free hand. She attempted to open her mouth to yawn and breathe deeply enough to oxygenate her senses. Abby finally managed to get a hand to her face and then pry open her right eye. It wasn't dark out. On the floor, immediately in front of her, was vomit. She could smell it now. Abby wondered if someone had chained a log to her head. It felt so heavy and barely moveable. When she did try to move it, the pain was intense. She propped her free hand and found enough strength to push up enough to see beyond her nose.

There was an old single bed frame. She could see into the bathroom because the door was open. Abby attempted to crane her neck in the other direction, toward the drip, drip, drip sound. Above an old sink and a drippy faucet, a chipped and cracked mirror leaned forward like a phantom spy.

Weakness was engulfing her again. Abby slid back down and grabbed at her head. It was as though a wild stallion was rearing and his hooves came down with force on her head. Then the fingers of darkness closed her eyes once again.

Sherry switched channels. "It should be starting in just a minute or two." She snuggled on the loveseat with Phillip. "Thousands of people will be watching. And to think we are so involved with something capturing national attention!"

"I'm not expecting this to conclude like a Jack-fell-down-the-hill-and-Jill-came-tumbling-after debate." His thoughts dragged into words.

"Worried a little about Abby, are you?"

"Yes, and a heap more than a little."

Anchorwoman Stella Delsey appeared on the screen. Bright-red lipstick matched her red and ruffle-sleeved dress and accented her fair complexion. "Good morning, panel contestants. We will be addressing a very interesting subject today." Her voice boasted with enthusiasm. "Some are referring to the unusual event, which happened April first, as a miracle. Others look at it as a very unfortunate April Fool's Day joke. Some believe a crime is behind what happened. Some give praise to modern interventions and the evolution of the brain. Others say, like in Bible days, Jesus is the miracle maker who delivered a young man from a legion of demons." Stella smiled for the camera and then turned toward the panel participants.

"What a surprise today to welcome Charley himself to this panel. We are glad you decided to show up. I'm sure all across this country people are anxious to see for themselves the young and changed man you claim to be."

Charley smiled. He leaned against his chair as though cushioned by unseen arms. "It is with joy I come today."

"Yes, I can tell. You seem very happy to be here. And, of course," Stella continued, "Jasper is here to explain his view on how he lost most of his prize Angus cows early that morning."

Jasper charged from his seat, like a disturbed bee from its hive. "Why you no-good, Bible-thumping fool! You would rob me of my cattle!"

Two men from the panel, shaken from their ivory seats, pulled the crazed Jasper off Charley. Jasper's sandpaper hands grabbed and yanked savagely at a white shirt, ripping it off a young officer's chest.

Next the camera zoomed in for a quick look at Stella, who's porcelain face strained as though it were about to break; then it resumed videoing the skirmish between Jasper and his two challengers.

The officer, and the other distinguished-looking gentleman, though noticeably disheveled, finally stood victoriously with the disgruntled Jasper's hands pinned behind his back. The video captured the moment's gallantry before homing in on Jasper's blood-red face. He sputtered, "I demand that man pay for what he did to my cattle!" Within seconds, two uniformed men came out of the background crowd, handcuffed the angry, bearded man, and dragged him away. Curses spewed from Jasper's mouth as he kicked and balked before thousands of viewers.

The camera's lens yawned in relief as it aimed and cradled around Charley, whose head was bowed silently.

Stella broke the silence, yanking the leash of her viewers. "Thank you, Mr. Richards." She forced a smile. "After such a heroic intervention, Chief Deputy Jason Richards, from our law enforcement, hardly needs an introduction to our panel today."

Jason looked down with gawkiness at his bare chest. He smiled back, red-faced, at Stella. "I'm happy to be here today, Stella. I've always liked a little action with any show."

"So I see." Stella's eyes raised as she drew in a deep breath. "Also, thank you to Michael Routes. You men did a marvelous job recouping order here."

Michael was attempting to rearrange his mussed-up, thick head of hair as cherry-red blotches colored up his neck. The slight sag in his plump cheeks tightened with his pleasant and round-lipped smile. "My pleasure to be here, Stella. I think that guy ran off with a handful of my hair."

Stella nodded, returning the smile. "Looks like you have plenty left anyway." She looked back into the camera. "Michael too will join us today. Michael, as most of you know, is chairman of the County Commissioners for Perjure County."

With a tilt of her head, Stella continued. "Now let's introduce the other panel voices. Dr. Soothers is here to verify that the dramatic change in Charley indeed did happen. He will attempt to explain the change in Charley's mental health."

The psychiatrist shifted his torso, posturing himself like a peacock before a group of ugly ducklings. "Ah, yes, Stella, I believe we are seeing remarkable strides in mental-health interventions. I am proud to be represented here."

"And we have two clergymen represented here today. Let's welcome Reverend Richard Staunch, who is chairman of the ministerial. He pastors the God's Love Fellowship Church in Mirage County."

The reverend blew a breath through dilated nostrils. His lips penciled a thin smile. He sat straight-backed, taking the spotlight like a veteran ready to receive a gold medal.

"Thank you, Stella. Glad to be a part today."

"Also with us is Reverend Paul Marvel from the New Vision Church in Perjure County, where the event happened in the first place," the anchorwoman added with a nervous twitch of her chin.

Paul's right cowboy boot was dangling beneath his crossed leg. His demeanor appeared as youthful and genuine as the first tulip in the spring's sun.

"Thank you, Stella. I am delighted to be here and attest to Charley's testimony."

Stella tossed her sun-bleached head of hair in front of the camera. "And last, but by far least, I introduce you to Lorsey Zany. Lorsey is here to represent the PMHA.

Lorsey, would you be kind enough to explain this to all those viewing our telecast today?"

Lorsey pursed her dark painted lips. She fluttered her eyelashes and ran a hand through her long, black-dyed hair. "Why, Stella," Lorsey's words poured like honey onto toast, "I am proud to introduce our organization, PMHA. We are the People for the Mental Health of Animals."

"Thank you, Lorsey. I'm sure we are all looking forward to your input in our discussion today." Stella smiled impishly.

"Oh, this oughta be good." Phillip groaned. "Like a circus sideshow! Will the next contestant please stand up!"

"What does animal mental health have to do with Charley's recovery?" Sherry drew a blank expression.

"Good question. I doubt, however, this woman thinks she is just a pawn on a chessboard. No. No. She looks like she is about to prove she is the queen who cannot be cornered."

———

Voices? Abby moaned. She lifted her face from her arm, which lay heavily across something cracked and white. *A toilet? Why am I sitting on a floor and resting against a toilet?* She tried shaking the grogginess from her head. She needed to think. Then the voices came back.

"I paid those lugs good money and Charley still made it through those doors," a low voice growled.

"And he sits now before thousands of television viewers talking and in his complete mind," a second, more monotone voice answered. "You were worried about what the girl might say at the debate. Kidnapping her has only put us in deeper."

"Well you're a lawyer. Come up with something. Anything. Make it look like an accident. I don't care."

"I thought you gave strict orders not to kill her? Now you want me to find a legal way to dispose of her?" said the second voice again, spitting out the words.

Abby stared into the toilet bowl. For a bleak moment it looked like a bottomless chasm. An involuntary shudder went through her whole body. She had to think quickly. She had to do something. But what? With a deep breath and both hands now propped on the toilet seat, Abby pushed up. Her legs followed.

She was in a very small bathroom. *The window isn't even big enough for me to fit through.* Abby took a few steps to the door, holding on to the wall, just in case her rubbery legs gave out. She put her ear against the door.

"Whose going to write the suicide note?" the first voice said with low, basement-grating words.

"She is."

Abby swallowed hard. She guessed the men planning her suicide were a fair distance away from her. That didn't make the chance of escaping this place any easier. She didn't have a clue where she was, nor where she might run if she even had a chance to. Her hand shook its way to the door knob. Carefully she tried to turn it. Locked from the outside. Abby's face paled. Her life was in the hands of the plunger now, and she need only wait for the violent move.

"Then call those lame-brain lugs back. They've got some dirty work to do," the first voice demanded.

———⁓⁓⌯⌯———

"Charley." Stella used her baby-side voice, as though Charley were a lap puppy. "I think you are aware that Jasper is blaming you for the death of his cows. Did you chase Jasper's cows into the icy river?"

"No. I did nothing to those cows," Charley answered without flinching a muscle.

Stella paused as though she were mentally fingering through index cards. "Two very strange events happened simultaneously on April first." Stella let out a strange little belly laugh. "We are trying to determine this evening, through the help of our panel, the reason for these occurrences. Maybe one or maybe both of these happenings were nothing more than a big April Fool's joke. Problem is, Charley, you are sitting here very much changed. I'm not sure that can be explained away." Stella leaned forward, kind of hungry looking. "Charley, tell us what happened to you on the first day of April."

"My story hasn't changed, Stella." Charley looked up. An invisible infusion of peace and confidence pumped throughout his countenance. "Just like I said before, I had been tormented by hundreds of voices. These voices chased me. I ran in fear. But a man of God came to visit me. He introduced me to Jesus. It was Jesus who set me free. It was Jesus who sent those voices away. All I know is that Jesus made me the new man I am today."

Dr. Soothers harrumphed. "I'd like to add a few words here, Stella, if I may."

"Yes, go ahead, Doctor," Stella obliged.

"We had been seeing positive changes in Charley,"he began with a left-lipped curve to his smile. "One must understand, however, that when a person shows such severe dissociative symptoms as Charley had clearly demonstrated, results from psychotherapy can vary. Sometimes after a long period of intensive treatment, as I would now venture to claim, dramatic results have been known to occur in such an instantaneous manner."

"Could you elaborate a little more on what you mean by dissociative symptoms and the associated treatments?" Stella's right hand flew to her chest. "And," she continued, "are you claiming that Charley has been cured by these therapeutics?"

"Well," the doctor continued in a calculated drawl, "dissociative symptoms result from being detached from normal mental activities and functions. People become detached from themselves because they have no sense of identity." Dr. Soothers, still sitting stiff-backed in his chair, glanced over at Charley. "Charley, like others with these symptoms, had switched to alternate personalities. He could actually feel the presence of these other people living in his head."

"Oh my." Stella gasped.

"Yes, and consequently, he put a greater distance between himself and his identity."

"And so," Stella interrupted, "how did you treat Charley?"

After a long, premeditated exhalation, Dr. Soother's continued. "Though Charley was mute, he sat in on talk therapy with other clients. He was also on psychotropics and was treated for anxiety."

"So Charley is cured?" Stella pushed for answers.

"Time will tell. Sometimes personalities change to more positive beings. It is possible that he has now switched to better personalities, which appear more normal and acceptable to society. In any case," the doctor concluded, "the change is better."

"Reverend Staunch," Stella addressed, "you look anxious to comment on what Dr. Soothers has so masterfully presented."

"Absolutely," the word squeaked out. He cleared his throat and attempted to loosen the white collar, which could possibly become a lethal rope wrapped so tightly around his skinny neck. "I couldn't agree more with the good doctor. The word *psych* is a Greek word meaning "breath" and "life." Indeed psychotherapy is a marvelous method of caring for the soul. No doubt in this process Charley has been learning to center in on his inner self. He is giving himself permission to do what he needs to do!"

"So," Stella butted in, "what about God? Do you think this is a miracle of God in anyway?"

The reverend looked up above his glasses as a scornful chuckle rumbled from his mouth. "There are branches of religion that chase after the eccentric. You know some churches teach that miracles are like bumps all over a goose. Everything that happens is not a miracle from God. It is usually not God's will to heal. If He chooses, yes. But God has given men brains down here. Men have made great breakthroughs in science and medicine. In that sense, yes, I believe God is in this, Stella. Have no doubt about that! There is spirituality in balancing our emotional, mental, physical, and spiritual energies with harmony. Spirituality is an empowerment to change and to find a correct identity. I think we see God in this way by what is happening to Charley."

Stella smacked her rounded red lips together just as the camera zeroed in on her face. "Well, I think these deliberations are challenging and interesting. And"—she smiled—"there's more to come, right after this break."

Abby heard the many steps coming toward the bathroom door. She slumped to the floor, sensing her heart was about to give out. *Play dead.* The thought came to her, as though she were being approached by a bear. *Like that would stop these men.* She was about to dismiss the thought, *but maybe I could pretend I am too drugged to write a note.*

The door was opening. The thud of feet close to her head. "She's still out of it," the first voice grumbled.

"She'll be easier to throw in the trunk this way. We'll get her to where she needs to be. She'll come out of it soon enough. Let's get her wrapped in that blanket."

"Okay, men. You know what to do. No money until the job is done right. And, if it isn't done right this time, you guys will be the next victims," the first voice said, now more rabid sounding.

Abby purposed to keep her body limp. Rough hands under her neck, pulled her hair painfully away from her scalp as they lifted her upper torso. The other arms forcefully lifted her from under her knees. They dumped her onto something wool, which she guessed was the blanket, and rolled her around in it.

"On the count of three then," an unidentified voice added, "One, two, three." Abby was lifted off the floor like a dead person in a body bag, only she was sagging in the middle of the material.

"Okay. In the trunk with her," the unidentified voice sounded again.

"Wait, did you hear something?" a new voice asked.

"I don't think so. It was probably just Oscar checking up on us," the first unidentified voice guessed.

"No! Quick. Throw her in the back seat and let's get out of here!" The new voice raised an octave higher.

Inside the blanket Abby was being heaved toward something. Then unbearable pain shot throughout her head, followed by a feeling of floating in darkness.

Under the flicker of her eyelashes, Stella's lips opened wide into a welcoming smile. "Well, ladies and gentlemen, we are back. We have an excited group of contestants here, each biting at the bit to fill your ears. I'm going to ask the young minister, Paul, for his thoughts now," Stella said raking her fingers through her hair. "Paul, you listened to Reverend Staunch and Dr. Soothers. Both seem keen on the same philosophy, that mental health interventions are miraculous and even spiritual in themselves. Do you feel that Charley is the changed by-product of psychotherapy?"

Everyone's gaze shifted toward Paul.

Reverend Staunch's glare carried sparks ready to ignite into flames.

Paul's blue eyes, as a river soaking in the deep of heaven, met all stares with the very calm of resting waters.

"Of course not, Stella. I do not agree that Charley is a product of any mental-health intervention. God can heal through doctors and any human intervention, but God is not limited to human limitations. Jesus Christ is the captive's Redeemer. Jesus Christ did set Charley free. And it was a miracle."

Paul's eyes met Dr. Soothers. "Sir, you mentioned that people actually lived in Charley's mind. Those were demons. Charley was living in the kingdom of darkness. These evil forces owned him. On April first, Charley met Jesus Christ. Jesus is not just another personality that has produced a more positive change in Charley's life. Jesus Christ has delivered Charley from the kingdom of darkness and transferred him into the kingdom of light. Charley does have a new identity now. His identity is now found in Jesus."

"Oh," Stella exclaimed. "Interesting. So tell me, Paul, are you implying then that Jesus sent those demons into Jasper's herd of cattle, causing them death by drowning?"

"Yes! The Bible tells of another man, like Charley. This man was homeless and lived among the tombs. He didn't wear any clothes. He was filled with the hatred and the anger of demons. This man could rip off any chain or any shackle used to bind him. Great was this man's torment. People feared this man. Jesus stopped by this graveyard. Only Jesus loved this man. This man fell down before Jesus and cried out! And it was Jesus who commanded the demons to release this man from mental, emotional, and physical anguish. The demons begged Jesus to allow them to enter a herd of pigs. When the demons hit the pigs, the pigs rushed down the steep bank into the lake and drowned. I say today, Charley's testimony is that Jesus Christ set him free from demons. The demons rushed Jasper's herd of cattle into the icy river!"

"How awful for that Jesus man to murder all those innocent pigs and cows! I think criminal charges should be ordered at once against this man!" Lorsey screamed, springing up like a jack from a jumping box. "He defamed animals. He didn't care about their mental agony or physical suffering. I expect the law to intervene here!"

"Well," Commissioner Michael answered, licking his lip while pondering his next word, "as for Jasper's cows, I think we need to determine who is responsible for this outlandish crime. Already beef farmers across the surrounding counties are worried their animals might be the next victims."

"Such discriminating, barbaric acts against animals must be stopped!" Lorsey hissed loudly as she curled her fingers into cat claws. "Are you prepared to act on this evidence, Officer Richards? You heard the preacher. Jesus is guilty as charged!"

"Well, Lorsey," Jason grunted, "legendary figures like Jesus aren't exactly available to handcuff. I think Daniel Boone probably shot a raccoon or two, but who can find the man now to arrest him?"

"You blundering idiot." Lorsey's face twisted like a mop being rung. "We're talking about animals being plundered and terrorized by human maniacs right here in Perjure and Mirage Counties!"

———————

"Oh goodness." Sherry winced. "I think some demons need to be released from that woman! What a frightful face she just made!"

"I don't think you'd like to meet her in any dark alley. Probably not even on a cloudy day," Phillip interjected. "She's a few fumes short of a working engine."

———————

"Charley, after listening to the other contestants, tell us what you think really happened," Stella cross-examined.

"I have already told you what happened, but you did not listen. Do you want me to tell you again that it was Jesus Christ who did this marvelous thing? Can you believe then that this is a God thing? I tell you it was Jesus who set me free!"

"Oh, come now." Reverend Staunch stood and pointed a bony finger at Charley. "You talk like you are one of his disciples or something. You are identifying with a time in the past. Your head is still not on straight!"

Others were standing, agreeing with the Reverend, pointing fingers, and bashing Charley with harsh words.

Charley stood tall, facing his accusers. "Have you all forgotten that Jesus Christ is very much alive today? Perhaps you, too, should consider becoming His disciples."

"Ha! I am learned and taught of His laws. You are just an unlearned boy of obscure heritage! How dare you speak against my authority!" Veins were bulging from Reverend Staunch's neck. "Nothing you say here today is credible!"

"If your Jesus is alive today"—Lorsey growled— "He should be lynched! Maybe you should lead us to your master."

"If it were Jesus who caused such a riot, I mean if He were really here today, then I can assure everyone that we would certainly ask Him to leave. We don't need such disturbances occurring in these counties," the commissioner asserted with a shake of his head.

Stella squirmed. Her cheeks were inflamed to nearly the red of her blouse. "Enough now!" she called out. "This whole matter is still under investigation. The county board, law enforcement, the ministerial, health and human services, city council, as well as animal protection, will all be meeting again behind closed doors to hash this out further. Be sure justice will be served. But for today, our telecast is over!"

———⁓⁓⊙⊙⊙⊙⊙⁓⁓———

"What have you got, Caleb? Are you sure it's her?" Phillip's voice thundered into the phone receiver.

"A couple hours ago we spotted a van with confiscated plates parked behind the old Edge Water Motel. I witnessed two men throwing what appeared to be a body wrapped in a blanket into this van. I'm sorry, Phillip. This might not have a good ending."

"Get to the point! Where is she now?" Phillip's hand shook.

"My men and I are following the van."

"I'm coming! Where are you?"

"We are approaching the Blue Spruce Overlook. But it is not a good idea for you to come here."

"I'm coming!" Phillip slammed down the phone.

Phillip's heart was hammering. Was it Abby's body in that blanket? It was all his fault. Who knew that what started out as a great story for Abby to write could have ended this way? His car was now speeding away from Edge Water and toward the Northwood's Crossing. It was a shortcut—one he had taken many times before when he had been a cop.

———⁓⁓⊙⊙⊙⊙⊙⁓⁓———

Abby was moaning. She grabbed at her head, expecting to find a drill boring through her skull. And someone was demanding her to wake up. She turned her head to the side and it burned against something rough, like tree bark. Her eyes squinted against the bright sun light. It was tree bark. She had been propped up against a tree.

"It's about time you woke up," the voice shouted again. "Here," he ordered, ramming a pen between her fingers. "You've got a note to write."

A man had squatted on one knee beside her. Despite her weak and bobbing head, she managed to steal a glance at him. A dark-skinned man with high cheek bones and cold eyes stared back at her.

"I can't write," Abby sputtered back at the man.

She noticed more legs coming toward her. Long legs. She looked up. A tall hatchet-faced man with a pony tail glared down at her.

He snapped open his pocketknife and put the shiny blade in front of her face. "Well, we can make this easy or painful. The choice is yours." He spit on the ground in front of her.

Abby tried to stabilize the pen between her thumb and finger, but it slipped to the ground.

She saw the blunt handle of a pistol coming toward her face.

Whack.

Abby felt her head sink in faintness.

"Why did you do that? She was finally waking up," were the last words she heard.

Phillip parked his vehicle behind a clump of trees near Blue Spruce River. He stooped down beside the narrow dirt road entering a wooded area which led to the look-out pass. *Yep, that's where they're taking her.* Pain stabbed at his gut. Were they planning to dump her corpse into the river? Or, was there any chance she was still alive? He didn't dare let his imagination run wild. It made him sick wondering what these evil men might be doing to Abby.

Phillip walked as far up the road as he dared to go. He couldn't risk being seen. There was only one of him carrying one pistol. He had no idea how many of them he might encounter.

The path was slanting upward, and he veered off of it and into the woods. He could use the trees to help propel him forward. Phillip was racing with the sun. He could hear his heart pounding in his ears with each step he took.

"You knocked her out. We need her awake to write the note!" a disgruntled voice shot through the woods.

The words stopped Phillip in his tracks. His airway constricted. "She's alive." The words squeaked out of his mouth. She wasn't far away from him. He stood taller, listening through the woods for the squealing of brakes. Caleb and his group should be arriving soon. He needed help to save Abby.

Phillip eased ahead quietly. Watching. Listening.

"Well, we aren't going to be able to wait for her to wake up again. We're gonna have to kill her with or without a note." Another more serious voice was in command.

Boom! The loud whine of a gun shot pierced through the woods. Tears stung Phillip's eyes. "No, God. Please no. I can't be too late."

He struggled with weak legs to find a place behind a large cliff-like rock. He could see them now. A long-legged man, gun in hand, had skirted behind a tree. On the ground lay two motionless bodies. Phillip swallowed a big bunch of air. He had to get there just in case there was breath left in Abby. He stayed low to get to the other side of the lookout. Maybe there he could outsmart the man, sneak up behind him.

Phillip scraped himself on a sharp rock edge. Dusk was setting in, making it more difficult to move in the stony and jagged cracks and crevices. *Where were Caleb and the men?* he wondered.

The clearing was in close range now. Phillip cursed under his breath. The man with the gun wasn't in sight. The two bodies were still. He moved a little closer. The smaller body was Abby. A glint of her red hair shone through a low sun ray. She looked lifeless. Phillip groaned.

Bang! Another bullet whizzed by him. He thought his own heart had stopped for a moment. He steadied his shooting arm. He poised to shoot back.

Out of nowhere several men in SWAT clothing were rushing to the scene ahead of him.

"Phillip, you almost got yourself killed. And you could have jeopardized our efforts here!"

Phillip turned around, never happier to see Caleb. "I'm sorry buddy, but where is the man with the gun?"

"I shot him. He was aiming his gun at your head, and it left me no choice."

"Oh, I guess you saved my life. Maybe Abby's too."

"Well," Caleb replied, "first we shot the guy who was aiming to shoot Abby. So, you see, both men are dead. Dead men don't give out information."

"You're thinking these aren't the real crooks here?" Phillip asked, feeling his heart slinking down.

"That's my guess."

"I'm sorry. I really am. But if Abby is alive, she can give you the information you need. I need to find out," he said spinning on his heel to go.

The wail of an ambulance could be heard coming up the trail as Phillip raced toward Abby.

"She'll be fine," one of the responders shouted up at Phillip. "She's got a big egg on her head and looks pretty roughed up, but I can't see anything life-threatening."

"Abby." Phillip sniffed back tears as he knelt beside her. "What happened? You have no idea how relieved I am to find you alive!"

Abby looked up at Phillip, her eyes glazed over. "Phillip, what are we doing out here? Who are all these people?"

———————

Sherry woke with a start. She sat up in bed. The moon was full, so big that it shed enough light to see the steady and even heaving up and down of Phillip's chest. She had always felt safe next to him, but something was different tonight. Sherry slipped out of bed to crawl downstairs. Sherry stopped at the bottom of the steps. Her heart battered against her chest. The door was opening, and she hunkered in the corner. Her hand went quickly to her mouth. *Jamie and Jack. Where have they been?* Sherry was thankful for the sufficient light afforded by the full moon. The couple stepped inside the door.

Jamie was dressed in a long black dress. "Wasn't it wonderful, Jack? I am so glad you were with me tonight celebrating the Great Rite."

Jack stood thunderstruck, his hands buried in baggy pant pockets. "Yeah, it was amazing. That lady goddess knows how to please her horned lover."

"Yes, they know the union of life. Every spring they renew their commitment to each other." Jamie threw herself on the couch and put her legs to rest on the end table. "Last spring I was initiated to the coven." She reached for Jack's hand. "We are in union with them, Jack."

He sat down beside her; his eyes were question marks. "Those chanting in a circle, they were angry. Were they talking about that pastor we visited?"

"Yes, that squirrel-like one who speaks of this Jesus as though He were all-powerful God."

"So what were they saying?"

Jamie scooted deeper into the soft couch cushion. "A black curse. A black dragon curse." She looked with big eyes into his. "These are powerful curses. They aren't used too often for that reason. But that man is a strong Christian. So it will take hard hexes and much unity on our part to put him down. And it will take a very weak moment on his part. I hate Christians."

Tears were streaming down Sherry's face. "Oh Lord," she prayed. "She's my little girl. I couldn't bear losing her this way. I can't lose her. You are my new found friend. You are powerful. I am asking You to help my daughter know the truth."

———

Abby opened her eyes. Darkness and a strange bed under her caused a shiver to course through her body. She tried to sit up. "Oh," she moaned grabbing her head, "Someone must have hit me over the head with a shovel."

The curtain around her bed opened. A man stepped in.

"Don't scream, Abby. You're safe at Edge Water Hospital."

"I don't understand. Who are you?" she asked as her breathing accelerated.

"I'm Phillip's friend and I'm with the FBI. My name is Caleb."

Abby caught her breath. She was staring hard into the handsome, strong, and chiseled face of the man who was staring down at her. "Caleb." She swallowed the words.

"Yes. Perhaps Phillip has mentioned my name a time or two." His face lit up with a smile. "I met Phillip several years ago when he worked for law enforcement. He has an amazing intuition. I was a rookie with the

FBI, trying to solve a case. Phillip had already put the puzzle pieces together. He helped me out. I owe him."

"He is amazing," Abby agreed. "But why am I in the hospital? What happened?"

"I'm trying to find out why you are here. You were kidnapped, Abby, and I need to find out by whom. The doctor believes you are suffering from some amnesia right now, but he doesn't believe it is permanent." He smiled down at her. "How are you feeling? Do you remember anything, yet?"

"I feel like a stack of baloney lying on a hard piece of bread. I don't remember much, except this headache feels very familiar. Did someone clobber me?"

Caleb chuckled, and his eyes danced. "You did get pretty banged up. You have two significant lumps on your head. The one on the top of your head looks like someone did clobber you with some sort of a blunt object. The doctor thinks you hit your head on something, causing the bump on the side of your head."

"Why are you staying with me here at the hospital?" she asked, trying to shift her body into a more comfortable position.

"Bet you never thought you'd have body guards," his voice teased. "It happens to be my shift now." He stood and smiled once more for her and then disappeared behind the curtain, leaving her alone to hear only the loud beat of her heart.

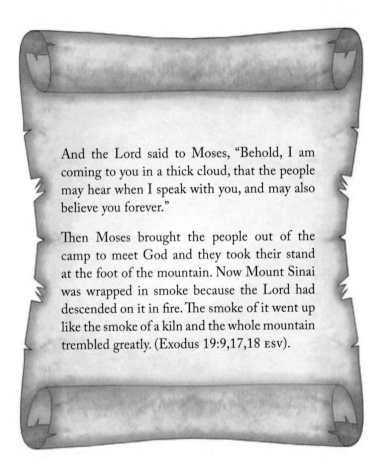

And the Lord said to Moses, "Behold, I am coming to you in a thick cloud, that the people may hear when I speak with you, and may also believe you forever."

Then Moses brought the people out of the camp to meet God and they took their stand at the foot of the mountain. Now Mount Sinai was wrapped in smoke because the Lord had descended on it in fire. The smoke of it went up like the smoke of a kiln and the whole mountain trembled greatly. (Exodus 19:9,17,18 esv).

Chapter Seven

"Thank God she's okay!" Phillip's heart whirred like a hummingbird before nectar. "But she doesn't remember much. It may take some time," Phillip added, squeezing Sherry's hand.

"I agree with you." Sherry looked up to meet his gaze.

"About what?"

"That we have God to thank." Sherry stopped to stare at the floor for a moment, as though she were thinking, meditating, recouping her thoughts. She looked up and locked eyes with him.

He could see his reflection cowering in her eyes.

"Phillip. We really need to talk. I'm so proud of you for your heroic actions to save Abby. She was in grave danger, and you knew it, and you wouldn't rest until she was safe." Sherry paused, staring down briefly at the floor again. "If only," she added looking back up into his eyes, "you would see that your children may be in danger too. I'm worried about our kids. Some things are going very wrong. I need you to think about this. I need your help."

Phillip continued to stare into her eyes. This morning, he noted, her eyes appeared larger than normal. Sadder too. An arrow hit his heart. He should be here for her today. She needed him. But he was in a hurry again. He needed to stop by the hospital and check on Abby before hurrying off to work early this morning. He couldn't bear to keep looking into Sherry's eyes for they were like kilns of fiery sorrow. Instead, his hand briefly caressed her elbow. "We'll talk later, I promise."

⸺⸺∿∿◦◦❧☙◦◦∿∿⸺⸺

Abby stared down at her breakfast tray. Nothing looked appetizing, especially the lumpy oatmeal. She took another bite of toast. If only she could remember something—anything at all would help. Instead her brain felt like a flat tire running on gravel.

"Hello, Abby."

The voice grated at her nerves. Abby winced as she looked up to meet the cold eyes behind the words. "Sheriff," she acknowledged, trying to hide the fear in her voice.

"Yes. I am here to get a report on what happened to you. I understand you were kidnapped."

"Apparently I was." She swallowed hard.

"I'm sorry about that. Edge Water has the reputation of being a very peaceful town, and this type of thing is unimaginable. Do you have any idea why someone would want to harm you?"

She wanted to scream at him. How could he call this a peaceful town when someone had murdered her sister? Abby sucked in a deep breath. Even if she would have been able to recall the past several days, she would not tell Oscar. She didn't trust the man.

"Well," his voice deepened. "Tell me what you do remember."

Abby paled. The voice. Why did that voice make her heart race? She glanced away from him. "I remember nothing."

The door opened. Caleb stood before them. His eyes were like burning stars staring at Oscar. "Can't you read?" he asked Oscar. "The sign on the outside of this door strictly prohibits anyone entering without an FBI agent."

"Well, I'm the sheriff. I would think that qualifies me." He chuckled fiendishly. "Just doing my job and trying to get a report from the young lady."

"Please leave. The FBI is handling this." Caleb's arms were crossed in front of his chest. He may not be as wide-boned as Oscar, but he was well muscled and fearless.

Oscar's brow furrowed and his mouth twisted as though he were about to say something he would regret. But he said nothing as he left the room.

"You okay?" Caleb asked Abby.

"Yeah. Thanks for sending him away. For some reason I don't like the guy. I never have."

"Abby, if you should remember something, one of us agents will take your statement." He blew out a relaxed breath. "One of us should be outside your room at all times."

"How long will I be here?" Abby questioned.

"For only a couple more days. We have a top-notch neurologist coming in to review your case tomorrow. Meanwhile the nurses are monitoring your neuro signs."

"Oh, is that why they wake me out of a good sleep to shine a flashlight in my eyes and ask me to touch my nose with my eyes closed?"

"Yep." Caleb smiled. "But they're just doing their job."

———

Oscar looked to each side and behind him as he scurried into the alley behind Nelson's Drug store, and soon disappeared behind the city's recycling bins. A tall, gray-haired man with a nicely trimmed mustache stepped forward to meet with him.

"Thanks for meeting me here, Shamrock. Did you bring the stuff and your white lab coat?"

"Yes and all of this is going to cost you."

"We already agreed on a price." Oscar seethed.

"I'm taking a great risk. I've already lost my right to practice medicine, and have served prison time for taking a lesser risk than this."

"Your disguise looks good. I especially like the mustache. Right at change of shifts the place is less guarded. I'll make the call pretending to be Dr. Schultz and ask the nurse to give Abby something to make sure she sleeps and some morphine. You slip into her room about 10:45 tonight, which will be at shift change, and push a lethal dose of the stuff into that IV port. And not to worry, the nurse will take all of the blame."

"If it's so simple why don't you do it?"

"You're a doctor and—"

"*Was* a doctor," the man interrupted.

The room grew mysteriously smoky. Tongues clicked off. Hearts drummed together in fearful crescendo. The stranger stepped through the door, and all eyes strained to see. Deputy Jason Richards pulled his pistol from its sheath.

The figure came closer. His long hair shined through the smoke.

"Stop where you are! Put your hands in the air where I can see them," Jason demanded.

The man's arms went up. As he continued to move forward, the smoky substance thickened. "I bare no weapons except the truth, which is in my mouth," the man cried out.

Jason moved ahead, attempting to get a picture of the man's face. "Who are you?"

"I am a voice for God."

Jason tried to move closer to the man, but the heavy cloud of smoke became a blindfold, wrapping itself around Jason's face.

"Why are you here? And where is this thick smoke coming from?" Jason waved his hand to push the smoke aside. Then he realized the smoke wasn't eating up his oxygen. No person was gagging or coughing from the thick haze. He felt his blood thicken cold. "This isn't smoke. What does this thick vapor stuff consist of? Is this biochemical in nature? I demand you identify yourself and inform us what this substance is!" Jason aimed his gun at the stranger.

"I am here as a voice crying out the truth," the man again answered. "The glory of God has accompanied me. That is what you see."

"You are a blasphemer!" Reverend Staunch said, pounding his fists together. "We are about to have an important meeting here, and you are not invited."

"I think everyone needs to clear out of this place now until we know what we are dealing with here," Jason raised his voice in alarm. "We could be dealing with anthrax." Jason analyzed as he blew out a jagged breath.

"I have been compelled to come," the man stood firm. "God has sent me to address the leaders of the local churches and all who offer council in these counties."

A low gurgle of disdain and mockery oozed like frothy sludge to a river's edge. But the man spoke out with a forceful voice, "The Lord asks of you today, 'How long will you spiritual leaders, who call yourselves men of God, limp between two different opinions? Choose this day whom you will serve! You have turned to the wells of this world. Only words fill your religious wells. There is no river for the young to drink from. You have made a mockery of the one true God. You are stiff-necked! You have a form of religion, but you deny the power of God! Your people have come to broken cisterns, where there is no life. You are lukewarm, naked, pitiful, wretched, poor, and blind. God could be ready to vomit you from His mouth. You listen to and follow lying spirits. Instead of truth and hope, you feed hopelessness to the hurting and abused, who are crying out for help! Your ears have grown dull, your eyes dim, and your hearts are hard. Your love is cold! Your children have been given over to the enemy. You are the workers of iniquity leading the blind. Wake up and repent for I will come as a thief and you will not know what hour I come.'"

A train whistled mournfully as it rolled like thunder through the town. The ground trembled under everyone's feet.

"Prepare ye the way of the Lord!" the man cried out. "Hear what He says. Do not harden your hearts. People need Jesus! They need the truth! Give them truth and not lies!"

"Arrest that man." The woman, Zany, stood to her feet in a screeching fit. "He's a danger to the animals!"

Many voices joined in, "This man is a mad, crazy fool!"

"He's drunk!"

"Yes, he's insane, harassing us! Threatening us!" Many men began shaking and striking with their fists. "Away with this Jesus fanatic!"

Jason waved his arms through the smoke. "Okay, stand back. All of you!" The young deputy pushed his way through the stirred-up mess. One swinging fist smashed hard against Jason's lip.

Jason backed up in a daze. He grabbed his radio and called dispatch for assistance. Then he called for Incident Command action. He had to cover every base.

Unable to restrain the raging group, Jason shot into the air. The blast created a deadening silence. "I said stand back everyone. I will arrest this man and have him jailed peaceably! And I repeat again. I am asking everyone to leave this building immediately. Go single file out the door!"

There was cursing. There was a low roar of voices. No person listened to the deputy.

Frustrated, Jason walked to where the hub of action had been incited. A man lay moaning and rolling in pain. "Well, help me get him up," the deputy ordered.

"Commissioner Routes?" Jason asked, stepping back in unbelief.

The round and stout public servant stood bent over. His face bloodied. His hands cupped over his nose. Blood was trickling through Michael Route's fingers.

"What is the meaning of this?" Jason's face contorted in bewilderment. "What happened to you, Michael? And where is the man I am to arrest?"

"He just vanished." Michael sniffed back blood. "He was a few feet from me, and then he wasn't. All I know is several fists from more than one direction found my face."

The sheriff and another deputy rushed into the Community Center holding guns in hand.

"He got away," Reverend Staunch hissed through clenched teeth.

"It's about time you get here," Lorsey howled. "There was this man defending Jesus. He's an animal killer, too! You need to find him. Think of all the innocent animals!"

"Oh, I don't feel so well." Michael's voice faded away, and he slid to the floor again.

"Someone call an ambulance," Dr. Soothers commanded, kneeling beside the commissioner. "Appears he has been pummeled all over his head and face."

"Did anyone get a good description of that intruder?" the sheriff asked, standing straight and broad.

"Well," Jason answered, scratching his head, "he was rather tall. But there was so much smoke, especially around him. I couldn't see his face."

"Smoke?" the badged man asked, scowling. "There's not a trace of smoke in here."

Everyone stood silently. Jason's mouth dropped. "But there was smoke. It was so thick I could only see a form. The closer I moved toward that man, the thicker the smoke became."

Someone said, "Yes. It was thick and blinding."

"Then why do I not smell smoke?" The sheriff's voice deepened.

The color drained from Jason's face. "I don't know. It was strange smoke. I could breathe just fine in it. But the presence of that man and the smoke around him took my breath away. I have called the emergency response team as well. I had no idea what the substance was, sir. I just acted quickly for the welfare of all involved here tonight."

"So what did this mysterious man want?" a younger deputy asked with a cocky, curled lip.

Jason scratched his head. "He kept talking about the churches and the public leaders only feeding the people lies." Jason swallowed hard. "He said he was a voice for God, and he's quite sure God is not happy with people around here."

The sheriff's muscles tensed. His arms crossed his chest in a take-charge kind of way. "Someone here should be able to describe this man. Surely someone saw him."

A voice yelled from the group, "There was too much smoke. It was very mysterious."

"I'm sure it's not as it seems." Reverend Staunch stepped between Jason and the sheriff. "This man had some sort of a smoke bomb, that's all. He was of a whacky cult trying to stir up more publicity. There are some out there trying to get our counties in an uproar. They want people to think that a miracle maker is walking about these parts. Next thing you know they will claim someone was raised from the dead."

The sheriff flanked close to Richard Staunch, whispering in his ear, "I have a feeling John has been resurrected from the dead. I can't think of another man who could pull something like this off."

The reverend's eyes bugged out as he mulled over the possibility. "It couldn't be. Could it?"

The emergency medical team rushed into the building.

Michael's face looked swollen in the light and in the absence of smoke. An EMT knelt beside Michael. "How're you doing?"

"I've felt better." He groaned.

The commanding officer knelt beside Michael. "Can you tell me what happened before they take you away? You sure you didn't get a good look at him?"

"Like Jason said, there was an incredible amount of smoke."

"Yeah, yeah, but who is responsible for assaulting you. Can you describe the man who did this to you?" Sheriff Grand demanded sharply.

"It wasn't that stranger who hit me. I was trying to walk up to him. But I couldn't get close because of the dense, smoke-like cloud. Then right before my eyes he vanished. He went in a funnel of that stuff. Then everyone went nuts. All these people were punching me. It was like everyone was blind or something. The smoke was gone, but they still couldn't see it was me they were striking."

"No, no." Minister Staunch's long starchy body hovered near the sheriff, sensing the problem was bucking wild like a bronco with no rope to hold on to. "Oscar. Sheriff, I saw that big bruiser take a swing at Commissioner Routes." The Reverend's eyes poured glue down on Michael. "You just can't remember right after that wallop!"

Doctor Soothers smoothed his thinning hair back with his right hand. He blew out a breath from the side of his mouth before talking. "The Reverend's got a point. The mind can trick the best of us. I'm sure tonight, in the heat of confusion, some deluded to optical illusions."

Doors flew open and gloved and gowned men wearing strange masks with plastic over their faces entered like a *Star Wars* invasion upon an unsuspecting planet. Sirens could be heard surrounding the building.

"This is no optical illusion!" the sheriff blurted out. "You have come to investigate some strange smoke. Well, there is none to check out!"

"But there was!" Officer Jason insisted.

"Furthermore," the sheriff continued, "that smoke must have made all these people whacky. The person responsible for this mayhem, smoke and all, has disappeared, and no one had the brains to stop him."

A man, overstuffed in a biohazard suit put a cone-shaped speaker to his mouth and bellowed out, "Everyone is now commanded to exit this building. One at a time. Leave through this east entrance. Form two lines outside. There are two tanks screened off where each of you will be showered and given fresh clothing. After that you will be directed to the information line. Next you will follow suit to triage nursing. This must be done quickly and in order. Do not panic. Just follow directions. We have paramedics, nurses, emergency supplies, helicopters, and ambulances available."

"Abby, I would like to introduce you to my brother, John." Mable's pale and puffy fingers reached out and petted the man's right bicep. "Oh, I know you probably do not recognize him with his beard and all, but you and Julie stole his heart way back when." She smiled. "Which reminds me, I have a picture of him building a snowman with you girls. Hold on while I dig it out of my purse."

"So I know you?" Abby stared into the man's tranquil, grayish-blue eyes.

John nodded as Mable searched frantically through her leather bag. "I found it, Abby. Now look here."

Abby took the picture from Mable's hand. She stared at it, mouth open, and then her eyes turned to John, studying him for a moment. "Oh, I do remember you now. I think I even remember this snowman." Abby's face dimpled into a big smile. "You made him almost come alive. You gave him your hat and one of your jackets, too." Abby's face saddened. "Look how happy Julie looked here." Abby looked up again into John's eyes. "You had a habit of making us laugh. I remember that about you."

John chuckled.

It was the same chuckle Abby had remembered it to be. His deep laughter had always sounded like water rolling down a rocky cliff and dancing as it splashed below.

"I suppose you've heard that Julie was killed in a terrible accident?" Abby's voice dropped to a whisper.

"Yes. I'm so sorry, Abby."

"She sounded happy again. I can imagine her laughing, like she did in this picture. She said she had found peace. She was coming home that night, and we were going to be a family again," Abby's voice weakened. "She would have loved to see you again."

"How are you feeling this morning, dear?" Mable asked, changing the subject. "You know Caleb and

Phillip have decided that after you get discharged from the hospital you will come and stay with John and me for a while." Mable rambled on, barely taking a breath. "You know it will be just for a while, until we know you are safe and all. And I'll prepare a nice meal for us and I'll use my finest dishes. I'll invite Phillip too. No doubt he is getting behind at the *Edge Water Times*. You were his right-hand star," Mable beamed.

"You know Phillip?" Abby turned to Mable with a curious stare.

"No, not really. I saw him at church only, but I am looking forward to meeting him in a more formal way. John just met him several days back."

"John!" Abby's voice wheezed without the force of wind. "Are you the John Charley spoke of? Are you the man who helped Charley be normal and to be free from those voices that drove him mad?" Abby sat straight up in her bed. Her face took on the color of the pale pink sheet over her.

"Yes, Abby. I was there when your nephew was set free from all of those voices."

———

Phillip was in a big hurry to close shop early. He had come to work early and spent hours piecing together the local news and advertisements for the paper. He had reread his recapping of the television debate several times. "Seems I am more biased for Charley and Paul even though I've tried to maintain a neutral position. Well, I will read it again tomorrow and try to neutralize it some more," Phillip mumbled to himself. He stood and stretched. "Thank God," he said between the stretch and a yawn, "Abby is okay." She had been so peacefully sleeping early this morning that he hadn't wanted to wake her. "I'll stop by this evening." He yawned again.

A loud rap on the door caused the hairs on Phillip's arms to stand up. He unlocked the door. A woman stood at the door entrance. He stared into her almost black eyes. "Have I met you before?" he asked, dumb-stricken.

"No, I seriously doubt that. But members of the city council have sent me here to deliver this report to be written in your paper." The woman spoke with her chin tipped high. Her jet-black hair was tied in a neat bun behind her head. She handed him a sealed envelope and turned to leave; her hips were swaying in a tight blue skirt. So arrogantly the woman carried herself that her high heels barely touched the floor.

"Wait a minute. What's your name? And what's this all about?"

"Knowing my name is not necessary. I'm just the delivery woman. You will see the signatures from the mayor and chair of the council board at the end of this article." With no further ado, and without another backwards glance, she left Phillip standing with the same questions stuck in his throat.

I know I've seen that dame somewhere. I don't think I trust her.

Phillip sat behind his desk again and opened the manila envelope. He jumped up when his eyes hit the large looming title: Did the Young Pastor, Paul Marvel, Commit Murder?

"What kind of game is this? I knew that woman brought trouble with her!" Phillip protested. He slapped his hand angrily against his desk. "Dirt-throwing fools!" Phillip could feel his pulse skipping recklessly. He forced his eyes to read on.

> Shortly after Charley Frank's recovery and the drowning of Jasper Schafer's beef cattle, the young preacher, Paul Marvel, just seemed to show up mysteriously. He claims to pastor the New Vision Church in Perjure County.
>
> In a five-county effort to investigate what happened on the early morning of April 1, 2008, city and county officials, along with law enforcement, have made every effort to uncover some helpful leads. The Bureau of Criminal Investigation has joined these county efforts.
>
> The county committee members obtained the following information about Paul Marvel and his wife, Victoria. Paul's first pastorate was located in Blames County in the city of West Chambers.
>
> Other ministers from that area were happy to see Paul leave the area. Reverend Tepid, from the West Chambers Bible Community Church, told reporters, "He was a strange man. He was like a cult leader. People that left his congregation claim he thought he was as powerful as God. He had many people brainwashed that way."

Some say, "Strange things reportedly and frequently happened in that church. In addition, strange and phenomenal happenings tore the community apart. These were linked to the cultish activities performed by Reverend Marvel."

Paul left his church shortly after a woman, who had attended his church, supposedly committed suicide. However, people who knew the deceased still accuse Mr. Marvel as the reason this woman died. Though he was acquitted of any murder charges at that time, the fact remains: Reverend Paul Marvel is still a suspect of this murder in the minds of many folk from Blames County.

Phillip sat down again. He suddenly felt like a giant invisible vacuum cleaner had been plugged in somewhere. And it was actively sucking the life out of him.

Phillip wasn't about to print this article. No, he couldn't, not without first checking the bridge's tower for support before crossing it. There was something broken, dangerously unsteady about these accusations. He needed to look into it. First, he would find the right links. He would not stop at just calling Reverend Tepid. He needed the names of every clergy, every official, anybody in Blames County who might have some helpful information. He'd for sure need the name of the woman who had mysteriously died and any names of her family members. He'd check with law enforcement and try to obtain a copy of the coroner's report. That is, if he could get through the obstacles. More than likely there would be bull-headed people, unmovable, like brick walls, opposing every lead he might take. Of course, he would talk with Paul, John, and anyone else that stood out as a good source of information.

Pure slander, that's all. I can smell it. This is a nest of rotten eggs; that's what it is.

Phillip called the law enforcement center in West Chambers. He jotted down a date. At least they had agreed to meet with him. He figured they would not release information any other way. His mind began wandering.

Sometimes it would be worthwhile knowing how to pray. Maybe I really do need God. I would be able to pray with Sherry then. She keeps begging about that. Oh, God, I don't know what to do about all this mess. I don't even know how to help my wife. I really don't.

Phillip closed the door behind him, finally out of the office. *Can't wait 'til Abby gets back to help. Thought I'd never get free today.* Without looking back, he jumped in his truck.

"What in the world is going on?" Phillip stared at the roadblocks. The entire west side of town appeared to be off limits. Colored streamers, yellow cones, and wooden barricades were everywhere. There were plenty of policemen parading around, redirecting traffic. Phillip impatiently backed up his truck and took a back-way road.

"Why wasn't I informed about this? Ambulances, fire trucks, tanks. Helicopters? What in the world has happened?"

Phillip slammed on his breaks. He was jumping out of the truck before it could come to a dead stop. His camera was in his hand. He may be tired, but duty called.

"Let me through," Phillip's voice fired over the roar of other voices. He pushed his way through a forest of arms and heads and bodies. People everywhere.

"You responding to our local emergency response?" Sheriff Grand's voice seethed from an angry twisted face.

"Shouldn't I?" Phillip counter offered. "Isn't it newsworthy?"

"Suit yourself. I think the committee had a little too much to drink. They are reporting a strange, mysterious man who walks in smoke and who talks with God." He eyed Phillip warily. "You haven't heard any rumors of such a man in these parts, have you?"

"If you ask me," Phillip's voice blared madly, "this whole flipping area has gone mad! There isn't a trustworthy man among the drunks."

Oscar's eyes darted back and forth, as though he were monitoring the situation at hand and keeping an eye on Phillip at the same time. "Well," he breathed heavily, "it concerns me that maybe bygones may not be gone."

"What?" Phillip exchanged a peppery stare. "You think I'm capable of just looking past what you did? Do you really think I believe this area is a safer place since you've taken charge?"

"We should talk things through. We need to be on the same page. I think we could glue some things back together over a couple of stiff drinks."

"Think again, Captain." Phillip's words were straight and unbending. "I need to get a few snapshots and maybe a couple other opinions on what happened here this afternoon."

Chapter Eight

"Your doctor called and asked me to give you a sleeping pill and a dose of morphine to ensure that you get a good night's rest," a young blonde nurse said as she checked Abby's name band. "That doctor Schultz sure is great, huh? Seems he really cares about you."

"That's odd," Abby said. "I'm really tired. I'm thinking I will sleep well tonight without a sleeping pill."

"He was pretty adamant about you getting this stuff tonight," the nurse's blue eyes engaged with Abby's. "How's your headache?"

"More bearable."

"On a scale of zero to ten, how would you rate the pain?"

"Maybe six."

"Well then," the nurse concluded, "the good doctor must have a reason for wanting you to take these medications."

———

Phillip felt exhausted, like his engine was running without steam. "What a crazy day. And I'll bet John was behind all of it. That man!" Phillip fumed.

It was already ten fifteen at night. He hoped Abby was still awake. He had planned to visit her earlier in the evening. If only he could plan his day.

"Knock, knock," Phillip said, rapping on the door.

"Come in," Abby's voice sounded groggy.

"Man, I'm glad I didn't come a minute later. You look like you are way out there in sleep land."

She yawned. "I know. I was tired before that nurse insisted I take a sleeping pill and another dose of morphine. But, it was the doctor's orders."

"Oh, he must have been concerned about something if he visited you tonight. What did he tell you?"

"Nothing. He didn't stop by. He called the nurse," she said, trying to keep her eyes from becoming glued shut. "I'm so tired."

Phillip's brow furrowed as he mulled over why a doctor would want Abby drugged. The thought troubled him. He shot up off his chair. "Listen Ab, you get some rest. I'll check on you tomorrow."

Phillip was about to rush out of the door, but instead he took a moment to stand beside Abby's bed. How he had wished to tell her about his day, about the crazy dame and the letter accusing Paul of murder. He needed to tell her about the mysterious man in a smoke-filled building. He needed to tell her to hurry up and get better because he needed her to write lots of articles for the paper. But, here she was, unable to keep her eyes open.

"She's drugged too much," he whispered, "and something doesn't seem right about this."

Phillip turned and took a step out of the door, bumping face to face into a man in a long white lab coat.

"Excuse me," Phillip said eying the man. "Mind if I ask you a few questions? I mean, if you are coming in to examine Abby, I have some questions."

"And you are?" Shamrock's mustache twitched.

"Phillip. Abby works for me. I want to know first," Phillip said as he continued a full-body scan of the man, "why you ordered a sleeping pill and morphine for Abby tonight? She is extremely drugged."

"I believe her primary care doctor ordered those medications. Now if you will excuse me, I would like a moment alone with this patient." The man gave Phillip a peppery glare.

"Why?"

"Why what?" The man was becoming impatient.

"Why are you here to see Abby tonight? She obviously isn't in a talking mood, and I would like to know why you need to disturb her."

"Have you ever heard of HIPPA and confidentiality laws?" the man huffed, blowing out an agitated breath.

"Yes I have," Phillip glared back and pushed his face closer to the man. "But how do I know who you are?"

"I'm Dr. Banks. I'm a specialist. A neurologist."

"Well, I'm not leaving until you do," Phillip asserted himself. "I find it hard to believe a physician would want to do a neurological examination on a patient this time of the night, and," Phillip continued without taking a breath, "especially on a patient who was ordered to be drugged."

Shamrock looked at the young FBI agent, Brad, who watched the scene from his chair. "Young man," he said. "I believe you were told that a doctor would be coming to examine Abby tonight."

"Yes, sir," the young man replied.

"Then could I ask that you have this man removed immediately?" Shamrock ordered as blood flushed through his neck and darkened his face.

"Phillip has a point. We are here to protect Abby, and doing an examination on a drugged girl doesn't seem appropriate. Could we see your credentials?"

Shamrock reached under his lab coat and into his pocket. He pulled a card out of his billfold, and handed it to the young agent.

"Dr. Jerry Banks."

"That's right."

Phillip grabbed the card. "Mind if I have Caleb do a background check on this card?" he asked. "And, what else is in that coat pocket, besides the stethoscope?" Phillip badgered on.

"None of your business!" The man's voice scraped iron.

"I'm making it my business," Phillip rebuffed.

"And, I'm making it my business!"

Phillip turned to the sound of his friend's voice. "Caleb, what took you so long?"

"I've been here watching this dude for awhile. Brad sent me a message a while back after questioning the nurse. I had a hunch." Caleb's teeth sparkled inside his wide spread smile under the dim hall light.

"We meet again, Shamrock," Caleb's voice grew stern. "Get your hands in the air, nice and slow. Brad search this man."

The man glared back at Caleb in cold silence.

"A live witness at last." Phillip chuckled.

———

Phillip and Caleb were both fussing over Abby. "You're doctor is discharging you from the hospital today. Apparently, the neurologist report was favorable?" Phillip questioned.

"I'm fine. I just can't remember." Abby sighed. "'Sometimes after head trauma it takes time for memory to be restored,' is what he said."

"We believe you will be safe with John and Mable. To be sure, we are going to have an agent staying there too," Caleb reassured Abby. "Don't fret about your memory. The doctor's right. When it does begin to come back, let us know immediately."

Abby couldn't take her eyes off Caleb's shining blue eyes and the whiteness that sparkled off his teeth with each smile he gave her.

"That's right," Phillip inserted, interrupting Abby's wistfulness. "And, it won't be long 'til we have all of those lawbreakers behind bars. They're losing ground fast. That phony doctor is shaking in his cell right now."

"What do you think he was planning to do?" Abby's eyes grew larger.

"He had more morphine in his pocket. If he could have pulled it off," Caleb continued, "he would have shot the lethal dose into your intravenous feeding, and the nurse would have been blamed for overdosing you."

"Like Julie, I would have been just another accident." Abby's eyes filled with moisture.

"But you weren't," Caleb said, putting a soft hand on her shoulder."

Admiration was swimming and splashing out from Abby's eyes. She wiped off the tears with the sleeve of her blouse. "Yeah, and I don't know how to thank either one of you. If only I could remember something that could help solve all of this."

"You will remember, Abby. In the meantime,"— Phillip returned to his boss voice—"You rest up. Rest up fast, though, because I will lose my mind if you don't get back to the office to help me write those articles."

"Looks like John and Mable are pulling up in the parking lot now," Caleb said while peering out the window. "I think Mable will make sure you get plenty of rest." Caleb turned and winked at Abby.

"It smells heavenly!" Abby sniffed in deeply. "Can't remember when I've been this hungry. And I love meat loaf."

Abby watched Mable stoop over and pull out a roaster filled with meat loaf. "You should have the best-cook-of-the-year award."

"I'm glad you have your appetite back." Mable looked up adoringly into Abby's eyes. "And I remember how much you love meat loaf. That's exactly why I chose to make it tonight." A chuckle rolled from Mable's throat. "Why, you could pack a big plate full of it away, even as a little girl. 'Course," Mable's eyes twinkled, "you needed a half-bottle of ketchup to do so!"

"I remember!" Abby smiled. "So many wonderful memories are coming back now."

Abby stopped talking. A fear grabbed at her heart like a huge trap viciously snapping, ready to break her, should she search into her past for good cheese.

"But," her voice returned weakly, "Even though I can never forget the very painful days of my childhood, I know Julie and I were happy when we stayed with you and John. We'd get off the school bus and run to the house. Such wonderful smells. We would be greeted by the smell of hot, right-from-the-oven caramel rolls or freshly baked cookies. And there was safety. We felt safe." Abby began to cry. She looked up into Mable's eyes. "Then they took Julie and me away and brought us back to where there was only pain and fear, where there was no safety, where our lives became separated forever!"

Abby's jaw trembled. "Here I sit needing to remember what just happened to me, but no matter how I try, I can't remember. And here I sit needing to forget all the horrible things that happened to me as a little girl, but I can't forget! Those things are still too real inside of me, where no person can see or even begin to understand."

Mable wiped her hands on the apron tied snugly about her ample waist. "My dear child, God sees way down there, where other eyes are unable to see. And His hands can reach down there. Abby, He's a good

God. He wants very much to heal the brokenhearted and to set the captives free. Honey, it wasn't God's will that your father and other people beat you girls and hurt you so badly. But be sure it is His will to heal you. He can reach down and remove that emotional cutting knife. Just like He did for Charley, He'll do for you. With arms wide open, He'll welcome you." Mable put her hand on Abby's shoulder and placed a soft kiss on her cheek. "It's always a miracle when a hurting child opens his or her heart to Jesus. Jesus comes to a broken heart who cries out to Him. That's when healing begins. That's when love has strong arms to hug and gentle fingers to heal. My dear Abby," Mable added while gently stroking Abby's face, "there's a love miracle waiting just for you."

Abby hugged Mable back. Shaking back tears, she managed to giggle. " Oh Mable, if He came to me like He did to Charley, and if He sent evil things flying into another herd of cattle, I think some very angry people would become totally unglued. I don't know if our little world here could handle another happening like that. I wouldn't want to write about it. That's for sure."

"Of course you would!" Mable let out a jolly belly laugh. "Just like Charley, you would stand up tall and be willing to shout it from the mountaintop. When God does a miracle, it makes a person free enough to waltz right through all of the obstacles."

"Well," Abby answered with a raise of her brows. "I'd say those obstacles come in the form of rabid people."

"It sure has caused a stir, hasn't it?" Mable's cheeks jiggled as she shook her head. "It's a shame folk have such a hard time giving God the credit for healing Charley."

Mable sighed. "People sometimes, even those in churches, have a lot easier time blaming God for all the bad things that have happened. Tongues flap and fingers point at God the minute something bad happens. But when God does something great, like He did for Charley, few will stand up and praise Him. Makes me wonder when churches will wake up and finally hear God's heart. God sent Jesus to shed His blood and die for people. Now that's some powerful love. That love wants to happen in every life. Jesus wants to walk to those who are hurting, ill, depressed, and in terrible bondage. Jesus hasn't changed. He still wants to set people free. And He would appreciate it if those who call themselves Christians would be about His business of helping people get free down here." Mable hugged Abby harder. "Oh, Abby, God really does love you. He wants to prove that to you. He wants to prove that to everyone!"

"Mable, I think your potatoes are boiling over!" Abby jumped up from her chair to come to Mable's side.

"Oh goodness, girl. I do talk so much sometimes I lose track of what I'm doing," Mable answered, grabbing some pot holders with one hand and turning the burner off with the other hand.

"Mable, I love to mash potatoes. May I help?" Abby asked with a slight grin tugging at her lips.

Mable reached for beaters and the hand mixer. Then her eyes tenderly sought Abby's. "Yes. That would be a great help. And, Abby, I cherish wonderful memories of you and Julie. All the memories of us. But just you mind the truth. God's plan is to give you a future and a hope. He said He wants to do great and mighty things, if you will ask Him."

<hr />

Unbelievable!

Phillip was walking through Walmart, looking straight ahead. He had to pretend this was just a leisurely, friendly Walmart jaunt. From his peripheral vision, he knew he had passed the clothing sections, the pharmacy, the gift and card area, the dog-food aisle. *There. Finally the garden center.*

The blend of color and aroma boomeranged through Phillip's senses. The spirit of spring danced throughout the garden center. He stared at hydrangeas with their big flowers. *Sherry would love it here.* He could picture his wife in her flower garden admiring the plants as they zoomed skyward.

"Phillip."

Phillip startled. He tossed his head back in defense of his embarrassment. "Sorry, John. Guess I haven't been in a garden center recently."

"Really caught up in it, huh?"

"Well, it is my wife's thing. But yep, I can see why she loves her flowers. They are relaxing and genuine. I don't see one of them holding a gun to someone's back. There's not a mean one in the bunch."

Phillip met John's compassionate and understanding gaze.

"I'm having a hard time with all of this, John. I know people can be crooked and greedy. But," Phillip said, rapping his knuckles on a table full of potted, mixed-colored marigolds, "they are dangerous enough around these parts to kill an innocent girl and then come after Abby. There are many faces behind this crime, and yet here we are hiding from what we cannot see. And law enforcement doesn't have a clue that Abby's sister was murdered and that it is the very same people who want to destroy Abby and Charley."

"Well," John answered as he swung an arm about Phillip's shoulder, "if you told law enforcement that Julie's death was a murder, do you think they would believe you? Could you back it up with proof?"

"Probably not. But I'm wondering if it shouldn't be mentioned just the same. They'd at least know we are suspecting foul play. Maybe they would do some more checking."

"Maybe this is a protected crime. One thing is for sure, we both know that things aren't always as they seem."

Phillip shrugged. "What I want to know is what you're hiding. If Charley's dad is a killer, isn't it time we reeled in the facts and get the guy behind bars before he does more damage?" Phillip snorted. "And thank God Abby is okay! But"—Phillip's eyes narrowed, and he hooked John's eyes with a suspicious gaze—"it doesn't seem right that you're holding back such important information. How do I know you are not part of this somehow? If you have the answers, why are you keeping me in the dark?"

John stopped walking. He stuffed his hands in his pants pockets. He stood before Phillip, confident and calm. "I think we will both have all the answers we need in a very short time now."

Phillip blew out a disgusted breath. His gaze hardened. "Meanwhile, the problems around us have become compounded more and more each day. Still your mouth is sealed. But they're not wasting time placing blame!" Phillip spat out a low curse. "Look at this letter. Some strange dame dropped it off at my office a few days ago." Phillip added as he yanked a paper from his shirt pocket. "See for yourself. Someone is going to get blamed for stuff. It won't matter who's really innocent in the long haul. If you want to cover your friend's butt, and ours for that matter, I think it's time you put your two cents' worth into the pot of soup."

John unwrapped the paper. He was silent as his gaze bored into the letter.

"You see!" Phillip's frustration shot through the quiet. "Up to this point, you have been the most mulish man I've worked with. I'd really appreciate hearing the truth and all of it!"

"I understand how you must feel, son, and I agree. Unfortunately, I don't have all of the answers yet."

Phillip could feel the rush of adrenaline burst through his entire body. He felt like a bridled horse being held back from the winning cup. "Then what the heck are we doing? Are you just some mysterious nut I'm following around? Which reminds me"—Phillip's

eyes narrowed again as he loomed before John's face—
"were you the mysterious and religious idiot people are
talking about who showed up in a cloud of smoke at
the Community Center?"

A slow grin played on John's lips. "Why? Would I
hit the front page of your paper if you could prove it
was me?"

"It was you. I already know that. And," Phillip added
crisply, "I protected your butt. The sheriff is suspicious
of you. I'll have you know that."

"Phillip. I can tell you that Paul is innocent of these
charges. He didn't kill that woman. And"—John's lips
pressed into a firm line—"I could tell you many things
right now, but I desperately need the proof to back
up my words. I don't know where all the land mines
are planted. I could tell you things, but if you chase
after this octopus and pull the wrong leg, the other legs
could wrap like a hangman's noose around your neck."

"Great! Just great." Phillip's breaths were coming
short and fast. "So what are you proposing to do?
There are dangerous people on the loose. And there are
curious people waiting to know what to believe. And
there is me. I am supposed to print up some answers. I
mean, we've got to get some answers!"

"And I am praying those answers happen soon,
Phillip."

John's arm looped around Phillip's shoulder again,
and he began walking them forward. "I believe answers
are coming, but we've got to be wise and careful. For
now, Abby is fine. Charley has testified before thousands
of people viewing that debate. The enemies are shaking.

Yes, and they are mad. That's why this letter was given to you about Paul. They are being defensive. They don't want attention right now, and they are desperately trying to get the lime light on others like Paul. They'd like to sink you and me, too, Phillip."

"So you are just praying about this. All prayer and no action?"

"That's how I know there will be action. When I pray, God works." A tidal wave of confidence peaked in John's voice.

Phillip's tongue felt numb and heavy, and he curled it around in his mouth awkwardly before he could get it to cooperate. "And where does this leave me? While I'm being surrounded by the unknown and dangerous, I'm also being pressed to follow a mysterious, religious nut who might just be crazy."

"I've been called crazy before." John smiled again as he stepped toward the door.

"By the way," he said, looking back at Phillip, "down here, it's more than just a fight against dangerous people. Rather, it involves a battle against Satan's dark kingdom. Satan uses people in his battle. That's why we need supernatural help, which comes from God's kingdom."

Phillip caught his breath. He shook off a shiver. There had been too much talk about the darker side of things. Devil stuff. Even Sherry was thinking the kids were chasing after some invisible devils. Or was she thinking the devils were chasing the kids? *Oh man, this is way too far out to be fetched!* Phillip's brows lifted into his forehead. "You make this sound like a *Star*

Wars movie. Only in this movie, the good people only sit around and pray."

"We pray to be led by the spirit of God."

"Okay then, it sounds like you are obsessed or possessed with this Spirit thing. I thought being possessed was bad." Phillip grinned, having delivered a perfect stab.

"Depends on what kingdom you permit to take over your life. It certainly could be very bad, Phillip." John's voice was deeper now. His laugh line had disappeared. "If we are owned by the kingdom of darkness, we are on the dark road of destruction. Some of the devil's gang are cruising along, unaware of their blindfolds, and content to believe the lies that are being fed to them. Others, like Charley used to be, are physically possessed by unloving spirits from the dark kingdom as well."

"Are you telling me there is good possession and bad possession?" Phillip asked, trying to find a way to pull a spear out of his own gut.

"Absolutely! The Bible says, 'Choose you this day whom you will serve.'" John held the door open for Phillip. "In God's kingdom, we must learn to know the voice of Jesus, which is the only true way. It is glorious to be possessed by His Holy Spirit and to be led by Him. His powerful possession is truth, and it is the life that triumphs over the other kingdom of death and lies."

"Oh, John"—Phillip arched his brow, seething a little that someone could doubt his ability to know the difference between a lie and the truth—"I've been doing what I'm doing for quite some time now. I can't remember a single time when I've been duped by anyone's lies."

"Maybe," John answered with a hint of insistence in his eyes. "I should stress to you that the lord of darkness is ever so clever. He isn't a dummy. And he is leading a worldwide hate war against God. He can best hurt God by deceiving what God loves most, which is His created humans. The devil needs to be a shrewd strategist to lead such an army of people to hell with him. He knows all of us very well. He studies us and schemes carefully on how to deceive us. He may just feed us a few little lies, which sound right. The bait will be coated and taste good. Soon he has us eating out of our own hand. We believe ourselves, and we certainly can't see that we are in his trap. Nope. If we've listened to wrong voices and have bought into them, we are deceived and blindfolded. The devil's master plan is to keep people from understanding how much God loves them; how powerful is the blood of Jesus to cleanse them from sin; how supernatural is the resurrection power of Jesus, which, through the Holy Spirit, is fully capable today of bringing people out of the grave of death and into His life. The devil doesn't want anyone to know of that resurrection power. He does a good job keeping even churched people from experiencing this great truth."

They walked into the parking lot. Phillip stared at the cement. It was obvious. He wasn't making any headway with John.

John opened the door of a 1998 dark green Buick. "You ready to see Abby?"

"But I didn't change anything on the records!" Sherry insisted. She could feel her face boiling to red.

Kevin leaned over her desk. His eyes flashed seriousness. A wide-boned face angled into an almost perfect V with the goatee at chin level. He slapped the papers on Sherry's desk in front of her. "See for yourself. It is inconsistent with the meeting report. The State picked up on this, Sherry! Now they suspect we were not compliant with Medicare dates. Do you have any idea what this is going to cost us?" His voice was sharp, slicing through her reserve.

"I kept a draft of this report on my computer. I know I did not change any dates." Sherry could feel her voice quivering along with a juddering heart. She clicked on the document and sent it to the printer. "Kevin, you know how careful I am with my work."

Sherry tapped her fingers on the desk, waiting for page seven to slip onto the printer tray. She could feel Kevin's breath blowing down on her. She couldn't bear to look up and meet his fuming eyes. "Page seven. Here it is." Her eyes scurried to paragraph three, and she began to read aloud. "The above dates were changed to be in compliance with Medicare Statutes." She grappled for some right words, for something to prove her innocence. "This isn't right. Someone has access to my computer!"

Sherry was grateful for a knock on her office door. Her head felt like it was in the spin cycle of her washing machine.

"Kevin," the honey-laced voice said his name. "Hope I'm not late."

"Not at all. I was hoping you'd join me for supper. We can talk over soup and coffee."

Sherry looked up to see him accept the woman's hand and hold it with both of his hands.

"Madame, I'd like you to meet my secretary, Sherry."

Sherry felt her spine freeze as she looked into a set of the coldest, blackest, hate-filled eyes.

———

"Oh, Mable. I haven't had homemade bread for so long." Abby's eyes rolled up in delight. "I think the last time I tasted homemade bread was when I lived with you." She clapped her hands and let out a breath. "These rolls are made with oatmeal, too, aren't they?"

"You remember that too. My, I hope all your memories of staying with me are good ones." Mable chuckled as she piled the warm buns in a basket.

"Only the best!" Abby switched over to a scanning mode. "Where is everyone anyway? It looks like we have everything ready, but where are the guests?"

"Well, ah, I thought they'd be here by now. John went to pick up Phillip. They should be coming right along any moment now." Mable's sweet, rolling cheeks creased with her smile.

"That's odd."

"What's odd, dear?" Mable asked, raising bushy brows.

"Just that Phillip usually drives himself around. Why would John need to go and retrieve him?"

"Well, I'm not sure, but John went that way to get those journals for you anyway. There are safety concerns, as well you know, Abby. You can trust John. He is a very wise and God-fearing man."

"I had always wondered what it would be like to have a kind father, someone who really cared about me. I almost dared to hope that John could become that figure to me. He sorta became that hero back then."

Mable's eyes held a hug in them and she opened her arms to Abby.

Mable was a soft pillow against Abby's face. "I am grateful to both of you," Abby sighed.

Sherry was able to shut off her computer, but there was no powering off the tears. They streamed from her eyes, like the pilgrims pouring freely from the *Mayflower*.

Sherry locked her office door behind her. She felt uneasy and unsafe.

Sherry grabbed at her head. "Father? Are you there? I do want to believe in Your Son Jesus. I was told You have given me Your very powerful Holy Spirit to live within me. If He is there, I want to hear Your voice, and I so desperately need help now."

"Hi, Phillip." Charley greeted him from the back seat.

"Charley. I'm glad John brought you along." Phillip turned to shake the young man's hand. "Hey, you did a great job on that debate show. I mean, everyone else was falling to pieces around you. You just sat there rock solid."

"It was awesome, Phillip. The whole time I was sitting there I was wrapped in such peace. 'Course, I knew John was praying.'"

"I could see that peace written all over you," Phillip admitted. "Glad you are going to be at dinner with us tonight."

"I wouldn't miss it. John tells me his sister, Mable, is the best cook around these parts." Charley chuckled. "John's cooking isn't bad, but I wouldn't mind tasting an improvement."

John reached into the back seat and tousled Charley's hair. "It's going to be liver and onions for you for the rest of the month!"

Charley rested his head back on the seat. "It's going to be great spending some time with Abby."

"I can't wait 'til she gets back to the paper. It's a mess without her." Phillip glanced back at Charley.

"She did a great job on the article about me and Jasper. She told the truth just like I asked her to do."

"This wasn't the average run-of-the-mill type story, Charley. She told the facts as they happened. But now the public is going to demand more answers. The media certainly isn't going to cover this thing accurately." Phillip grimaced. "There's another strange side to all of this."

"What's that?" Charley echoed.

"Just seems so strange." Phillip shook his head, like he wanted to line up the dice in his brain. "Christianity is a religion, isn't it? So why wouldn't all these religious people, like Abby's pastor, believe that God did this for Charley? He and others preach about God yet don't believe God is capable of doing the miraculous today. Seems they'd just as soon rip a person like Paul to shreds for daring to make a bold statement that God can do something powerful like deliver Charley."

John looked straight ahead, keeping his eyes on the road. Phillip could see the twitch of John's face before the movement of his lips.

"You were a cop," John said, breaking the awkward silence. "You were a good one, too. You probably know many wonderful law enforcers. But have you ever come across one or two who were crooked and pretending to be law-abiding citizens?"

"Oh." Phillip heaved a breath. "Say no more." He gagged, like he was about to swallow the same rotten ham sandwiched between lies. "I know a couple who would do anything to save their own hides, even if it meant protecting a crime."

An I-thought-so grin creased John's face.

"So how do you know the difference between those in the profession who are good and decent from those who are not honest? I mean, how do you know who is telling the truth and who is telling the lies?"

Phillip let out a whistle. "Sometimes it's hard. At least it isn't easy until I've been around them long enough to know they're double-dealers."

"And religious people can be double-dipping with the enemy, too. Talk is cheap. God isn't interested in cheap talk. It isn't religion that attracts God to a person. In fact, Jesus was often confronted by the religious Pharisees and scribes, who knew the law backward and forward. Seems they were the ones often pointing a finger of rebellion and accusation in the very face of Jesus and denying His power," John said with a shake of his head. "God is attracted to people who honor Him with their hearts. He is looking for people who fear Him and who are looking for a pure relationship with Him. Religion doesn't mean a relationship. He wants commitment and obedience, not smooth talk and double minds. So it doesn't surprise me that religious people could slander a real man of God."

Phillip arched a questioning brow. "So you can never be sure about the clergy people either until you are around them long enough to tell if they are who they say they are."

"Yep. The Bible says we can know if a person is in a true relationship with Jesus by their fruit. God tells us what kind of fruit He expects us to have if we are in a relationship with Him. This is the fruit of the Spirit, which is the very character of God. It says in Galatians 5:22 that 'The fruit of the Spirit is love, joy, peace, long suffering, kindness, goodness, faithfulness, gentleness, self-control. Against such there is no law.'"

John tapped lightly on his brakes to slow for the sharp curve. "I can assure you, Phillip, the Holy Spirit is producing all of the above fruit in the young pastor Paul's life."

Phillip could hear the smile in John's voice.

"You talk a lot about the Holy Spirit." Phillip sounded offended.

"Yes, I do." John tilted his head back with laughter. "Yes, I do. He is the very power of God, who raised Jesus Christ from the dead. And He lives in me. I should be excited about that. I have the same dead-raising power as Jesus did living in me."

Phillip harnessed his urge to throw up his hands in frustration. "You are like a turtle, John. You duck inside your secret shell and expect me to understand what in the blazes you're talking about. Believe me, I have searched out many trails. Some of them ended up being only rabbit trails." Phillip cranked his neck to look more squarely at John. "We can't be endlessly sniffing out a trail like a dog after a phantom raccoon. So I hope this Holy Spirit person whom you or I can't see has a good sniffer. I really do hope that."

John laughed heartily again. "He does, son. He really does. You will come to realize that one day."

Skirts of pinks and reds hung from the clouds. It was as though the whole sky was dressed for some kind of celebration. As Sherry stepped out of her car to visit with Pastor Paul and his wife, it felt like she might just step right into the warmth and beauty of the sunset's glory. She closed her eyes and took in a deep breath of the evening air, letting it soothe her frazzled nerves.

Victoria opened the door and welcomed Sherry in.

Sweet perfumed candles greeted her senses as she stepped into the small but quaint cabin home. "You have a lovely home," Sherry said, trying to blink back the tears that pooled at her lashes. "Thanks for letting me come early, before church starts."

Just a few minutes before, Sherry had felt the same old emotional knife stabbing, pushing deeper, trying to cut through her life vein. Now, an odd thing was happening. She was realizing, for the very first time, she no longer wanted to protect that knife. For too long now she had believed that blade of guilt and shame had a right to spear through her and make her bleed out emotionally.

Victoria placed a hand on Sherry's shoulder. "Please, Sherry, sit down. Would you like some coffee?"

Sherry shook her head, declining the coffee. She stood there wringing her fingers together. Everything felt locked up inside of her.

"Are you okay?" Victoria asked.

"So much has happened. I've never felt so uncertain of the future or as frightened as I do now. I feel like I'm still a mess inside. I feel guilt and shame and voices telling me that life is hopeless. It keeps me from believing. It keeps me afraid and unable to trust." Words began to flow like an uncovered spring. "Pastor Paul, it causes me to panic and think it could be too late for me. It causes me to think maybe He doesn't want to help me or to answer my prayers after all. But I don't want to think this way any longer. I don't want to be a miserable victim anymore."

Pastor Paul pulled up a chair and sat facing Sherry. "The spirit of fear wants to keep you hopelessly chained to your past. The devil is a liar. He hates it when someone is transferred out of his dark kingdom into the kingdom of light. So he tries to keep our chooser in his dark and hopeless kingdom. Sherry, when you belonged to the devil, he controlled your mind. He built up his kingdom and has put his mind-sets there. He doesn't want to lose his rights to you. When you gave your life to Jesus, however, you were given a mighty weapon of truth to pull down the devil's strongholds, which are in your mind."

"What am I to do?" She asked, her lips drawn thin.

"In the kingdom of God, Sherry, there are new protocols. Now you must learn to be led by the Spirit of God. In the past, you were led by the rules of the world and by your own reasoning."

A bright pink hue from the evening sun splashed and waved its farewell through a cabin window. It lingered on the young pastor's face. His expression was genuine. The words from his mouth were like a bowling ball knocking down the shaky pins in her heart.

"Sherry," Pastor Paul continued, "emotions lead people in the wrong direction. Emotions change with the circumstances of life. Our emotions can feel spiritual one moment and hopeless the next. Fear often happens when our emotions lead us into a depressed state. Fear is opposite of faith."

"But how can I have this faith?" Sherry asked. "I don't want this horrible fear any longer. I want to believe bigger."

"Yes." Paul smiled. "You want to believe bigger because there is a hunger and thirst for more of God in you. And that faith will come as you open your heart to the Word of God. The mind-sets of your past must be renewed. That's what the Word of God does. It renews our minds. Every day as you cry out for more of Him and as you feed on the words of life in this book"— Paul's hand tightened about his Bible as he pulled it up next to his heart—"the Holy Spirit will spark His words to life in your heart. This is the powerful Word of God, which will renew your mind and which will transform your life."

"But there's more!" Sherry cried. "Something terribly evil is happening. It's like there is a plot against me, my children, and you, Pastor Paul." An unexpected moan escaped from Sherry's lips. "I overheard my daughter and her boyfriend. She's involved in some kind of coven. There's a group of them meeting somewhere in the area." Sherry's head sunk, and she grabbed at it with both hands. "My babies. Will God save my babies? I don't know how to help them. I can only sit helplessly by and love them and beg God to save them."

Sherry accepted a Kleenex from Victoria's hand. "That's not all." She sniffed back a sob. "They have prayed a black dragon curse over you and your family," her voice muffled with sobs. "It's just the most terrible thing. I'm so sorry."

"Sherry, may I pray for you?" Pastor Paul asked sincerely.

Sherry nodded.

"Father, in Jesus name and by the authority in His name, I ask that the enemy's assignment against Sherry be stopped. I command fear to release its hold on Sherry right now, for it is written that Jesus came to destroy the works of the devil. Jesus, be the Lord of Sherry's mind and of her emotions. I ask for warring angels to be released now in her defense. I ask for the power of Your blood to be about her and her family. Protect them, Lord. Let Your peace flood Sherry. Let Your perfect love come and replace that fear. In the name of Jesus I ask these things."

"Sherry," Victoria spoke softly, "God understands how much you love your children. He loves them even more."

"And," Pastor Paul added, "He wants the fruit of your womb to be blessed. He said the fruit of your womb is a reward from Him. You can pray for your children, Sherry. Never forget that the one in you, who is the Holy Spirit, is greater than the enemy. That's His promise. It's His Word."

"I'm so sorry you and your family have been pulled into this, too," Sherry said, choking on her words. "Jamie said that dragon curse is the very worst curse."

"Sherry, so long as I walk obediently with the Lord, He protects me from curses and evil. The devil can't touch me with any of those curses." Paul smiled with confidence. "All through the Bible there are promises of blessings to those who obey God. On the other hand, curses are promised to those who will not obey God, who choose to live apart from God, and who willingly rebel against God's authority."

Sherry's eyes widened. "I don't want those curses either," she cried. "I don't want them on my children."

"You have realized that your life is empty without Jesus. You responded to Him with instant obedience the day you, by faith, asked Jesus to be your Lord and Savior. Now, Sherry, you must learn to be submitted to His lordship. He will show you how."

"Yes, but I don't think I understand what it is to obey Him." Sherry trembled at the new realization.

"It simply means that He will be King in your life," Paul began to explain. "It is choosing to put Him and His kingdom first. It means you will no longer seek to obey what fits into your plans. Nothing must be more important than to instantly obey Him. Obedience is submission to Him. Disobedience is seeking our own way, which is sin. Not to submit to God opens the door to rebellion, which is how the devil is able to bring in a curse."

"Bu…but," Sherry stuttered, "how do I know what to obey? What if I do it wrong?"

"The Holy Spirit is here for that very reason. He is to lead you into all truth. The Holy Spirit will help you. God knows your heart yearns to walk in obedience toward Him. Ask Him to help." A smile danced in Paul's eyes. "It is what He shows you, that you must be quick to obey. As you allow Him to speak to you from His Word, you will begin to understand more."

Victoria's eyes sparkled with merriment. "Oh, Sherry, when your broken heart cried out yes to God, the Holy Spirit came to dwell within you. Your life is not meant to be broken and empty any longer. He came to give you a powerful new beginning." Victoria squeezed Sherry's hand. "See, He came to completely save you. That means He wants to be your deliverer and healer, too. He wants you emotionally healed as well. Then you will be able to hear His voice and learn to obey Him."

Victoria handed Sherry a booklet. "This is a Bible study guide. Would you be willing to study through the Bible?"

Sherry read aloud, "The Gospel of John." She opened it and flipped through a few pages. "Yes, I want to understand the Bible."

"Great!" Paul said. "And, Victoria can write down a couple verses about fear for you to pray each day. It would be helpful for you to pray them several times a day. He has not given you a spirit of fear, but of power, of love, and of a strong mind."

At the sound of the doorbell, Paul jumped up.

Through her tear-soaked eyes, Sherry was able to recognize faces as they began to fill the small house.

Victoria extended her hand to each of the visitors. "I want to be sure everyone here knows Sherry. A couple weeks ago Sherry visited our church. She received Jesus as her Savior and friend that day. Please welcome her here with us tonight."

All the visitors surrounded Sherry offering handshakes, smiles, and hugs. A young man with a ponytail squeezed Sherry's hand. "I'm David," he said. Immediately, Sherry recognized David as the drummer. His exterior still looked rugged, tough, but Sherry was more drawn to his eyes. They were bold eyes yet tinged with gentleness.

Another couple, about Sherry's age, greeted her. "I'm Jake, and this is my wife, Barb." Barb's effervescence was like a wand blowing bubbles of joy.

A young woman, whose face was delicate and lovely, introduced herself as Rachael.

Paul began reading from his Bible. "These Words of God are from Acts 16:26. 'Suddenly there was a great earthquake, so that the foundations of the prison were shaken, and immediately all the doors were opened and everyone's chains were loosed.'"

Joy sparked from Paul's eyes. "Two men, Paul and Silas, were beaten and thrown into prison for proclaiming Jesus. While shackled in that prison, their faith in Jesus remained strong. They were filled with the Holy Spirit. They had experienced His resurrection power, which is powerful to break any shackle! Their feet may have been fastened in stocks, but they were praising God and praying. That's what we want to do here tonight, praise and pray. See, there were other people shackled in that prison with Paul and Silas. As Paul and Silas praised and prayed, a marvelous thing happened. God sent an earthquake, and it shook the foundation of that prison. Hear this!" Paul cried out from his heart. "Please hear this. As these two men praised and prayed, this verse says 'all the doors were opened and everyone's chains were loosed.'" Paul took a minute to grab eye contact with each of his listeners.

"God's people need to know this! Paul and Silas knew this. That is why they dared praise God. That is why they were praying. They knew that it is God's will to break the shackles that hold people in bondage. They knew God could always open a door! He can always open a door! Paul and Silas were not afraid to suffer for this truth."

Sherry's heart was beating with an eagerness to embrace every word she was hearing.

"We are here to pray tonight. We will not settle for a lukewarm slumber bath. We are going to pray for prison doors to be shaken open, and shackles and chains to fall from the captives, for people to be set free from sin and bondage. This is the will of God. This is His heart. This is our commission."

A stunning silence happened as those about Sherry fell to their knees.

It was as though something, as glorious as heaven might be, flooded into that little living room. Sherry felt it settle around her. She could scarcely breathe for the presence was divine, pure, all-searching, all-knowing, and powerful. It bade her to humbly seek her knees. She could not close the pages of her life. They lay bare and open before the eyes of Jesus. That was okay. Sherry knew all the shackles of her past had fallen off. She knew that before her, He was opening the right door. She knew what she wanted now. She wanted so much more of this divine presence.

"Thank God you are okay, Aunt Abby." Charley's face beamed at her. "Phillip told me all about the adventures he and Caleb had rescuing you."

Abby put another forkful of meat loaf in her ketchup pile and swirled it around until it was well coated. She was smiling back at Charley. "I sure am grateful for that. Too bad Caleb wasn't here to taste this delicious meat loaf."

"You know, you're face just lit up when you mentioned Caleb's name," Phillip said with a grin. "I think I noticed a soft pink blush come over your entire face a couple days ago when your eyes met his."

Charley's green eyes twinkled like the shimmer of rain on spring leaves. "I think he is a great guy."

"Very brave," Abby whispered.

"Wait a minute," Phillip said, wearing a hurt look on his face. "What about me? Aren't I B-R-A-V-E?" He drug out the word.

"Yes, you are brave," Abby said, faking a yawn. "And besides being a pain right now, I can imagine that you are behind on everything, and that there will be a heaping pile of paperwork stacked up on your desk waiting for me."

"You got that right," Phillip chimed in. "I'm miserably behind in that office."

"It may be a few days before you need worry about that paperwork, Abby. Safety first." John answered before tasting another sip of water.

"Well, one thing is certain." Phillip wiped his mouth with a napkin. "Not to worry, the work is not about to go away."

"That's comforting." Abby sighed. "Now if I could just remember more. I have a faint recollection of feeling drugged. There was vomit. My vomit. And"—her voice raised an octave—"there was a toilet. It was an old cracked toilet." Her head sunk a little. "Everything else is still spinning around in my brain."

John's heart reached out to her. "Yes, you were drugged. Honey, they didn't want you to show up for that debate. They didn't plan for Charley to be there, either. But he was."

"I told them the truth, Aunt Abby, even though they didn't want to hear it," Charley added with a thumbs-up.

"Don't you worry," Phillip added. "We are close to nabbing the whole lot of those villains. Their plots are about to be dismantled. You can be sure of that." He stared a moment at his empty plate. "Just a few puzzle pieces missing. Right, John?"

"We need to be praying and listening for the Spirit's leading," John answered.

"Pfft," Phillip muttered.

"Would you care for more meat loaf, Phillip?" Mable asked.

"How could I pass that by? John, your sister is a fantastic cook."

"Aw," Mable cooed. "Bet your wife is just as good at cooking." Mable raised her eyes. "My goodness, John, we should have invited his wife tonight!"

"Well, Sherry, had other plans tonight," Phillip answered. "She was getting together at Pastor Paul's place for some sort of prayer meeting." Phillip stabbed another potato. "I'm sure she would have loved being here otherwise."

Phillip's eyes took on a more serious depth. "Sherry seemed troubled the other morning. She started telling me something about Jamie and some kind of witch stuff. Then she burst into tears. I was in a hurry as usual and told her we'd talk later. That's when she said she'd be gone tonight. Said she needed to talk to Pastor Paul."

"That must be very hard for her," Mable said, shaking her head. "I'm glad she is getting help from Pastor Paul. That's a mighty big burden to carry inside of her."

Phillip scooted back in his chair, squared his shoulders and changed the subject. "John, from what I understand, you already know who is behind this whole bizarre plot. Where is Charley's father?"

"Remember, this is an octopus, Phillip. You can't just grab one leg, or you'll be strangled by another. We need people praying for the right opportunity to happen, for the whole creature to be exposed." John laid his fork down and rested back on his chair. "The time isn't right. As you know, the law requires red-handed proof, which I am not prepared at this time to give."

"You sound like a lawyer or something," Phillip harrumphed.

"I was," John chuckled. "Today, however, I work for a better judge."

Shadowy clouds pulled their dismal curtain between Sherry and the moon's beam. They seemed to be saying,

"Lights out!" Sherry yawned under their hypnotizing games. She signaled to take a short cut home.

Words to a chorus they had sung that night rang through Sherry's mind and heart. *Come. Now is the time to worship. Come. Now is the time to give your heart.* It had been an awesome night. She had never heard people pray the way this small gathering had prayed tonight. Pastor Paul had said, "Obedience is the highest form of worship." His words left a fear in her heart. It was a different kind of fear, a kind she could not explain. She wanted to learn obedience. She wanted Jesus to be King in her life.

Willingly we choose to surrender our hearts. Willingly our knees will bow. Her heart was beating to the song's rhythm now. "Jesus, I want to surrender my heart to You. I want You to be King."

A winged-creature swooped and dropped low. Sherry attempted to dodge it, but she felt and heard the clobbering smack against her car. "Oh! Shoot, did I hit it?" She stepped out of her car. Big, circular owl eyes peered up at her. It was attempting to drag its battered body away. Sherry groaned. "Now what am I suppose to do with you? Why were you stupid enough to fly into my car anyway?" She groaned again. "And look at my rear view mirror!" The glass had been scattered. The mounting bracket sagged as much as the owl's broken wing.

"Who can I call this late? I'll have to call 911 for you." The wounded creature's eyes seemed haunting and tormenting to Sherry's well-being, and a shiver ran over her entire body.

Sherry reached into a pocket and grabbed her cell. As she lifted the phone to her ears, her eyes saw a moving object on the road ahead of her. A cold tenseness poured its icy contents over her and through her until every cell in her body was seized by fear. She wanted to scream, but the words were glued cold in her throat.

Sherry's eyes became fixed solid on the figure caught between the headlights of her car and the woods.

Sherry remembered that Victoria had written down some verses for her to pray whenever she felt afraid. "Lord, help!" she cried. "Help me not to be afraid."

As the figure came closer, Sherry realized it was a woman. She appeared hurt. She was stumbling around. She was fragile. "You okay?" Sherry blurted out.

"I need to get to safety," came the weak, feminine answer. The woman was moving closer, near enough now for Sherry to see long blonde hair hanging lifelessly, except for the areas where it stuck to a long, slender, and bloodied face.

"Well, I can drive you somewhere safe." Sherry sucked in some air with her words.

"Please. That would be great." The woman teetered weakly in front of the headlights.

"You're hurt bad! Oh my, what happened to you?" Sherry asked as she ran to the woman's side. "Who did this to you? I need to call for help."

"No!" the woman shrieked. "Please no."

"Can't anyway," Sherry said, letting out a frustrated puff. "Absolutely no signal here. Should have known my cell wouldn't work out here in the back woods."

Sherry stared. The woman's eyes were near swollen shut. Her lips had been beaten so badly they covered at least half of her lower face. Her face had been battered out of proportion. "But you need a doctor."

"My husband is a very influential man. He will be looking for me. I can't take any chances. Please just drive me away from here," she whimpered.

Sherry steadied the woman into the car and closed the door behind her. As she was about to leave, Sherry turned and noticed the owl had drug itself into the ditch. Still she could see the whites of its eyes—eyes that were glaring at her. Another pair of eyes flashed like burning embers into her memory. Sherry cringed, remembering the hate-filled eyes of Kevin's visitor.

"I can drive you to the hospital in Edge Water," Sherry suggested.

"No. I can't be seen by anyone from around here. I'm looking to find someone. His name is John Wiseman. I heard he is back."

"I've never heard that name," Sherry answered with a confused shake of her head. "My husband has been meeting with some man named John, but I know nothing about the man, not even his last name."

"Could he possibly be the man helping Charley and Abby Frank?" The woman sat up straighter, and hope jumped from her eyes like sparks from jumper cables.

Sherry swallowed her words. *Who is this woman?* Sherry began to drive, trying to catch a few moments to collect her thoughts. She wasn't sure how to answer this stranger. She wasn't sure if she should answer any question involving Charley and Abby.

"What's your name?" the woman asked.

"Sherry." She felt safe with such a short answer.

"Oh yes, Sherry. You must be Phillip's wife." The woman sighed, and her body relaxed.

Sherry slammed on the breaks, bringing her car to a screeching halt. A warning, brighter than a police siren, flashed in her mind. "How do you know Phillip? How do you know Abby and Charley and me for that matter? And who are you?" Sherry's voice heated up with boldness.

"I'm Lexi." The woman's head hung. "And you work for my husband, Kevin."

Sherry's heart felt like a flat tire on the freeway. It was thudding, bucking. Her body was like a car on the road, spinning recklessly with a flat tire.

"Relax, Sherry. I'm on your side." Lexi's voice jolted Sherry back to her senses. "I just need to talk with John."

"And I need to know what's going on!" Sherry straightened her back and locked eyes with Lexi. "This whole thing with Charley is setting off a rush of bizarre happenings. Your husband included! He has been down-right nasty to me lately. And look at you! Did he do this to you?"

"Sherry, trust me now. I need to speak with John. Or could you just give him this?" The woman reached in her pocket and pulled out an envelope. "You must give it only to him. It is enough now that John knows. It's best this way. Just drop me off at the junction of Forty-one. I will find my way to safety from there."

Sherry felt numb. "But I don't understand. Can't you please shed some light on all of this for me?" Sherry could feel her spine prickle with fear. "Please, Lexi. There was this woman who came to the office this morning. She was very evil—dark-black hair and black, hateful eyes. She was haunting. It was almost like she could have been the devil's wife. She was with Kevin."

Lexi blanched and scooted around uncomfortably in her seat.

"Yes, that would be Jezra," Lexi whispered.

"Jezra? Who is she?" Sherry swallowed hard.

"That's her real name. Though, she goes by aliases. And," Lexi said with a shiver, "she is a high priestess. You know right, Sherry. Jezra is a very evil woman with dark powers. And my husband is captivated with her and her powers. She hates me, too."

Suddenly Sherry remembered where she had seen Jezra's face. "Could she also be the woman who goes by the name Lorsey Zany, representing some animal welfare person?"

"Yes. She plays many roles. Jezra is involved in the most radical forms of activism. It is part of her rebellious nature."

"That's weird," Sherry said with a shake of her head. "Why animal activism?"

Lexi's eyes took on the evening's chill. "She hates God's authority. Everything that is done in the evil kingdom is an attempt to strike down the very authority of God. So, you see, Sherry, because God gave man dominion and authority over the animals, some, like Jezra, will try to reverse what God said. In this role, Jezra is planting the idea that what God said isn't true. She wants people to rebel against what

God said and believe that animals are equal to man and not to be owned by a man. Kinda like scientific creation, she would want people to rebel against God creating a person in His own image. No, she would say man created himself or evolved into himself. That sort of thing."

"She looks the part. Dangerous and crazy is how I picture her."

"Well," Lexi continued, "she doesn't always play the crazy part. Sometimes she can morph into a subtly dangerous woman. Jezra can have people eating out of her hand and following her. She has an unusual gifting to deceive people."

Lexi glanced at Sherry. "It's kind of like the Bible story of Sampson and Delilah. Jezra could convince a guy to lay his head on her lap or even on a chopping block."

"Oh my." Sherry risked a return glance at Lexi.

"Jezra will go right into a church. There she will look and smell like a saint. People will think she is, but they had better watch out. She will get into heads that aren't on straight and run away with them."

Sherry could feel the blood rushing in her ears. "Church?"

Pin-dropping silence followed. Lexi stared out of the car window for a minute. Then she added with a heavy voice. "Jezra got an applaud from my father-in-law, Richard Staunch. Jezra, with all of her seductive powers, was welcomed with open arms into his church. Then my husband welcomed Jezra into his open arms."

Chapter Nine

Abby stood outside Mable's charming country home. She felt better. She was energized in the morning sunshine. She felt motivated by the Eager River, which reached for and captured the sun rays in its little dance. It moved right along, enjoying the playful breeze. Abby breathed in deeply. Everything smelled fresh, laced with beauty. Everything was new. She was drinking in the river's energy. She should be moving on now, too. First, she needed the key information, which was still blocked from her memory. Who wanted to kill her? Would she be shocked to find out who that person was? When would she be safe enough to return to work for *Edge Water Times*?

Abby's fingers tightened around the journal she held in her hand.

"Morning, Aunt Abby!" Charley's voice tossed sweetly in the spring breeze.

"Where have you been?" Abby quipped. "Mable had the best flapjacks! I'm sure she saved some for you."

"I've been out walking around the river. So much to think about and pray about." He choked back some unspoken emotions. "Guess I'm trying to imagine what life down here could have been if I had been a normal child. Still, I want to experience right now everything life is meant to be with God in it."

Abby listened. She watched his eyes scan the horizon.

"Me too," she answered, still staring up into the blue. "What would normal feel like?" Abby breathed deeply as a breeze played with her face. "I love to write, Charley. But I can't rewrite the book of my past. I wish I could because I hate the old book so much!"

Charley gathered her with his eyes. "I believe in new books, Abby. Mom did too. I think you can begin to write a new book."

Abby's hand lifted Julie's journal to eye level. "I don't know, Charley. So much of what I have been reading is about the hallmark of pain. Why have our lives been branded as worthy only of hurt and rejection?"

"Abby, can we sit down over there at the river's bank? It's so pretty there. And could you read me some from Mom's writings?"

Abby nodded. She hooked her hand in Charley's elbow, and he gently guided her down to the river.

"Charley."

"Huh?"

"I can't tell you how wonderful it is to have you this way. I mean, you are such a beautiful person. It's as though you are a gift from Julie to me. Maybe you are her angel?" Abby's eyes had grown large and serious.

"I'm not an angel." Charley laughed. "But I am family. We have each other, Abby. Hey, here's a great spot to sit. I love soaking in the sun. Out here it's like there never was a problem."

"Look, Charley. This journal starts in December of 1992. You were born in December!"

Abby paged through the journal to December 18. "You ready for me to read?"

The blue of the river with its glint of sun had invaded Charley's eyes. "Yes, I am."

There are few words to describe childbirth. I labored all night. "It takes time," the nurse had said over and over again. While I waited for that time to arrive, I thought I might simply faint from the pain. I wonder if it would have been easier if I could have had someone to sit by me and love me through all of it. Even the nurse had a sneer on her face. Once she said, "Kids shouldn't be having babies." I think she thought I was evil. I could tell the doctor did not appreciate being there to deliver my son so bright and early this morning.

Neither did the long wait make me happy. Finally at four this morning I began pushing. I delivered a baby boy at four forty-five. It's still dark outside. It's now six in the morning. He is absolutely gorgeous. Yes, it was all worth it. Childbirth is worth the reward! He has a full head of dark-brown hair. I love his button nose and his round cheeks. I counted his fingers and his toes, and they are all there. He is hungry, and this is an unbelievable feeling holding him so close to me. He is such a part of me. I love him already, and I want to hold him this near my heart forever.

Abby cast an understanding glance at Charley, watching as a tear graced down his face, then another tear and still more left shimmering trails on his skin. He sat beside her. He looked so innocent, so undeserving of all that had happened to him.

"She loved you so much, Charley."

"Yes," Charley mouthed the words. "What a wonderful day it will be to see her again. Then I will tell her how much I love her, too. I never really got the chance to mention it down here. Read some more to me," he said, hanging his heart from his sleeve.

Abby turned the page. It was still dated December 18.

How could they take my baby? He's mine! A policeman and a woman from child protection came right to my bed and took my baby from me. They said I was too young to have a baby. They said I had no home and no place to bring the baby. They said I could never take care of him or provide for him. They said I was always in trouble with the law. "Don't worry," they said. "We will find a good home for him. He needs a home with a good family." They said a troubled teen mom would not be good for Charley. They said "We're sorry," but they were not at all sorry. They said they were still searching for a person from my family worthy to care for my baby. They said I was still a kid and would be placed back with my foster parents. I don't want to go back to my foster parents. They are cruel. I wish

Abby and I could still be with Mable. I know Mable would have been here. She would have taken the baby in, too. She and John moved to Chicago somewhere. If only I knew where to reach them. I would call them. John could help me get Charley back. I don't know if I can go on living knowing my baby is in someone else's arms. Worse yet, what if someone is mean to him? I want my baby back! I simply can't live without him!

A sad silence lingered between Abby and Charley. They shared quiet tears. They huddled together under a questioning sun.

A dark cloud covered the sun's face. Was the sun crying too? Perhaps it was ashamed, sick from witnessing so much injustice, from trying to put light into places where darkness was winning, from trying to warm hurting hearts.

"Julie's life only got more complicated from that point on. She was so little and so lost in such a big world. She ran away shortly thereafter, and I never saw her again," Abby cried. "She was such a beautiful person. She was good all the way through. She was not a troubled teen. She was so much more than that!"

"I have a picture of her," Charley whispered while blinking back tears. "Let me show it to you. I have it in my billfold. John had snapped a picture of her right before she headed this way to be reunited with us." Charley reached in his back pocket and pulled out a brown wallet.

Abby put the picture close to her face, studying it carefully through misty eyes. "Oh, Charley," Abby cried. "She's more beautiful than even I can remember! Absolutely breathtaking. Look at her smile! She really was happy again."

"This is how she looks in my heart," Charley said tenderly. "Long, wavy blonde hair and such a youthful and sweet face. I can imagine she shines right alongside the angels in heaven now."

Abby's breathing became irregular. "Oh, Charley, your mom looks so young and excited in this picture. Julie knew she was coming back to you! She had finally found John!"

"John said she was very happy. She was coming back to both of us. John said she had felt very badly about leaving you, too. She had always tried to protect you and felt like a mom to you."

Abby's heart throbbed remembering Julie's little body standing between Abby and her father. Abby felt her body shaking. "She took his fist for me, Charley. So many times, she stood there bravely as Dad's fist bowled her over."

"That's what Jesus did for us, too, Abby. He took the fist of death for us." A sunbeam, like a spray of fire, flamed over his face as he stared heavenward.

"Abby, look! Look at that cloud," he said pointing to the sky.

They watched as a dark cloud attempted to curl around the sun and take it prisoner. But the brightness of light pierced through the cloud's hideous attempt, unrolling a smoky tail. The sun continued to spew out enough powerful light to fracture through the cloud's angry, serpent-like head, dispersing it into several gray pieces.

A smile burst through Charley's frown. "Did you see that? The sun's light exploded right through that dark cloud. The devil is like that dark cloud, always trying to hide the light from us. But he isn't going to win. His kingdom is darkness, and God's light is going to shatter him."

Abby continued to stare into the sky. "Yes, it does seem more peaceful now that the evil-looking dark cloud broke into tiny pieces. But what about all the dark clouds that hid any hope of light from us as children? Why is evil allowed to keep kids from knowing the security and love they deserve?" Abby asked, nervously pulling a dandelion out of the soft soil.

"That's like asking why Hitler was allowed to kill all of those Jewish people, some which were our ancestors. How could people be so deceived as to listen to such a crazy man? If people don't hear the true voice, they are going to be listening to the wrong voices and be making wrong choices." Charley said, picking up a stone and tossing it into the river.

"But how can a woman feel a baby moving its tiny body inside of her, and experience its birth, and still not love her baby?" Abby whimpered.

"Maybe," Charley said slowly while staring at his hands, "she doesn't know how to live loved. Maybe nobody put a blanket of love over her."

"What?"

"If a mother doesn't know how to live loved, I suspect it might be hard to give love." Charley locked eyes with Abby. "I know it sounds strange, but a person needs to receive love before they can build a relationship on love."

"Well, Julie never had a chance to live loved. And we just read about how much she loved you. In the end she lost everything and she ended up in an ugly pine box."

"Abby, I believe that even in the face of hate and pain, Mom believed in love and she chose it. In the end, Mom's prayers were answered. It didn't matter to her when they laid her body in that old box. She wasn't a misfit any longer. She was happy because she had experienced real love." Charley struggled to hold back his tears. "She wasn't really in that box. I like to think of her going right into the loving arms of Jesus."

"If I can just believe she found happiness! I hope she knew how very much loved she was."

"Abby, she did find out that she was not an unlovable, only to be used, outcast. John had explained to her how much the devil wanted her to believe that about herself. He told her about the big love of God, that Jesus came to heal the heartbroken with outstretched arms. Jesus understands because when He came to walk on this earth, people rejected Him, too. Seems that only those who are broken will open up their hearts and lives to him." Charley's hands cupped over his face.

Their hearts were entwined so differently now. Before Charley's miraculous healing, they were like two strangers. Now they were inseparable family.

Abby remembered how she hadn't been there for Charley when he needed her most. Now he was here for her, letting her pain beat along the same path in his heart.

—⁓⟡⟡⟡⁓—

"Why didn't you call me right there and then?" Phillip shouted.

"I tried. I didn't even have a signal on my cell out there on those back roads," Sherry cried. "Anyway, what was I supposed to do? This woman was scared. She was very scared. She didn't want to be seen by the wrong people. Her life was in danger. That's all I know."

"You should have called the cops!" Phillip slammed his hand against the wall. "This was a domestic assault. If you really wanted to help her, you should have brought her in to make a report of domestic abuse. There are shelters for women like that. You know that, Sherry. For crying out loud, you were an abused woman yourself. There's no excuse for what you did! Well, you need to make a report this morning. It can't wait."

Sherry stood with large, tear-washed eyes. Her mouth parted without words. Her heart raced about unsteadily. Her breathing was rough and uncontrollable. She didn't dare tell him everything. She wondered what he would do if he knew this woman was Kevin's wife. Sherry guessed Phillip would take the bull by the horns. Only this bull, Kevin, might be more dangerous than Phillip could possibly conceive. *So I must be careful. And I need to get the envelope to John.* Sherry gulped. She didn't have any idea how to find him. *Paul would know. I'll call Paul.*

"Are you listening to me, Sherry? You must make a report. Listen to me!"

Sherry began to back up, trying to separate herself from Phillip's angry words. She didn't know what to say. She only sensed grave danger, and saying anything could make matters worse. "Phillip, the woman didn't want me to report anything. She didn't want to be found. I think she was afraid her husband would find her if a report was made out. It could have put her in greater danger."

Sherry began backing away from Phillip. Quietly she opened the bedroom door and slipped inside. Sherry locked the door behind her and threw herself on the bed. Her face and tears found refuge in a pillow.

———

Phillip paid for his fuel and asked the young man at the cash register for direction. "I need to get to 6060 Broad Road, South." Phillip felt his heart hopping like a rabbit being chased by hounds.

From the car window, Phillip watched the buildings blur by. He grimaced. It was about time to uncover the whole puzzle. Neither Abby nor Charley would be safe until all the pieces came together. Today he was just looking for another piece. Someone was blaming Paul for murder—why? How many legs did this octopus have?

Phillip wondered why it felt as though there was a heavy weight stuck right in his gut. He sure carried a short fuse lately. It wasn't like him to let things get on top of him so. He certainly had no good reason to yell at Sherry.

Maybe when things settled down a little; yes, after some of this stuff hitting the fan blows off, maybe then he should think about doing something about his temper problem.

Phillip had dressed in his best black suit. His shirt was bleached white. It was spotless and without any wrinkle. *I look the part at least. I can't let them try to buffalo me. I am all about getting the business done right.*

At the sheriff's office, Phillip stood outside the door. He took a deep breath and let it slowly out, counting to seven. Then another big breath in. "I can do this."

"Come on in, Mr. Acumen." A long, slender hand reached for his. "I took it upon myself to check you out. I hope you don't mind, but we can't be too careful." The tall, too skinny of a bodied man stood before Phillip. They were about equal in height, but there were three times as much of Phillip as there was of Sheriff Nathan Plots.

"I'm just the owner and editor of *Edge Water Times*, sir. I have been handed a document along with a request to publish it. I'd like for you to read it and comment on it if you would. I have some standards to go by, Mr. Plots. I don't purposely print things to destroy the character of good people. I'm sure you understand that." Phillip felt annoyed at the amused look he was receiving from this sheriff. "I have met Reverend Paul

Marvel. He didn't strike me as the sort of person who would murder an innocent person."

"So you consider yourself talented enough to judge a book by its cover?" The sheriff raised up his shoulder, flashing his badge.

"Maybe I do. I've had practice smelling rats. Minister Paul doesn't have that beady-eyed look or the smell of perfume over rot."

"Yes." The sheriff grinned through pale lips. "You strike me as the kind of man who can read through any cover." He picked up the coffee pot and refilled his mug. "Care for some coffee?"

"That would be nice. Thanks."

"I talked with your friend Sheriff Oscar Grand yesterday," Mr. Plots said while pouring coffee in a mug for Phillip and without looking up.

Phillip felt something take a punch at his gut. He gulped back the pain trying to keep his composure. "So you know Oscar?" Phillip asked.

"No. Can't say that I know the man. Um, do you use sugar or cream?"

"Just black. This really has nothing to do with Oscar. I'm not sure why you called him," Phillip said, accepting the cup of coffee.

"I find it peculiar that you are interested in the possible murder of a woman from West Chambers, that's all." The sheriff stirred two heaping teaspoons of sugar into his coffee with only a sneaking glance at Phillip.

"And I find it interesting that the ghost of this woman is accusing a preacher from my home area of murder. There seems to be a lot of hate being smeared against this young man. I don't want to print all these secondhand charges about the pastor without something a little more concrete."

"Hmm. Yes. Your sheriff friend said you like to put your nose right in the middle of things."

Nathan plunked down on his chair. "Take a load off. Have a seat."

Phillip sat down, taking time to choose the right words. "It's my job, I guess." He studied the long-faced sheriff, sitting with lofty confidence. The guy had a little age on him. Thinning hair, combed straight back, gave the sheriff's face a bonier look.

"He say anything else?" Phillip inquired.

The sheriff gave an amused sigh. "I don't think that man trusts you. Sounds like Edge Water has a few dark secrets. This must not be the first time you've been snooping. Maybe you make him nervous. I could tell he's annoyed with you getting involved in things."

Phillip could feel his tank fueling with anger. "I can assure you my business here is because I run a reputable business. I don't believe this article is the truth. I want to print it only with the other side portrayed accurately. The murder investigation addressed in this article should be public knowledge 'round these parts."

Nathan blew out a no-nonsense type of breath. He squared his glasses on his nose and read the document.

"So is he?" Phillip asked with a husky voice.

"Is he what?"

"Is Paul Marvel a murder suspect in the minds of many folk here in West Chambers?"

Nathan gave Phillip a pacifying smile. "There was talk of it. But he was acquitted. It was an odd kind of thing. The whole thing seemed more of a political thing between churches, if you get the drift."

"What were the autopsy results? Surely there was some proof that Paul was innocent."

"I attend the West Chamber's Bible Community Church, which was only a block away from Paul's church. But..." Nathan leaned back in his chair, his long legs propelling the chair into swiveling in a complete circle. He grinned sheepishly. "There was plenty of tension between the churches."

"Why so?" Phillip quizzed.

"Well, from what I hear, things were happening in Paul's church."

"Like what?" Phillip pushed for an answer.

"For example, Mrs. Olson, who was on her deathbed with last stage pancreatic cancer, claimed to be miraculously healed. And Fred Otter, who had been in a wheelchair for six years with a very crippling disease, suddenly was walking about town."

"Why would anybody complain about those things happening?"

"I'm not sure. Made a few people, who seemed more educated in the Bible, quite upset with the young pastor. They didn't believe any of it, even when both Mrs. Olson and Fred were walking around town openly admitting it had happened. So a few people from our church went there themselves to see if they could be healed from various things."

"Were they?"

"Mostly no."

"Okay, back to the point at hand," Phillip said, fiddling with his pen. "Tell me about the woman who died."

Nathan pursed his lips and nodded. "Her name was Ruth. She attended our church, so I knew her quite well. Speculation has it that Ruth visited Paul's church a couple of times, maybe to get some kind of healing for her mental illness. She was a very disturbed, middle-aged woman. Definitely mentally ill. Very driven type. Well, then one day she was found dead. I suppose because she had gone to Paul for help, people assumed he might be linked somehow with her death. The autopsy report showed drug overdose as the cause of death. So given her history and all, there was no way in the end to pin that on the young pastor."

"What's your pastor's name?"

"George Tepid."

"Ah, you think maybe he would have a word with me later today?" Phillip asked.

"I can give you his number," the long-legged man obliged.

"And what about Ruth's family? Is there someone there I could speak with?"

"Hmm. She has a cousin who sporadically attends our church. His name is Mason Olson. Otherwise, I'm not aware of any relatives in this area."

It was another one of those nice evenings—comfortable temperature, really pretty out. Abby loved it at Mable's. She, John, and Charley had gravitated to the river, which coursed proudly through the property. One of Julie's journals was opened on Abby's lap.

"Go ahead. I'm listening." John waited for Abby to read.

"It's been very hard for me to read lately. I can't imagine how awful it was for her to have her baby yanked from her arms. To be pushed around like a nobody. I don't know if I can read anymore. It's just too hard."

"May I read it for you?" Charley asked.

Abby caressed the journal near her heart and then handed it to Charley.

John watched the exchange.

Charley held the journal on his knees. He drew in a large breath of air.

December 23

No voice. I have no voice. I had none to listen. I had hoped that maybe in a court of law someone would give me a chance to talk, that maybe someone would hear what my heart says. Maybe I would be protected by some rights. Instead everyone else read me my rights. Simply stated, I have no rights. I tried to tell them all things they were saying weren't true after all, but my voice was not loud enough. I was told I had legal assistance. The legal aide man representing me said there was nothing he could do to get my baby back to me. The other lawyer was a very snotty woman. She dressed richly, marched around in high heels. They didn't make her look taller or more important to me. She handed the judge all kinds of documents. My last foster mom testified against me. I had run away twice. She thought I would be an unfit mother.

The mental health worker said I had a serious personality disorder, that I would never be stable enough to care for a newborn. But I would! They couldn't hear my voice crying for the chance to be a mom. I wanted to love. I just needed a chance to prove to everyone that I could love, that I wanted to give myself completely to loving my baby. Love. I experienced it only once myself. It was at Mable and John's.

When the judge looked at me, I knew he believed the other people. He had cold and condemning eyes. I had no voice for his ears either. He didn't want to hear me. I kept wondering, *Why does everyone hate me? Why can't somebody hear me?*

John is a lawyer. I know he could and would help me. If only he could have been here today. I was told he left. I was told he died in a car fire. I don't believe it. Mable is gone too. She left to care for her mom. At least I have a memory of love. It is a strong memory. It is enough to assure me that I could give love. I do love Abby, too. I've tried to show her that. I would choose love above hate any day. This Christmas I have a memory of love. And a picture of love, too. I will never forget holding my baby. Everything else I know is pain. Pain is the ugly wrapped package in my heart.

Here I am, my baby robbed from me because of the hate in people around me. And I am faced with the biggest question ever. Is life worth living without love? Could I run far enough to find love? If I could find love, then maybe I would find a voice. Then maybe I would find me. Then maybe someone would get my baby back for me.

Abby struggled to find a rational thought. No words could find her mouth at that moment. It was as though her very breath was being torn from her. So much was left unsaid. Like a half-baked cake, the very heart of her seemed undone. Yes, she was sinking in the middle of it all. Finally she dared to look at John. She lifted her red and swollen eyes to meet his. She felt her throat tightening. "You really are a lawyer, John? You could have helped Julie?"

John sat quietly, his eyes following the river. "Yes. I was a lawyer. Julie couldn't find me because I was in hiding." He turned his pain-filled eyes on Abby and then on Charley. "I had been chased off the case before Julie was even pregnant."

"But why?" Abby begged to know.

"It's a very long story."

"Please tell us." Charley asked, searching John's eyes for clues.

John's eyes reached to the sky. "I had been a lawyer for many years," he answered, still staring upward. "I always credited myself as an honest man. I thought I was smart, too. Didn't think I could ever be fooled. But I was." John's eyes dropped.

"You seem hurt by it," Charley said.

"It had begun as a child protection case. It involved a small child who had been hospitalized with a head injury and other bodily injuries. It had been determined as abuse. The father was sent to jail. All the while, however, he had pleaded innocent. The little girl's mom and dad had separated. The mom had moved back to our county, and I was representing her. The father was being tried for assaulting his child." John's gaze dropped again.

Abby thought John looked a little beaten down. Maybe a bit tired. Certainly what he was saying hurt him. She could only imagine him fighting for that little girl.

"Go on," she encouraged.

"The mother insisted that while she was away at work the baby's father had brutally beat their baby. She testified that when she had returned home that day, she discovered the baby unconscious and immediately called 911. She told me the baby's father had an anger problem and that he had pushed her around a time or two. She had the hospital records. The young man had come to the hospital claiming to have just learned about his daughter's injury. He went into a rage when his rights were read, and he tried fighting off the officers. They struggled to handcuff him right there in the hospital. He swore and spat at them, insisting he had not hurt his daughter. He said it was his girlfriend's new boyfriend who had been babysitting and who had assaulted the child.

"The documents, in favor of the mother's argument, were all there," John continued. "It seemed an easy enough case. The guy was obviously a loser. He had a record of driving while intoxicated. He had such a temper, which had gotten him some other domestic charges as well." John blew out a heavy breath.

"During the trial," he continued, "the woman reported instance after instance of abuse. Meanwhile, he kept yelling from his seat in the courtroom, 'Why doesn't someone check out the blanketty blank boyfriend of hers?'"

"So…" John's word became suspended in the air for an awkward minute. "So we won the case," he continued. "But we really didn't win."

John exhaled slowly. "Remembering back, I can't forget the look of horror on that young man's face. He was being blamed for what happened to his little girl. I can't imagine how he felt looking at her tiny, battered form and to have a jury blame him for it. What must he have felt to have them usher him away behind bars? The doctors had diagnosed his little girl with a significant TBI. He would have to carry the blame for the rest of his life."

"What's TBI?" Charley asked.

"It means a traumatic brain injury."

Abby shook her head. "I don't understand why God lets little children be hurt so by wicked adults."

"And," John said, looking into Abby's eyes, "I thought I had spared this little girl from another wicked assault. But unfortunately, I had been very wrong."

"Why?" Abby felt her heart trying to gallop out of her chest. "What happened?"

"The father had not been guilty of harming his daughter after all. All the while he had only wanted to rescue his daughter and get her away from abuse. Though he had been convicted and labeled as the abuser, it was soon to be learned that he had been telling the truth."

John stared into the distance. Washed with the feelings of the setting sun, John continued. "In less than a month's time, the little girl had been beaten again. This time she didn't survive. It was the new boyfriend who did it. The little girl's mother had been covering up for her new friend from the start. She was an accomplice to the death of her daughter."

"How awful!" Abby gasped. "This makes me so angry when adults hurt children! I don't understand what is lacking in their brains!"

John squeezed Abby's hand. "They lose their ability to nurture and care for their own children for various reasons. Often they have been abused, and then they turn to things like drugs to numb their pain. They may try to find courage at the bottom of a bottle or by popping, sniffing, smoking, or injecting chemicals. They don't start out thinking these mind-altering drugs might cause them to hurt their child. But drugs rewire their brains. Their brains need healing, Abby."

"But you had tried, John. You tried to fight for the little girl," Charley said, sucking in a breath. "It wasn't your fault."

"There's a chapter of mistakes in everyone's life, son. But God is merciful and forgiving. I have blamed myself plenty. Even to this day it is difficult not to think about it, but"—he heaved another big breath out—"God used it as a lesson in my life. I've learned to listen to God now and not lean on my own reasoning."

"Yes, I see you praying very often," Charley added. "You have been a great teacher to me. I've watched you closely."

"I've learned that I must wait upon Him for answers. But back then, I didn't spend time waiting upon Him and praying to be led by the Spirit. I went to church. Tithed. Opened my Bible once in a while. Said a quick prayer before running out the door every morning. I guess I felt like the average Christian pressured by all the demands of life. But after that little girl died, I woke up. I read from the book of Revelations about the lukewarm church of Laodicea and realized I needed to change, too. God wanted me hot and zealous for Him. Believe me"—John's voice began to fade—"I decided to learn to hear His voice."

"And that's why you ran away?" Abby asked, eyes propped open wide.

"I didn't leave then. Actually I was about to take another case. Your case."

Abby's face grew ghostly white. She felt like someone had just slid into the seat between her and death and was about to pull the plug. Her voice cracked. "Julie and me?"

"Yes. I got to know you girls when you stayed with Mable. Thank God the county still does not know that Mable is my sister. She had married and lived here before I came around. I'm glad I kept that a secret. Otherwise, it wouldn't be a hiding place right now."

"A hiding place?" Abby swallowed hard. "Are you still running, John?"

"Abby, I need to keep a low profile for now. I know some people are suspecting I'm not dead like I was reported to be."

"Oh, yeah. The car fire Julie mentioned about in her notes! Why was it rumored that you were in a car fire?" Abby squirmed on the grass beneath her.

"I was on to some things," John answered cautiously. "I had changed. Knowing the truth and standing up for it made some folk very angry. These were big people in big places. They were muckrakers, trying to smear me. They managed to get me barred from practicing law. Guess that wasn't good enough, though. They tried to kill me."

Abby gasped! "Oh my. Did they try to burn you up in your car?"

"They used a car bomb. It was a cold night. Fortunately, I used my remote starter to start the car. I wanted to warm it up. Let me tell you, it warmed up fast!" A faint smile creased John's face. "So I am reportedly dead."

"Why?" Abby continued to question. "Why did they hate you to that point? How could they be that angry over you being a good and honest man?"

"Well, to say the least, I opened a big can of worms. Your mom's attorney was her brother."

"Would that be Uncle Lester?" Abby's body tensed.

"I'm afraid so," John answered.

"He is an awful man. He was mean to us kids. He and my mom drank all the time." Her words trailed off.

"It gets worse." John's voice came up slow and sober. "He has evil friends. One of them is Charley's father."

Abby jumped up. She grabbed her face and covered it with her hands. "Oh, dear God. I should have guessed that," she mumbled into her hands. She could feel the flush of her rising pulse creep up her neck. Something like static was crackling in her mind, giving her head a crazy, spinning feeling. Something big was hiding in the shadows of her past. She just couldn't remember.

A scene from her past. *No! I can't see it. I can't go back.* Abby's right hand fisted and then pushed into her gut, bracing something hideous from being released. But the scene was still there. Who was that little girl crying in a dark bedroom? There were other little girls, too. Who were they? There were other places. There were children crying. There were faces. There were pleas for help. But the hands that grabbed them were not kind or helpful hands.

Abby began to pace beside the river.

John stood and leaned on a tree. His shadow lengthened before him.

Charley glanced at John. He could tell the older man was listening for the right voice. Charley had learned much from John. He knew John spent a lot of time waiting for his orders from the Holy Spirit.

Charley looked past John. Abby was wringing her hands and moving back and forth like an edgy tiger on the river's edge. Charley strolled toward her.

"Are you okay, Aunt Abby?"

"Charley, do you know who your father is?" Torment oozed through Abby's words.

"Oscar is my father. But we must keep this quiet. There is more at stake now than determining who my father is."

"That's right." John appeared suddenly at the riverbank. "You've got to trust me, Abby. I couldn't tell you before, or I would have. The timing just wasn't right. There's more you need to know."

"More?" Abby sunk to her knees in despair.

John knelt beside her and wrapped his arm around her. "You've got be strong now, Abby. You've wanted to hear the truth, and now you need to understand it."

Abby caught her breath. Through teary eyes she looked into John's face. "I need to know."

"Lester and his cronies were laundering you girls. There is a large group of pedophiles in these parts. I know it is hard to hear these things, Abby."

Abby felt weak. What she had buried needed to stay buried, yet her emotions were being trolleyed along like a car in wash. It was a powerful wash of emotions. She wobbled to maintain her balance.

Sensing her growing distress, Charley steadied her against his weight.

"Abby, this can wait." John's voice was as gentle as ever. "It may be easier to break it to you in small pieces."

"No!" Abby swallowed hard. "No. I want to hear all of it."

"Lester knows I know all about it. That's why he hired someone or maybe more than one person to kill me. But it isn't me I'm worried about."

John took his free hand and cupped it under Abby's chin, lifting it until her eyes met his. "Oscar and Lester know Julie can't talk, but they worry she may have communicated something to you." John pulled himself into a standing position and looked down tenderly at Abby. "I believe they are more dangerous now that their plot to kill you didn't work." John blew out a troubled breath. "We are all threats to them, including Phillip, who is working hard to uncover the story.

"What about Phillip? What if he says something?" Abby asked, jumping to her feet.

"I had a talk with him. He is on edge all right, but I don't think he will give out any information. He doesn't want anything to happen to you or Charley."

"Does he know about Lester and the sheriff?" Abby asked, her pulse skittering.

"No." John let out a frustrated breath. "I fear such information could put him over the edge and onto dangerous grounds."

"But he wants to help. He's good at what he does, John."

"Lester is the drunk attorney Phillip attempted to arrest a few years back. I think this guy is on Phillip's secret to-do list somewhere. Not only that, if Phillip would make any waves with this man, he could be on Lester's to-do list. He may already be. I don't know."

"Oh! Phillip told me about that sleazy lawyer. But I had no idea it was Uncle Lester." Abby stared wild-eyed at John. "We've still got to warn Phillip."

"Phillip is on another mission right now. He left early this morning for West Chambers," John wiped off his brow.

"Why?" Abby asked.

"Because these men are trying to cover up another crime they committed. Only this time they plan to pin the blame on Pastor Paul. This is a big network of evil, and it is a good thing that Phillip is about to uncover some missing information."

Abby glanced nervously around her. "But he could be in danger! Caleb!" Abby said loudly. "Shouldn't Caleb be the one going undercover there?"

"He is." A smile tugged at John's lips. "Only Phillip doesn't know it. Caleb admires Phillip's tenacity and skill in getting to the bottom of things. But, if the need should arise, Caleb is quick to action. All is well."

Phillip's mind was sending bungled messages to his heart. He heaved an exasperated sigh. He had gotten nothing more than a run-around from Nathan Plots. Reverend Tepid had left town on vacation. Mason

Olson had agreed to meet him over a burger. So here he was looking for Brad's Burgers. Mason said this was the best burger shop to be found anywhere, and Phillip was hungry. He welcomed the thought of relaxing in a booth, sharing his time with a big, thick burger covered in delightful fixings. What he did not relish was the thought of sharing this relaxing time with another bizarre person. Phillip seriously wondered if there were many sane people left on the planet.

Phillip found Brad's Burgers and checked his watch. "Noon. Perfect. Now where is this man? Oh, I already forgot his name. Names, names, names. Games, games, games," Phillip muttered to himself as he dug into his pants pocket for a paper. "Here it is. Mason."

"Yes," a strong voice, approaching from behind, sent a wave of the heebie jeebies through Phillip. "You must be Phillip," the tall, hefty man, whose face was completely overgrown by a brown woodsy beard, said. The man stared at Phillip, like a beast eying its soon-to-be kill.

Phillip became increasingly aware of his extremities trembling beneath him. He glanced at Mason's stretched muscle shirt pulled tight to make room for two very burly arms, both covered with numerous and colorful tattoos of dragons, guns, and snakes. Those arms looked like they could do some serious damage.

"You deaf?" the voice boomed.

"What? I mean, no, I'm not deaf," Phillip answered with a startling shake. "And, yes, I am Phillip." His smile was as weak as a cookie crumbling.

"Well. This is the place I told ya about. Hope you're hungry."

"I am," Phillip said.

"Let's eat then," Mason said with a head gesture toward the door.

"So the burgers are good here," Phillip made a spineless attempt at conversing with the brute now plopping himself down on a chair beside a small table.

"Can't get in those booths too easy. Hope a table works for you."

"That's great. Not a problem," Phillip's voice yielded.

"So you gonna do something about what happened to Ruth?" The man cast Phillip a menacing glance.

"I, ah…well," Phillip stammered. "I don't even know what happened to her. It would help to know that first." Phillip squirmed, wondering if he should now duck under the table for protection. "I came here to get the story. I mean, I've been asked to print a character-damaging article in the *Edge Water Times* about a young pastor being blamed for this woman's death."

"You gonna write something bad about that pastor?" Mason leaned over the table with a mean squint in his eyes.

The waitress showed up.

"We are having burger specials," Mason said, finalizing the order.

"Anything to drink?" The waitress seemed impatient.

"You want something to drink?" Mason's eyes locked with Phillip's.

"Water would be good," Phillip answered, wishing he could avoid Mason's eyes. "Oh, and coffee. I could sure use another cup of coffee."

The waitress walked away.

"It ain't the pastor's fault. You leave him alone! You understand?" Mason blurted, not caring about the stares coming from tables and booths around them.

Phillip's mouth hinged open. Shock pulsated through him like a live-wired current gone mad. Gaining only a fraction of his composure back, Phillip squeaked out, "I came here to get some information to protect the man. I've been asked to print an article about Paul that would hurt him, but I didn't want to do that."

Mason relaxed some. He slouched a little in his chair, causing him not to appear so ominous. Phillip began to breathe a little easier, too.

"Care to tell me more?" Phillip asked.

"Yep, I sure do." Mason bent across the table, lowering his voice from a roar to nearly a whisper. "That man you guys call a sheriff, he's a low-down. He is responsible as sure-as-shooting."

"Oscar Grand? Why would he be involved in the death of Ruth?" Phillip was whispering back.

The burgers arrived. They were big and tasty looking.

"Because of his son," Mason said, grabbing his burger between both hands.

"His son? What son?"

"You know a kid named Jerry Bargains?" the man questioned with a mouth full of bun and burger.

"Jerry Bargains? Yeah. I've seen him around. In fact, I saw him hanging around Oscar, but I never thought he was Oscar's son." Phillip sat up straight, grabbing the edge of the table.

"Jerry is Oscar's son, just the same. Can't help but feel sorry for the kid. Oscar has been teaching that child bad stuff. I believe it was Oscar that killed Ruth. That's what I'm thinking."

"Are you sure? They don't even have the same last name, and what does all of this have to do with this dead woman anyway?" Phillip felt himself coming unglued. He had thought that Jerry kid looked like a loner. He had wondered why he tagged with the sheriff. But there had been no talk of Jerry being Oscar's kid.

As Mason took a bite and chewed. His beard moved like a grass skirt out of sync.

"I don't understand!" Phillip exclaimed with a shake of his head. He stared at his burger stacked in front of him, but he wasn't ready to tackle it.

"Well, listen then. I'm trying to tell ya. Jerry is Ruth's son, too."

"You've got to be kidding."

Mason washed down a mouthful of fries with a swig of his water. "And I don't think what happened to her was an accident." Mason eyed his disappearing burger again. "Ruth wasn't as crazy as everyone made her out to be."

"Have you talked with Sheriff Plots?" Phillip heaved a frustrated breath before biting into his sandwich.

"Sure I did. Didn't help anything, though."

Phillip could feel the anger climbing up his neck. "And so you are telling me that Sheriff Plots knows Oscar and Ruth have a child together?"

"Sure enough he knows. You know what I think?" Mason bent over the table to stare into Phillip's eyes.

"No. What do you think?"

"I think there is something big, black, and messy going on. It's a networking of some sort, and it appears to involve some important people like chief executive officers and important businessmen. One was even a congressman. There are a lot of people talking with their backs turned. They have these secret meetings."

Phillip had taken another bite into his burger, and it felt like a wad of it was sticking in his throat. He gave a forceful cough to lodge it loose.

"Want me to thump you on the back really hard?" Mason offered. "That works better than any Heimlich."

"N-no," Phillip stuttered. "I'll be fine. I'm very interested in what you are saying."

"Well, some disgusting, big tumors are gobbling up the innocent, and there ain't no one stopping 'em. Nobody's trying to find a cure. Nobody dares 'cause the big guys hold the controls. Understand?"

"I think so. Sounds like you're saying that criminals in high places don't follow the same rules as everyone else."

"Exactly," Mason said, dipping a fry into the ketchup. "They don't get blamed. Some innocent wannabe gets the blame. That Jerry kid is a wannabe. He wants to be just like his daddy. He's growing bad. I'll bet ya the rest of my fries that kid will be doing his daddy's evil work. Probably already has. Oscar don't love that kid. Oscar doesn't love anyone. Oscar uses people and loves himself."

"So what other information do you have about Ruth?" Phillip asked, jotting down some notes.

"My mom's brother was the congressman. He was a senator—a very proud man and a party animal. He got a very young girl pregnant. The kid didn't even know she was pregnant until it became too obvious. So it came back to bite the senator. He was never re-elected." Mason chuckled. Phillip saw the flash of teeth through Mason's beard.

"Serves him right."

"You should know him, Phillip. You know Jasper Schafer?"

Phillip felt the hair raise on his neck. He could barely restrain himself from bounding out of his chair! "Jasper Schafer? The beef rancher? He's Ruth's father? He's a senator?" Phillip shuddered. "He must have been a senator long before he moved to Perjure County?"

"Was a senator many years back. Yep, it was a long time ago. He still had a temper back in his younger days that could raise the temperature in the North Pole to cooking hot."

"Unbelievable!" Phillip's eyes bugged. "I can testify to his temper. It's as fiery red as the hair on his head."

"Yep. You got it. He's the snarly kind. I can imagine he has getting even on his mind right about now. Watch your back. He knows all the legal ropes."

"Sure, but his options are limited as far as I see. I mean, given Charley's history, what rope could he use?"

Mason wrinkled his brows. "Is Charley that kid who claims to have had all those demons?"

"Yeah. The whole thing was on television. Jasper was blaming Charley for the loss of his beef cattle."

"Man, you are not hearing me!" Mason's voice dipped deep and low. "This whole murder thing has got to be driving Jasper and his buddies mad. He don't want the past drug into his present. That Charley kid will be no more than a media decoy in old Jasper's twisted mind. It's gonna be hyped up to keep the jelly brains satisfied. Jasper and the other big tumors will paint their butts and cover their dirty tails again." Mason dunked another fry in ketchup. "If someone like yourself isn't brave enough to protect that young pastor, he'll be served on everyone's dinner plate by the media. The media is so controlled by the far left, the corrupt, and the politically correct, it has no choice but to turn lies into mashed potatoes. There ain't no way the big tumors will let the media feed people the truth."

Phillip's head was spinning. *John's right. It is an octopus.*

The waitress dropped by with the bill.

"Ah, can ya get me some more water? Oh, and a piece of warm apple pie with ice cream," Mason said, his eyes brightening up. "How 'bout you, Phillip?"

"I could use a refill on coffee, please," Phillip suggested, shifting his weight on the chair. "Thank you."

Phillip scratched his head. "This is one big ball of thread. And it's rolling in so many directions. Let me think here." Phillip inhaled deeply, held his breath for a second, and then exhaled. "So you and Ruth had known each other for a long time?"

"Not exactly," Mason said impatiently. "Let me finish the story."

"I was told the girl Jasper got pregnant was very young, barely fourteen years old," Mason said, shaking his head. "She named her baby, who was my cousin, Ruth. The senator moved the young girl and baby Ruth somewhere. Nobody knows for sure where or why. Jasper didn't keep in contact any longer with his family. No one met his young mistress. Her name hadn't even been mentioned to my knowledge. Rumors happened. It was said that girl was strange; that she was messed up in some really dark stuff. To this day not one person can explain where she disappeared, but Jasper ended up trying to raise Ruth. Some years later Mom received a notification from child protection regarding Ruth." A pleased-to-report glint leaped from Mason's eyes. "See, your friend Jasper got himself in some trouble. The court was seeking a family member who might be interested in fostering Ruth. Of course, my mom was happy to do that. So Ruth came to live with us. She was sixteen and pregnant."

"One correction." Phillip twisted his neck to get the catch out of it. "This Jasper is no friend of mine."

The waitress brought the apple pie covered in a generous pile of ice cream. Mason licked his lips. "They have the best food here."

Phillip held up his coffee cup for another refill. "Thanks, ma'am."

Mason put a huge forkful of pie into his mouth. He took time to savor it, closing his eyes and smacking his lips in appreciation.

Phillip yawned and glanced at his watch. He opened his eyes wider to see Mason wolf down another bite of his apple delight.

"I might need another piece," Mason said, smacking his lips together again. "Anyway, when Ruth came to live with us. She was a very frightened girl. She'd even hide under things sometimes. It took a long time for her to learn to trust Mom or me."

"So that tells me the kid had been pretty badly abused."

"Yep. But 'cause Mom was helping her, Ruth was able to keep her baby."

"Oscar's baby?" Phillip interrupted. "Why wasn't Oscar charged with the rape of a minor?"

"Nobody knew whose kid it was. After being rescued by the county, Ruth had been receiving psychotherapy for severe personality disorders. She had been receiving medications for severe mood swings. Sometimes she was very depressed and quiet. But mostly she seemed extremely anxious and frightened. This anxiety got worse if anyone questioned who the father might be. So that ceased to be a question."

"So she was labeled as mentally ill?" Phillip asked, resting backward in his chair.

Mason swallowed his last bite of pie and wiped his mouth with a napkin.

"She was a scared, hurting girl. Ruth shared very little of her abused childhood."

"It's hard to imagine." Phillip stared out the window. "There's always another side to every story, too."

Mason's elbows thumped on the table. His eyes focused on Phillip again. "Ruth was always nervous, but especially for the baby. I even remember her pacing back and forth, always checking out the windows. She'd come back from school wide-eyed and grab the baby to herself. She thought someone would come and snatch her baby. She was afraid of Oscar."

"So Oscar was aware of the baby?" Philip asked, still trying to digest all the new information.

"Ruth didn't say so at first, but by her actions, we guessed the father must have been aware. When mom passed on," Mason continued, "Ruth moved to a little apartment of her own. I saw her from time to time, and it was apparent to me that her fears were growing bigger. Others at church noticed, too." Mason wrinkled his face together. "Can't stand how they snubbed her. Talked down to her like she was a pathetic rug. A bunch of gossips they were. Made her out to be a real basket case."

"How'd Oscar finally get Jerry?" Phillip asked, digging in his wallet for a credit card.

"Ruth ended up in the hospital. Supposedly it was an attempted suicide by overdosing on her antidepressants. About the same time, Jerry, who was nigh fourteen, ended up with his dad. Not much was said. Sorta hush hush, if ya know what I mean."

Phillip rested his elbows on the table. He looked square into Mason's eyes. "So how does Pastor Paul fit into this mess?"

"She had begun going to his church. I could never figure it out, but she seemed to be changing into a happier person."

"How do you know that, Mason?"

"She had me over to her place for dinner, just two days before her death." Mason's eyes drilled holes in the wall he was staring at. "She was happy. I had never known her to smile before that day. She said that Pastor Paul was real and caring. She told me, 'I feel healed down deep where I've been hurt for so long. Jesus is healing me from all that pain.'"

"She say anything else?"

"Yeah, she did. Ruth informed me that Oscar was Jerry's father. Said she wanted me to know that. She told me that he was a dangerous man and mixed up in dangerous stuff," Mason answered with a husky, angered voice. "Then she began to cry and told me that she loved Jerry so much. She said there wasn't a day goes by that she wasn't praying for him. Ruth showed me some Bible verses she had written down on index cards. Pastor Paul had given them to her. She told me they were God's promises to her. She said she prayed those words to God every day for her son."

"Oh." Phillip heaved a desperate breath. *Where do I go with this story?*

―――――⌘―――――

Abby drove down the long driveway. Dawn was drawing its chalky fingers through the mist of darkness. She shivered, remembering she had been awakened in the night by voices; voices from her past had visited once again. The monster wasn't dead. Even though she had hoped for a good night's sleep, Abby had felt that beast's chilled hands in the night. The monster and his friends had come to her bed. Familiar and hateful, they had clawed at her soul. They had robbed her of sleep.

One insidious dark creature, with strong, iron-like jaws, had screeched out its name. "I am Molech. The fruit of every womb belongs to me. You were mine then. You are mine yet." The words had been pushed with the wind of his breath, laced in burning smoke. The stench of his breath had been wretched, like burning flesh. His horrid mouth had opened, and Abby had felt her strength wane. She had felt herself disappearing into something as deep as her past. Sinking, sinking—she had been sinking. Then a light. John had opened her door. He had been calling her name. *Thank God you came, John.*

"Abby, are you okay?" John had asked her. He had been standing in the doorway so tall and surrounded by a peaceful light. He had spoken some other words, too, demanding darkness to leave Abby's room in the powerful name of Jesus.

The voices left at the sound of John's voice. She had been lying in bed, soaked from a cold sweat. It had felt like those voices had been choking the breath away from her. What a relief it had been when they fled. She couldn't explain this to John, though she had desperately wanted to. She couldn't tell anybody.

"Abby?" John had called out her name again.

She remembered at that point she had begun to relax. A strange and peaceful quiet had come to her thrashing heart.

"I am okay now, John. Thank you," she had answered him.

Abby knew John had been praying. When he had finished praying and had closed her bedroom door, she knew the monster had fled. In its place, it seemed as though celestial beings had surrounded her. It was like her bedroom had been filled with mighty warriors. *Perhaps they had been angels*, Abby wondered. Had God's angels chased away the monsters of her past?

Under the awakening sun, Abby was now cruising toward Edge Water.

Everything seemed calm, peaceful. Except, there was a twinge of guilt in her gut. She had left without telling John and Mable that she must find Phillip. There was so much to tell him.

The sun was peeking up boldly in the east. Abby's hands squeezed tighter around the steering wheel. The sign said "Edge Water. Population 10,500."

Abby wondered, *Will Phillip be busy at his desk this early in the morning? Maybe Caleb would be there!* She would get there early and get the coffee going. She had catching up to do. She had important information to give them. Abby shivered. She knew that information involved a part of her past, which somehow had bars around it. Would she need to find the key to the prison of her past? Even if she had the key, would she want to unlock the yesteryears?

Charley walked the river path. So fresh was the morning air. The vegetation was drinking in the dew. Every tree branch lifted its green sparkles in praise. He couldn't help but worship the Lord. He couldn't keep his lips from praising God. The river gurgled its praising echo beside him. Charley's quest was to learn to pray. He had written down Bible verses on index cards, and now he was praying back the powerful words to God. "For the weapons of my warfare are not of the flesh, but have divine power to destroy strongholds. I can destroy arguments and every lofty opinion raised against the knowledge of God and take every thought captive to obey Christ."

A fallen tree stretched before the path. Charley sat down on it to rest a moment. He knew he was surrounded by God's divine presence. It was happening more frequently lately. He had been soaking in the Word of God, and the Word was becoming a powerful presence pulsating through him and gloriously surrounding him.

He sunk on his knees and folded his upper torso over the downed tree. "Apostle Paul said that he wanted to know you, Lord, and the power of your resurrection. I want to know you that much, too, Jesus. Once I was so lost in shame and torment. But with such great power, You delivered me! It was the power of the Holy Spirit, who raised Jesus from the dead. And I want to experience more of that power. I want to be filled with that power. I want to be led by Your Holy Spirit. I want to only hear His voice."

Charley lifted his hands heavenward. "Oh God, You love so much. Your love was in everything you did. You can love through me. Please love through me."

A figure moved stealthily through the brush. His pistol was in his hand. Steam fogged from his mouth. His pupils were dilated, and he tweaked under the influence of methamphetamine. "No brother of mine is gonna take my father away from me. I'll show him," the tormented kid cried.

Another verse graced aloud from Charley's lips: "In the fear of the Lord one has strong confidence and his children will have a refuge. The fear of the Lord is a fountain of life, that one may turn away from the snares of death."

The greasy-haired kid stopped. He stared, bug-eyed, into the clearing at the young man bent over a tree. A wicked grin crooked his face. *Man, I didn't think it would be this easy.*

Charley was crying out the Word, releasing its power into the atmosphere about him. "The Lord shall cause your enemies who rise up against you to be defeated before your face. They shall come out against you one way and flee before you seven ways."

The young man's breathing became ragged. "Who do you think you are?" he cried out. "Don't say those words to me!" The kid stepped out into the clearing. Gun in hand, he staggered forward.

Charley stood up. More words released themselves from his mouth. "Behold, I have given you authority to tread upon serpents and scorpions and over all the power of the enemy and nothing shall hurt you."

The kid stood before Charley. "Just who are you talking to?" the kid asked and then cursed, pointing a dirty finger at Charley.

"These are the words of God. 'I have set the Lord always before me; because He is at my right hand, I shall not be shaken.'"

The young man began to shake violently. "Who is this Almighty God that I should know Him?"

Charley quoted another verse. "For the kingdom of God does not consist in talk, but in power." Charley took a step toward the kid. "God has not delivered me into the hand of my enemy, but He has set my feet in a broad place."

"Stop! Don't torture me!" The young man dropped to his knees. "Who are you? Who is that large man?" The gun fell from the boy's hand. His hands cuffed over his ears as he screamed. "Stop it! Stop torturing me with those words!"

Charley stepped forward, picked up the gun, and tossed it in the river. He turned toward the kid, feeling the weight of the boy's chains.

"Jesus came to destroy the works of the devil. You can be free. Jesus is the way, the truth, and the life. The truth would set you free!"

"No!" screamed the kid, who now rolled into a ball of anguish.

"You are loved by God. He came to die for you, just to set you free. He said in His Word, 'For God so loved the world that He gave His only begotten Son, that whosoever believeth in Him should not perish but have everlasting life.'"

The young man began beating the earth with his fists. "No, He doesn't love me. Not even our very own father loves me."

Charley stood near him. "Our father?"

"Yes. We share the same father. I've just wanted him to love me. Is that too much to ask?"

He cried from raw emotions.

"Your heavenly Father loves you. He brings liberty to the captives. He opens prison doors to those who are bound."

"If there is a God, even he could not love me. Do not talk to me about love!"

Charley stooped down beside the young man. "What is your name?"

"Jerry. My name is Jerry, and my father is Oscar Grand. I am your brother! And I came here to kill you. I would have killed you if that giant man hadn't come and put that bright light around you."

"Let me help you up, brother," Charley said, extending his hand to Jerry.

Chapter Ten

Sherry sat in the quiet of the early morning. Her Bible lay open on her lap. She was studying from the book of John. It was as though the words from the chapter jumped right out of her Bible just to talk to her. Sherry loved to read, but never had any book inspired her this way. She had been purposely meeting God in the mornings just to hear Him talk to her. This morning the words from the Amplified version were so powerful, she read them aloud and then wrote the verse in her journal: "It is the Spirit Who gives life (He is the life-giver); the flesh conveys no benefit whatever (there is no profit in it). The words (truths) that I have been speaking to you are spirit and life."

Sherry took a sip of hot coffee and picked up a pen and paper to write out her thoughts.

—⁓∘✦✧✦∘⁓—

Phillip yawned as he came down the stairs. He hadn't been able to sleep well. He'd have to go to the office, even if it was Saturday morning. There was so much catching up to do. And he had to get the articles written. The paper needed to be ready by Tuesday morning. In his head, the story was not ready. The story was like a haystack in the path of a twister. He had but a few short days to rake up what was scattered to the wind and bale it all together again.

In all respects, Phillip felt he had encountered the same gusty funnel. Before he would be able to accomplish anything, he needed to find a way to pull himself together, too. He wasn't in the best of moods. Pieces of him seemed scattered in the wind. It was his responsibility to fix things. He wasn't happy about his lack of know-how this morning! He wasn't happy about anything this morning.

"Sherry, is breakfast ready? You know I have a busy schedule. I've got to go to work. This whole story is getting messier by the day. Abby's been gone. I'm stuck with the whole cart of it dumped over my head," Phillip grumbled.

"Okay, dear. Will oatmeal do?" Sherry asked, setting her notebook and pen down. "It will only take me a couple of minutes to get it ready."

"I don't have a couple minutes," Phillip cranked on. "Never mind. I'll pick up an egg-and-sausage biscuit from McDonald's." *Least there's coffee.* He grabbed his thermos to fill it.

Sherry was by his side. "I'm sorry, honey. I didn't know you would be heading to the office so early this morning."

Phillip twisted his upper torso and then his neck to get all the sleep pinches out. "Too late to worry about it now."

"I'm so sorry this thing has become so overwhelming, Phillip. Do you suppose Abby will be back soon?"

"I sure hope so. She knows the paper needs to be out by Tuesday. I'm thinking she will be there soon, maybe even today." Phillip headed toward the door.

"Phillip, tomorrow is Sunday. Will you be coming with me to church?" she asked, her blue eyes big.

"No! Can't you see how busy I am? I'll be in the office tomorrow, too. Maybe for a month of Sundays!" Phillip slammed the door behind him.

The coffee pot was spitting out its morning wake-up call. Abby washed Phillip's coffee mug and set it beside the brewing mixture. Now she stood aghast in front of his desk, staring at the stacks of dishevel. *Where do I begin?*

She sunk in his office chair. She grabbed a handful of pictures. "Good grief. What are these all about?" People hovered around the community center, some of them dressed up in bloated suits and masks. "Looks like I have a lot of catching up to do."

She shoveled through the pictures. And there he was: Oscar's picture in the foreground, people rushing behind him in their crazy suits, tankers and ambulances. Abby grimaced and set the pictures down. *The likes of that man is the last thing I need to see today. I don't like what I feel either. It feels like murder. I think if I met Oscar right now, I would have no choice but to murder him. Why should he run free and my sister be dead because of him?*

Abby stood up. She began to pace. Her emotions were rolling in smoke, like a large boiler furnace burning on the inside with no chimney escape to vent. If Abby's fumings should be fanned, there would be no stopping the flames. They would rage and leap. They would consume in their hatred. How she hated! She hated what Oscar had done to her sister. She hated what evil men had done to them as little girls. They had had no voice back then. But now, somewhere a fiery voice waited. Deep inside of her, its smoky form waited for the moment of combustion.

Only a few blocks away was the sheriff's department. Abby could almost picture Oscar sitting in his chair, sipping leisurely away on a cup of coffee. *Did he murder Julie? Or did he hire someone to do his dirty work?*

"I can't let him get by with it!" Abby braced herself for action. "Nor will I. It is time for me to defend Julie's blood."

Abby grabbed the stack of stamped envelopes on Phillip's desk. "First the post office. Then, Oscar, I am about to get in your face."

Sherry drove down the long driveway. Plum trees and crab apple trees budding bright green lined up on both sides of the road kindly welcoming her. Pastor Paul had given her excellent directions to John's place. She pulled up into the yard. The homey house was perfectly tucked into a grove of trees. When Sherry stepped out of her car, her ears hummed with the song of the river's journey.

A tall man with a full growth of beard and long, silvery hair stepped out of the door. *So this is the John I've heard so much about. He fits the picture.*

"I'm Sherry," she said, extending her hand.

"Ah, at last I meet you. Phillip has told me much about you."

Worry burrowed across her brows. Phillip hadn't exactly appreciated her lately. In fact, she had felt completely ignored and misunderstood by him. "Oh, I see," she whispered. "He has been very busy lately, and I've seen little of him."

A rolly, jolly-cheeked older woman, still tied to her apron, squeezed around John and stepped out onto the porch. "Oh, my. Yes, we are so pleased you came, Sherry. Won't you come in and have a cup of coffee and a fresh-baked caramel roll?"

"I'd like that very much," Sherry answered with a wide smile. "You must be Mable." Sherry smiled. "And you were the pianist! The day I visited the church a couple weeks ago, you were the one playing the piano."

Mable's arm was around Sherry, quickly whisking her into the kitchen. "Yes, that was me! Abby called us from the office in Edge Water," Mable continued in a blur of words. "She's there to help Phillip catch up. My," Mable said, shaking her head until her cheeks jiggled, "Phillip has been up to his ears in problems since Charley's deliverance." Mable placed a bright blue coffee mug in front of Sherry. "You take cream or sugar?"

"I use a little cream," Sherry answered, sucking in a breath of contentment. It felt so good to have someone fuss over her. The loving attention from Mable was like a big hug from the sun itself on a rainy day. Sherry's heart leaned back on an invisible recliner as the busy and spunky Mable fussed and pampered it.

"Here you go, my dear. Milk for your coffee, and please help yourself to a roll!"

"You are so kind, Mable. Here I sit soaking in your generosity." Sherry blushed. "While I have been enjoying it, I haven't even offered to help you carry the rolls or the coffee. I'm sorry."

"Goodness, girl, you are blessing me by just being here. Don't you dare fret that way. You just sit right there and enjoy yourself. I don't have much else to do but have coffee with friends." Mable's smile pushed her wrinkles backward.

Sherry smiled back and grabbed a gooey roll. "Not sure I can afford the calories, but if these taste nearly as good as they look and smell, I'd be a fool not to have one."

John pulled out a chair and placed himself in it near the table. Mable was quick to pour him a cup of coffee.

"That Charley is still out walking the river," Mable cooed on. "Now there's a boy forever changed by God. He gets saturated every morning with God," she added. "But I'm expecting him home soon. He'll be happy to see the rolls all baked and waiting for him."

Sherry sighed softly, admiring the sweet home. Mable had a way of bringing sunshine to every corner of it. *The kind of sunshine I desperately want to mark my home.*

Sherry glanced at John from the corner of her eyes. He was like she had imagined him to be: confident and strong, yet gentle.

"John, the reason I came here was to give you something." Sherry reached into her purse and pulled out a letter. "I think it is very important. It's from a woman named Lexi. She asked me to give this to you. She was terribly hurt but wouldn't allow me to take her to a doctor." Sherry's voice began to choke up. "Her husband, Kevin, is my boss. John, Kevin has been very angry, and I'm becoming afraid of him. Then, this week a very hateful woman came into his office. Lexi told me that woman's name is Jezra. She is as wicked as the devil's wife. Lexi told me she goes by other names too."

Sherry watched John's expression as concern etched across his face. "Yes, Sherry, she is dangerous. But she is no match for God."

"Lexi said Jezra is a high priestess. Does that mean she is a devil worshiper?"

"Yes, which is a big appendage in this whole octopus, Sherry."

Sherry broke into tears. "I think I know why she hates me. She knows I'm Jamie's mom. My daughter is sixteen years old, John, and she's messed up in something big. There is a coven around here. They are sucking in my daughter. I just know this woman is a leader. Jamie is biting into something much more deadly than a poison apple. I don't know how to save her from its grasp."

"With God, nothing is impossible, Sherry. Never forget His hand is not shortened that it cannot save. At your disposal is the mighty weapon of prayer." John's gentle eyes bored peace into Sherry's soul.

Sherry handed John the envelope. "My husband would be furious if he knew I had this letter from Lexi. I told him about her. He was very angry that I did not take her to the police. But this woman was desperate. She was afraid for her own life."

"You did the right thing. I have been praying for Lexi. This young lady has been a rebel, even though she came from a good Christian home. Her parents are no longer around these parts, but I am certain they are praying for Lexi every day." John unfolded the letter.

Mable refilled Sherry's coffee mug. "My goodness," Mable said as she busied herself making another pot of coffee. "Lexi's beauty got her in deep trouble. She was really popular in high school." Mable blew out a breath. "I can imagine she still is very pretty. For a while she and her family went to the God's Love Fellowship Church. Her folks were dissatisfied with the church. They had become hungrier for God. So they moved out of state to be with family and to find another church. Their daughter was determined to stay with Kevin. So a hurried-up wedding happened, and her parents left heartbroken and without their daughter."

"I can imagine how much that hurt them," Sherry said, clutching her coffee mug.

"Poor child," Mable said with empathy dripping from her eyes.

John nodded his head. "But from the sound of this letter," John added, "I'd say our Lexi is coming home."

"Coming home?" Sherry repeated.

"Yes, she's wanting to know the truth. She finally wants to meet the Jesus she had been taught about as a child."

"Praise the Lord!" Mable's voice twittered with excitement.

"Yep and I will be picking her up for church tomorrow." He smiled.

"Oh!" Sherry exclaimed. "And I have decided I need that church. So I'm coming on Sunday, too. Pastor Paul has already helped me so much. I feel as though God just dropped me off at the door of that old, rickety schoolhouse."

"Yes, He did," John agreed. "I'm thinking God will be bringing others, too. There are many hurting people around us. They have bit into lies, but underneath layers of deception and pain, they are hungry for the truth. There are people praying, Sherry, and thereby God's hand is moving. It is His desire to heal people from all their hurts and to set them free by that truth. That's why prayer is important. It moves God's hand."

The door burst open, and Charley stepped in. Alongside Charley came a greasy-haired, thin kid.

Sherry gasped, noticing the boy's rotting teeth.

"John, I'd like you to meet Jerry Bargains," Charley said.

Jerry's head hung low.

John stood and walked toward the boy. He gave the boy a grandfatherly hug. "It's good to finally meet you in person, son."

"Are you John?" Jerry coughed away the spasm in his throat. "I'm sorry, man, but there are people hoping you are dead."

A smile swiped through John's beard. "Yes, indeed. But God had other plans."

"You were the mysterious man at the community center, weren't you? I think my dad is worried you might be alive after all."

John chuckled.

"You really smoked 'em all," Jerry confessed. "Wish I could have seen it for myself. Folks were humming mad." Jerry's mouth gaped open. He stared hard at John. "Why did you do all that?"

"I had a message from God to those folk. He's been hearing the cries of hurting children and the prayers of saints. He wants to answer those prayers and bring light into the darkness that holds folk captive in these parts. He wants to set people free, just like he did for Charley here."

Jerry teetered a little trying to stand up taller and take note of what this powerful man was saying. "Ah, you talk like you know God. I mean, how can you know God that much?"

"It's simple, son. He wanted us to know Him. So He made a way for us to get to know Him by sending His only Son, Jesus, down to earth to pay for our sins. That way we could become His sons and daughters, too." John wrapped an arm around Jerry. "You see, He wants to be a Father to us. Only, He is a Father who really went out of His way to pour love on us."

"Nah." Jerry's head slunk down. "He couldn't want to love me."

"Why not?" John asked, hugging the kid harder.

"I think my mom died because of me. Dad came and got me a couple years ago. He told me Mom had tried to kill herself because she hated me." Jerry heaved a breath. "My going away didn't help much. She killed herself anyway. Dad said she left a note explaining why she did it. Guess it was because she had born the likes of me."

Jerry looked up to meet John's gaze with panic-stricken eyes, struggling for words. "I came here today to kill Charley. I thought my dad would be proud of me."

"Jerry, even if you have never experienced love by your earthly father, the heavenly Father loves you more than you can imagine," John said.

"He's so real," Charley whispered to Jerry. "Jerry, I never knew our father, and I never knew a father's love either. But Jesus came to me with great love. He really loves you too, Jerry."

"That's right," Mable chattered. "You are both loveable. Now you and Charley get your butts over to the table for a big glass of milk and a fresh caramel roll." Mable's arm was around Jerry, and he followed her to the table like a hungry puppy.

Jerry stared hard at the roll. His eyes lifted up to meet Mable's as she poured milk into a glass. "Why are you doing this for me?"

"Because you probably haven't had breakfast, either. Just like Charley, who missed his breakfast again. My goodness, it's after ten in the morning already. Soon lunch time. And this is the first I've seen the whites of your eyes all morning." Mable gave Charley a playful swat on his shoulder and then turned and winked at Sherry.

"Just can't help myself. It's so peaceful out there by the river. And Jesus walks beside me on that river's trail. I mean no disrespect. I get lost in time out there."

"Goodness, Charley. That isn't an excuse. It's a reason. And if Jesus is the reason you spend all morning out there, then that's reason enough for me to hold breakfast for you." Mable chuckled.

"There's a powerful man out there," Jerry said, and he swallowed a mouthful of his roll. "The man had light all around him. He was standing over Charley protecting him. I didn't dare shoot." Jerry took a long drink of milk while shaking his head in unbelief. "And, you"—he turned to Charley—"you were talking to the man. And the light from that man almost blinded me."

"I was talking God's Word, Jerry. I have written many verses down. I pray them back to God. Those are the words you were hearing."

John straddled a chair next to Jerry. "And, son, God's Word puts angels to work."

"Oh!" The words leaped out of Jerry's mouth. "That big thing was an angel?"

"I'm thinking so." John's smile widened his face.

Sherry's eyes misted over watching the boy eat the quickly disappearing caramel roll. She could feel her own stomach churning, almost twisting in revulsion. How could a father do such a thing to his own son? The kid was a loner for certain. How could a father not know that? This poor, hungry, skinny kid! Where was his father? Sherry stared harder at Jerry. *Why, he must only be Blake's age.*

"How old are you?" the words slipped from Sherry's tongue.

"I'll be sixteen this fall," Jerry answered with his mouth full of dough.

"Oh, I was right. I guessed you to be about Blake's age. Blake is my son."

"Blake Acumen?" Jerry asked, focusing his eyes on Sherry.

"Yes. You know him?"

"Sure. We go to school together. He's my friend."

Sherry swallowed hard. *Oh no!*

"Oh, he told me." She gulped hard. "He said he had a new friend named Jerry. I was happy about that because Blake spends so much time alone. He doesn't seem to have friends. So you must be that new friend, huh?"

"Yep. I don't have any friends either. Except Blake now."

"Have another roll, son," Mable encouraged Jerry.

———— ∿∾⟡⊙⟡∽∿ ————

Abby grabbed the mail from the post office box and then locked it. Even before she spun around a cold settled into her bones. Abby whirled around only to be eye to eye with Kevin. Her heart spooked from the coldness in his eyes. She wondered how he had become so evil. Always he had been arrogant and demeaning to her, but something was seriously ominous about him now. Abby tried to keep her breathing in check. She stared back, refusing to bow to intimidation. Her eyes trailed down to his neck and followed the heavy, silver-chained necklace. Attached to it was a ring. Abby's stomach began to feel queasy. The ring had a distorted goat head, and there was something devilish about it.

Kevin took a step backward and then walked around her without a word. But Abby picked up on the many threatening, unspoken words. Her tongue was frozen to the roof of her mouth. For that she was grateful. If he would have said one single word to her and if she would have responded with a mouthful of what she felt, the results of this encounter may not have fared well.

Abby realized her hands were shaking. She glanced backward. Kevin was ordering something at the counter. Quickly she stepped outside. Abby felt a great need to run, but her trembling legs refused for lack of strength.

Once outside, Abby breathed in deeply. She dared her mind to come to attention. In doing so, Abby remembered the mission she was on. She must face another dangerous man! Abby's heart was like a whisk beating at its batter. Let the thrashing continue. She had come this far; she must see Oscar. He would be put on the defensive. He would regret killing her sister!

Abby stopped in front of the sheriff's office and took in a deep breath.

"Okay, I need to get control here. So breath in." Abby inhaled slowly, counting to five, and then exhaled slowly, counting to seven. "There. Be brave now. It's time to face the sheriff!"

Abby yanked open the door and marched into the sheriff's office. Crooking her hands on her hips in front of the main desk, she announced her arrival. "I'm here to see Sheriff Oscar Grand."

A young man stared up, apparently humored by her boldness. "Well, it's Saturday, and he doesn't do Saturdays," he said with an amused smile. "But I'm here," he said, sizing her up. "I haven't got anything better to do today than help pretty young damsels in distress. You are in distress, aren't you?"

"No," Abby snapped back, blatantly avoiding his questions. "Then I will be back to talk personally with the sheriff on Monday."

"Well, if you leave your name, I can give him a message," the guy suggested, grinning fondly at her. "Leave your phone number, too."

"I should say not!" Abby answered hotly, and she stamped her foot. "Thanks for your help." Abby turned on her heels and sped out the door.

Abby walked fast. Only a block to her office. Something didn't feel right. Sure, maybe it was just an unfounded feeling, like that of an animal being hunted down. What should she feel like after being drugged and assaulted? But that happened in the night while the dark shadows waited and plotted to sink their black fingers around her. This was bold daylight. She should be able to control her fears better. Why were her emotions doing this tumbling thing, like water over a falls?

Who would be brave enough to hunt her in the daylight hours? What was it about Kevin that frightened her so? The ring? Now she remembered! "The ring!" Abby shrieked. It was coming back to her. She had seen that ring the night she was abducted. "A ring and a knife!"

Abby could feel the blood rushing away from her head. Her body drained of strength. "My memory! It's coming back!"

What a twist of events. The ring had shown up. She had been going to face Julie's assaulter. She had been planning to step up to the plate and face whatever he pitched her way. She thought she had a good hold on the bat. When the pitcher stepped up to the plate, he wasn't whom Abby had expected. And he threw her an unexpected curve ball.

"Just a few more steps," she huffed out. "Thank God just a few more steps!"

Abby turned quickly at the corner of the building, crashing into a solid body. The wallop sent her legs to crumbling. "No. Please God, no!" He had her in his grip. She was losing it.

"Abby! Abby! Snap out of it. It's me. It's Caleb."

She felt a cool breeze fanning over her face, and she looked up to see Caleb's face. He was waving a folded paper over her. "

"Caleb?" she asked, feeling color coming back to her face.

"Yes. After I was notified that you foolishly left Mable's home, I have been following you around. Maybe after your memory fully returns you will remember how dangerous those men are."

"I had to come here. There's so much I need to tell you guys, and Phillip needs help to get it all in the paper."

"Abby. Are you okay?" Phillip's voice blared through her thoughts. He was kneeling beside her. "I didn't know if I should call the paramedics or not. You're as white as a ghost. What happened?"

She turned to meet Phillip's concerned gaze. She sat up, staring helplessly into two sets of eyes. "The ring. Phillip, I remember the ring. Kevin is wearing it. Kevin is the one who abducted me. I ran into him in the post office. I'm so afraid."

Caleb scrambled to his feet, and then he was gone.

Phillip blew out an agitated breath. "I should have guessed. Sherry! Sherry works for Kevin. She's been trying to tell me how frightened she is of him. Well, Caleb's after him. Kevin will live to regret he ever touched you." Phillip stood, offering Abby his hand. "There's more I need to tell you. Kevin is probably only a part of the whole big, black picture. Let's go inside the office and catch up on things." And as he opened the office door for Abby, he asked, "Do you know that the sheriff, Oscar Grand, is the man responsible for killing that Ruth woman?"

"What Ruth woman?" Abby tried to focus through the blinking stars she was still seeing.

"Well, you better sit down. This is a long story," Phillip let out a long breath.

"And getting longer," Abby said as fear blanched her face again. "Oscar is Charley's father."

"No way! Who told you that?" Phillip asked as he leaned back against his desk.

"Charley did and John agreed. That's not all. Lester, the attorney, the guy who cost you your job in law enforcement, he's involved in all of this." Abby felt distress washing through her body. "He's my uncle..." Her words faded away.

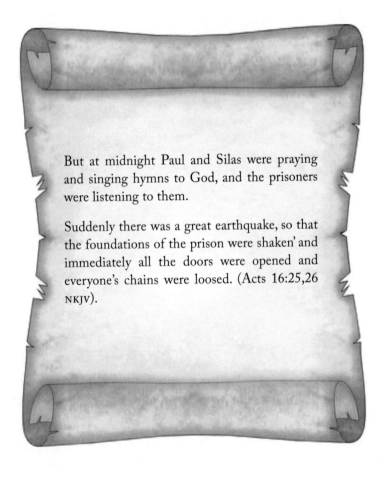

But at midnight Paul and Silas were praying and singing hymns to God, and the prisoners were listening to them.

Suddenly there was a great earthquake, so that the foundations of the prison were shaken' and immediately all the doors were opened and everyone's chains were loosed. (Acts 16:25,26 NKJV).

Chapter Eleven

Abby did not like Monday mornings. She especially hated getting up in the wee hours of the morning without a stitch of sleep. Exhausted, she sank in her recliner.

Late last night, Abby had finally completed the newspaper article for Phillip. She had faxed it to the office. Though the document, incriminating Paul to Ruth's murder, was going to be printed, Abby's completed assignment would refute that story. But it had cost her. Instead of a relaxing Sunday afternoon, she had been pushed to write such a convincing article to restrain the public from believing the accusations against Paul. Phillip had given her several pages of handwritten information to wade through. Such a difficult task had not only taken time and painful effort, but it had robbed her of sanity. It had left her rankled and completely unable to sleep.

This time printing the truth might cost her a whole lot more than loss of time and sleep. This article could become a huge, sharp rock lodged in a killer bear's paw. The mad bear just might become very hungry for revenge. How many people might end up as kibble to satisfy the salivating beast?

Abby walked to the counter and poured herself a cup of coffee. The FBI agent had made the brew sometime during the night. Apparently he had been unable to sleep too. She looked out of her kitchen window. Just the early hints of dawn. Still she could see the agent sitting in a patio chair in front of her house. She sucked in a breath of relief. At least she was safe.

Through the long hours of the night, in mental travail, Abby had decided to arrive at the sheriff's office first thing this morning, before Oscar had a chance to pour his cup of coffee. She must attempt to unsaddle Oscar's evil plans right in front of the deputies and dispatch workers.

Now haggard, with her strength fading, she sipped nervously from her coffee mug. Abby's eyes trailed to the stack of journals on the desk beside her recliner. She picked up the next journal. Maybe reading more about Julie would energize her enough to clobber the man responsible for such a travesty. Julie was Abby's reason for revenge.

Abby noted Julie had begun this journal one year before her untimely death.

> I opened my eyes one morning last month. That alone was a miracle.
>
> But I had determined never to open my eyes again. I was too lonely to want to be left alone any longer. People around me always ignored

me. Religious people judged me. I thought God hated me too. I thought everyone would be happier without me. I had really given up on ever finding hope.

I used to cut myself. I found that bleeding drained me of the energy I needed to keep from feeling the bigger pain inside of me. I couldn't face the huge hurt inside of my life.

When I was introduced to stronger drugs, which numbed me, I no longer needed to cut myself. Until last week. I am a bit ashamed now to even write the fact. But the truth is, I decided to cut myself once more. I wanted to end my life. I slit my wrist and waited to die.

It's been many months since I've written anything. I had grown weary of sadness and could no longer write about it. Now I must write again!

When my eyes opened last month, a man stood beside me. Heaven was there with him. It was all over him. He told me his name was John. I cannot find words to explain my joy when I learned it was John! I had been searching for John for years, only to have him find me in that hospital bed. I'm not sure how I got to the hospital. I thought I had ended it all. I thought I was dying. Someone brought me to the hospital. God made sure of that. What a miracle that He didn't let me die that day. I would have died without knowing Jesus. I would have never discovered the life and hope for which I had been searching for…for so many years.

John placed me in an apartment. I now have a home of my own, where no person can abuse me any longer. John gave me some money to buy new clothes. He picks me up and takes me to church. I've been hearing so much about Jesus. I didn't want to hear at first. I think I had been very mad at God. I'd been blaming God for taking my baby away from me. I just had so much hate growing in me. It was hard to believe in love of any kind. But I couldn't run away from this love. I saw it in John. I felt it in church. It wanted me. That's the biggest surprise! This love wanted me! God wanted me. He kept me alive to prove He wanted me.

So last week the preacher talked more about the love of Jesus. Jesus isn't mad at me. Jesus isn't ashamed of me. He loves me. He paid for the chance to love me by shedding His blood. The whips cut Him! The pastor said I could be healed from all my pain because those whips cut Him. By His stripes of pain, I can be healed inside and out.

Jesus died for me to earn the right to love me, like no other person could ever love me. He didn't stay dead. He was too powerful for death. His love is too powerful, too. It makes me want to live and never try to destroy my life in any way again. It's what I needed all along. I needed a miracle of love.

Anyway, I went up to the front of the church after the preacher's message. I went up there with my whole heart open to Jesus. I wanted His love more than anything. I had to have that love and all of the forgiveness that comes with His love.

That's when my eyes really opened up to life. His love is a miracle. I mean, I am really alive now! And His love is challenging me to forgive all who have hurt me so deeply.

Abby sat for a moment, her mouth hanging open, her eyes in a trance like stare.

"Julie, how could you even think of forgiving people like Oscar and Lester? That can't be possible. I don't feel anything but hate for them for what they did to you and me!" Abby blew out an angry breath. "I hope Jesus doesn't expect that of me."

Phillip wrung his hands. John had been right. Printing the truth was not going to be easy. Phillip felt entirely out of his comfort zone. He worried that he was about to create a war zone.

Phillip reread Abby's article.

Is Someone Guilty of Murder?

It has been said that there are usually two sides to every story. In this case, there are two very separate stories.

In the first story, by the efforts of a five-county investigation and with the help of the BCI, readers were encouraged to not only identify the Reverend Paul Marvel as a cultist leader but also as a suspect in the murder of a West Chamber's woman.

In an effort to explore this story, staff from the *Edge Water Times* and FBI investigator, Caleb Mettle, obtained information from Mason Olson and Sheriff Nathan Plots, who are both from West Chambers. Mason is a relative of the deceased woman.

Paul Marvel and his wife, Victoria, did pastor a church in West Chambers before taking over a pastorate in Perjure County. According to the first article ("Did the Young Pastor, Paul Marvel, Commit Murder?"), Paul is accused of doing some strange things. "He was a strange man. He was like a cult leader. People that left his congregation claim he thought he was as powerful as God. He had many people brainwashed that way. Some say strange things reportedly and frequently happened in that church. In addition, strange and phenomenal happenings tore the community apart."

During our interview, Sheriff Plots had this to say: "The whole thing seemed more of a political thing between churches. There was plenty of tension between the churches." We asked the sheriff to explain what strange things had happened under the leadership of Reverend Paul Marvel. The sheriff explained,

"Mrs. Olson, who was on her deathbed with last-stage pancreatic cancer, claimed to be miraculously healed. And Fred Otter, who had been in a wheelchair for six years with a very crippling disease, suddenly was walking about town."

Were these healings the "strange and phenomenal happenings that tore the community apart?"

Not everyone was healed. According to the sheriff, "Some people from the West Chamber's Bible Community Church went to see for themselves if they could receive healings from various things." However, they did not receive healings.

What about the deceased woman? How was she involved with Paul's ministry? We asked her cousin, Mason Olson, for his opinion. "She had me over to her place for dinner just two days before her death. She was happy. I had never known her to smile before that day. She said that Pastor Paul was real and caring. She told me, 'I feel healed down deep where I've been hurting for so long. Jesus is healing me from all that pain.'"

Mason Olson also informed us that Sheriff Oscar Grand, from Mirage County, and the deceased woman, Ruth Bargains, from West Chambers, had a son together. Mason said, "Ruth informed me that Oscar was Jerry's father. She said that she wanted me to know that." Jerry Bargains now resides with Sheriff Grand.

Furthermore, Mason informed us that his uncle, once a senator in West Chambers, is none other than Jasper Schafer from Perjure County. Mason reports that Jasper is the father of the now-deceased woman, Ruth Bargains.

The FBI is asking for more investigation into the death of the mysteriously deceased woman, Ruth Bargains.

Phillip's fist pounded against his desk. He had no choice. Abby had emailed it to him. He had run it through the printer. It would be out in this week's paper. It would be on the stands tonight.

———⟶⟶

Sherry finished emptying the dishwasher. She felt her throat tightening with apprehension again. This feeling kept coming and going.

In between these moments of uneasiness, Sherry thought about how wonderful church had been. Pastor Paul had said that many people have the wrong definition of life. People think life means living it their own way. That's not life but the pathway to death. Jesus said He was the way, the truth, and the life. "Be sure you know the right definition for life!" Pastor had warned. Sherry was grateful her kids had been there to hear those words.

Sherry blanched remembering the struggle to get her children to church. It had turned into an ugly battle. Phillip had thrown up his arms and yelled at the kids, "Obey your mother!" Then he hurried off to the office, leaving her to finish the fight. She winced remembering the hard stares and the rebellious comments. Jamie had said, "I don't want your religion, Mom!" Sherry's head dropped to her heart. She thought she had heard Jamie whisper, "I hate your church, Mom. I hate you." Sherry had seen a deeper coldness settle into Jamie's eyes. Even Blake had seemed more distant. It was almost as though he was being pulled out of reality. Sometimes he seemed just there in body. Something about that boy was bone chilling.

After the service, Pastor Paul had opened the altar for prayer. Sherry had prayed that her children would hear and respond to the preaching of the gospel. But they had remained, like stiff skeletons, in their chairs.

John had brought Jerry to church. Jerry had sat by Blake, but the neither of them had seemed interested in the message. Jerry didn't go to the altar either.

Lexi was at church. She had seemed an entirely different person than the woman Sherry had helped earlier that week. Throughout the service, Lexi had hung her head and wept. When the altar call was given, Lexi did not go forward. Sherry had sensed a great fear in Lexi, who had just remained trembling in her seat. Sherry had almost been compelled to touch Lexi on her shoulder and invite her to the front.

Sherry began wiping down the counters. She must not get discouraged. She was just learning to pray to a powerful God, who answers prayers. She must have faith now that God would hear the cries for her children.

What was this odd alarm striking so painfully in her gut? It came in gusty spasms, making her queasy with anxiety.

"I think I need to pray to You, Jesus. I don't understand what is happening. I just feel like I need to pray and ask You to protect someone. Something seems terribly wrong. So would You please be there for whoever at this very moment is in trouble? Please protect them. Lord, and be with my kids. I am asking You to protect them right now. Please put those warring angels around them. Amen."

Sherry wiped a sheen of perspiration from her forehead.

The phone was ringing. She didn't recognize the number. Her hand trembled as she picked it up. "Hello?"

"Mrs. Acumen?" A young voice seemed to burst into frightened pieces. "This is Jerry. You gotta come to school. I tried to stop Blake, but he had a gun."

Sherry dropped the phone.

———

Deputy Jason Richards repeated to Abby, "I do not know where Sheriff Grand is. He didn't come in this morning, and he didn't leave a message."

Abby pointed her right index finger into Jason's face. "Well, you can radio him and find out. I need to talk to him, and this can't wait."

A woman from dispatch answered an incoming call just as Phillip swung through the door. "Abby, what is going on? Why are you here?"

The woman said, "What? When?" Her voice was shadowed in alarm.

Jason's hand went up, cautioning Phillip to lower his voice. Jason stood to attention. His hand fingered his holster.

Phillip felt his face turn white. He knew the smell and the sound of trouble.

"There's been a shooting at the high school. The injury appears serious!" The woman's voice quaked.

Jason was out the door even before the last word was uttered.

Phillip followed. His rush of adrenaline was urging his body not to crumble on the way.

Abby's strength waned. Drums were pounding madly inside of her. She willed herself to chase behind Phillip.

There were no words. A dreadful quietness accompanied them. They could hear the wail of an ambulance as it approached the school. A crowd was gathering. Phillip stuck close to Jason, who was aggressively pushing his way through the crowd.

Abby saw Caleb pushing his way to the front, where the action was.

Paramedics were dropping down on their knees before a body that lay in its own blood, so still and pitiful.

Phillip saw Sheriff Grand directing people away from the scene. *How did he get here so fast?*

"What happened, sir?" Jason was asking Oscar.

"The kid came out with a gun. I had to shoot him."

"No, you didn't," another voice sobbed.

Phillip turned to the other voice. Oscar's son, Jerry, with a white and tear-soaked face, was bending over the injured kid's body.

Then a hysterical voice, like an unsettling blast of dynamite, shattered Phillip's resolve. "Let me in! I need to find my son!"

Phillip's lips thinned. The agonizing cry was from his wife.

"Let her in!" Phillip yelled, recognizing it was Sherry pushing her way in.

"No!" demanded Oscar. "Someone keep that woman away."

Phillip felt the hair bristle on his chest. He forced his way to the motionless heap of body lying on the floor.

The paramedics were working hard to save this life. The first responder had established an airway by intubating and had connected the tube to oxygen. One paramedic had a bag of fluids already running intravenously and was now busy slapping sticky patches to the boy's chest. An assistant was applying pressure to the kid's left side.

Phillip got his camera ready. He bent his knee close to the child. Then he gasped.

He dropped to both knees.

"Oh dear God, not Blake!" Sherry cried out loud. Abby rushed to Sherry's side.

"He's breathing," Abby said, wrapping her arm around Sherry. "They're doing what they can."

Jason began questioning a young man about Blake's age. "Can you tell me what happened here?"

"Yeah," the kid answered. "Blake pulled out a gun."

"Do you have any idea why?" Jason asked.

"He's one of those wannabes. He and that Jerry kid hang out together. They probably planned this together."

Phillip groaned.

Jerry stood. Angry words pushed from his white face. "It isn't like that. Dad, you know why he did this! This is what you wanted to happen!"

Mouths hung open. Every eye turned toward Oscar.

"Son," Oscar lowered his voice, "you are disturbed and confused right now from all of this happening."

"No! You asked him to come here with that gun. You promised to protect him. This was your game! You were planning to kill him. You were planning to kill me, too, so I wouldn't rat on you. But I didn't bring the gun. So you didn't want it to look like murder!"

Abby turned white. She pushed her way next to Caleb. "Caleb, it's him! I remember that voice. It was Oscar's voice in that room. And the lawyer called him Oscar. And the lawyer is Lester. They were planning to kill me! We need to get his gun!"

Blood pushed up, coloring Phillip's face. He jumped to his feet and stomped toward Oscar. His arms went out. His fingers were extended, ready to strangle the very air from the sheriff's being.

Caleb followed behind Phillip.

Jason grabbed Phillip. But Jason was no match for the wrath of this father.

Phillip's muscles corded for action. He was upon Oscar.

Oscar heaved a worried breath and pushed his weight against Phillip.

Sherry screamed, "Phillip, stop!" She rushed to the site of action.

Phillip's fist landed in Oscar's gut, bowling him over. Oscar tumbled hard, knocking Sherry over like a domino under him.

Phillip pulled Oscar up like a rubber toy and heaved him to the other side. "Sherry, are you okay?"

She moaned in a whisper, "Please, Phillip. We need to be here for Blake."

Wiping back tears, Sherry shot up another frantic prayer to God. "Help!"

Oscar was standing up again. A gun was aimed from his trembling hand at Phillip. "Jason, arrest that man."

"I'm not going anywhere until I know my son is safe." Phillip clenched his jaws.

From behind Oscar, Caleb sprung into action. He grabbed Oscar's right arm, which held the gun, and pushed it upward.

The gun went off. Its blast shattered through the air.

People were backing up in fear.

Caleb was wrapping Oscar's arms behind him. "You are under an arrest. You have the right to remain silent."

Abby found her breath again. Oscar would no longer be a danger to her and he would pay for all the things he did to Julie and Charley.

Phillip helped Sherry up, and she steadied herself against him.

The paramedics were rolling Blake out on a stretcher. Sherry reached out her hand and touched her son's face.

"Baby," she cried. "God, please help my baby." Sherry's head sunk deeper into the hollow of Phillip's chest. "My baby." She sobbed.

Phillip looped his arm around Sherry's waist and supported her as they followed their son out of the school building. "We'll meet him at the hospital, Sherry. You coming, Abby?"

"Yeah," Abby answered, trying to keep a rein on her own troubled emotions.

"Can I come, too?" Jerry's voice trailed behind them.

Phillip turned and locked eyes with Jerry. The kid's greasy hair was combed back into a form of style. Jerry's moist eyes were pleading wells. "Sure, son. You can hop in too."

Late Tuesday night, Lester, Jasper, and Kevin met under dim light.

"The FBI is involved now. We've been outsmarted, and I don't like that one bit! They have all the evidence they need. They have Oscar and Shamrock behind bars." Jasper spit between puffs on his cigar.

Kevin threw the *Edge Water Times* on the table in front of them. "I picked this up. See for yourselves what just came off the press. They have several big mouths on their side, including Mason and Abby." He spit on the floor. "Oscar wasn't very bright. He should have let me finish that dame off while I had her in my arms. It would have been so easy."

Silence, like the hand of death, entered the room. The paper was passed around for each man to read.

Lester broke the silence. "Where's Oscar's boy? We have no choice but to eliminate him. Hopefully it's not too late. The kid could blabber!"

"It is too late!" Jasper cursed until his face blotched to the same color of red as his hair. "Too late to think of eliminating any other person. There've been too many stupid slip-ups. Too many talking people. I'm betting Abby's memory is back. That's why Oscar got nabbed. Mason had to open his mouth and get me right in the middle of this mess. If we don't come up with an escape plan soon, the FBI is gonna swallow us and spit us out in prison cells." Jasper pounded his fist on the table. "Lester, we trusted you. You let us down. Way back when you thought you finished John off. Get it? None of this would be happening today if you had made sure the man was dead!"

"Save ourselves! That's the only thing we have left to do," Kevin snarled.

"You're both right," Lester said. "It's too late to put together another plot, except for a plan to save ourselves."

"That's right," Caleb said, pushing himself inside the door with three agents following him. "The problem is it is too late to save yourselves. You guys seem to have a habit of leaving trails everywhere you go. Now you are all under arrest. Guys, handcuff them," Caleb ordered.

"Where's Kevin?" Jasper's voice hit the basement floor.

"Looks like one of us did escape," Lester hissed back at Caleb.

Caleb looked at his agents. "Take these idiots in. I'm going after Kevin."

———∿∿•◦◯◦•∿∿———

In the old rickety school house in Perjure County, a handful of people had fallen on their faces before God. They were not content with quick and easy praying. They were not satisfied to stop praying until they could see God's hand was moving against the evil in their communities.

Tucked away in this small country church, such strange exchange with the divine happened.

Even when the night gave way to the dawn, these few men and women travailed on in prayer. They wrestled against the darkness and persisted until the light shone in.

These were people who had not just come to pray. These were people who were crying out to God for justice and for God to spare Blake's life. These were intercessors, praying for lukewarm churches to awake, crying out to God for people to be rescued from the kingdom of darkness and transferred into the kingdom of light. These were people who clung to God's promises. It was God, after all, who said, "If My people, who are called by My name, shall humble themselves, and pray and seek My face and turn from their wicked ways, then I will hear from heaven, and will forgive their sin and heal their land."

Their pastor, Paul Marvel, was not content with powerless preaching or powerless praying. This man's preaching was a testimony to such powerful praying that happened often, as it did tonight. He did not just preach the letter of the Word, for that would only kill the seed, and then it would not penetrate the inner heart of men and women. With a few people praying so earnestly for the Holy Ghost to be the entire influence, however, this man preached the Word with the anointing and demonstration of the Holy Spirit's power.

They did not seek a plan of their own. They were not bending their ears to any person. They were after the ear of God.

Great were their praises to God. Humble was their meeting with God, and passionate were their cries, which reached to the very throne of God.

———

Family was gathered in the waiting room of the Edge Water Hospital. Abby and Jerry sat among them.

The hospital felt like a prison. The pale-green painted walls trimmed with floral and green wall paper did nothing to help the dismal atmosphere. The drab peanut butter cookies, left on a tray, offered them no hope of energy to get through the long wait. The prison was around them and in them. There was nothing they could do or say to change things. Blake was now at the mercy of a surgeon. They could only wait to learn of his fate.

Sherry took another cup of coffee. While the others sat and occasionally nodded off, she paced and tried to toss her anxious prayers heavenward. Sherry began to remember some verses Pastor Paul had talked about. It was a Bible account about the Apostle Paul and a man named Silas who had been thrown in prison. They were in shackles. Still they had praised and prayed. Pastor had said praising and praying was a powerful combination. It worked well for those men. It had worked so well that the prison had been shaken until its doors had opened and everyone had been set free.

I sure don't feel like praising God for what happened. I prayed for Him to protect Blake. Why didn't He? How do I praise Him now? Okay, God, I don't know how to praise You. I don't even want to, but I'm going to try with Your help. Thank You that You are God. I praise You for that. You said nothing is impossible with You. So I praise You. I pray that You could be with that surgeon and with Blake, too. Help my unbelief.

Through her tears and praise, Sherry felt a peace gathering around her and in her. She praised God some more. The words began to leap from her heart and out her mouth. "Praise You, Jesus."

Phillip looked up, his face framed by anger. "How can you praise Jesus when this happened to our son?"

Abby poured Phillip another cup of coffee. "God only knows. We need that hope right now, Phillip."

The door opened, and the surgeon, clad in a blue lab coat, entered the room. He shook Phillip's hand.

"Your son is one lucky kid. That bullet lodged within a hair away from both the heart and the descending thoracic aorta. However, he is still unstable and in very critical condition. He will be spending some time in intensive care, where he will be monitored very carefully.

We have a large family guest room near the critical care station. You are all welcome to use that room. It is best if only one or two of you at a time visit by Blake's bed."

Color rushed back to Sherry's face. "God answered my prayer!" She danced in a circle before them. "I feel like He has come to our prison of despair and opened its door!"

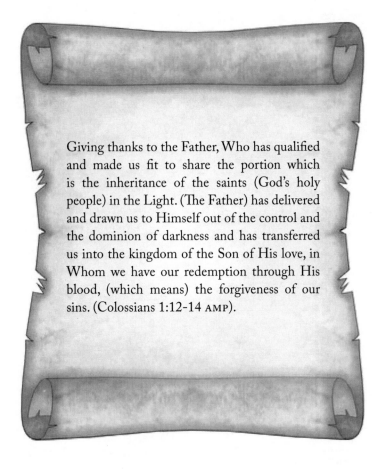

Giving thanks to the Father, Who has qualified and made us fit to share the portion which is the inheritance of the saints (God's holy people) in the Light. (The Father) has delivered and drawn us to Himself out of the control and the dominion of darkness and has transferred us into the kingdom of the Son of His love, in Whom we have our redemption through His blood, (which means) the forgiveness of our sins. (Colossians 1:12-14 AMP).

Chapter Twelve

Under the light of a full moon, Jezra sat in a lotus position. Her mind was centered, her breathing controlled. She sought to be the medium for her spiritual guide. He would guide her now through these menacing moments. *Jesus has not won!* The voice spoke. Then his form appeared. Robed in black, the face of her deceased and aged grandfather appeared.

Jezra smiled and relaxed. Her grandfather had willed her his powers before he had died. She had been his favorite. Certainly she could count upon him now to help her. "You must be very disappointed in what has happened," Jezra breathed heavily. "The FBI has taken Oscar and Lester and Jasper. I fear they will be charged with murder and with the trafficking of kids. I need your guidance. I could be caught and thrown in prison as well. And Kevin has fled."

"I am disappointed." Anger seeped through the form with thunderous expression. An ill-feeling wind pushed and fingered through Jezra's jet-black hair.

"What shall I do?" Her voice began to break under the chill of his words.

"It is simple, my daughter. The master demands sacrifice for the wrongs that have been committed against him. Tonight dress in white. Cover it in black and run to the Twisted Birch offering site. A priest shall await you. You will be the most pleasing sacrifice to your master's nostrils."

And eerie laugh proceeded from the mouth of the hazy guide swaying before Jezra.

Jezra gasped. "You are not my grandfather!" Her body began to shake until she was in a full seizure.

The form left her body, and Jezra lay limp.

———

At Phillip's house, a celebration was in full swing. Abby and Charley had helped plan this summer's get-together. New friends, Jerry, Lexi, Mason, and others from Paul's church, had been invited as well.

"It's been a delicious night!" Mable's cheeks jiggled with her laugh. "I haven't bit into such a tasty burger in a long time."

Mason, who stood like a giant caveman, was beaming. "I bugged them at Brad's Burger shop so often that they finally gave me their secret recipe." Mason's heavy arm swung, playfully slapping Phillip on the back, almost knocking him off his swivel chair. "That's why Phillip's burgers taste so good!" Mason's loud voice ricocheted about the room. "You did it, man! Those burgers are darn near as good as Brad's burgers."

"Hey, I'd sure like to be privy to that recipe," Abby said, forwarding a wink to Phillip. "Oh, and not to worry, it won't be printed in *Edge Water Times*."

"Well"—John chuckled as he stepped into the full moonlight afforded in the veranda—"I have a very newsworthy announcement to make."

Every eye turned to gaze at John. Every ear listened. It became pin-droppingly quiet. John had become a wonderfully mysterious legend. His silvery-blue hair flickered with the home lights. His presence was like a sweet zephyr.

"Seems all of these happenings have stirred up a lot of questions in the surrounding counties. People want to hear from some of these young heroes." John's voice whistled through his teeth. "So much so, the principal of Edge Water High has offered us their gymnasium next Saturday night. He thinks we will draw a huge crowd. It will be announced on several radio stations. Phillip has agreed to advertise it in *Edge Water Times*. And Abby will be happy to write up this article, won't you?"

"You bet I will, John!"

Jerry squared his shoulders. His face hosted an awkward expression. "What young heroes?"

A smile lingered on John's lips as he shared an affectionate glance with Jerry. "Why, you are one of those heroes, son!"

Jerry's eyebrows climbed up his forehead. "But I don't know how to talk in front of people."

"God will help you, son!" John dangled his words. "Blake will be there too, won't you, son?"

Blake's face lit up with emotion. "Me?"

"Yes, you. Kids need to hear both of your stories."

"And Charley," John added with a twinkle in his eyes, "I would like you to be there, too. There may still be some questions folk would like to throw at you."

"Okay, guys," Charley agreed quickly with a boyish eagerness smiling through his skin. "God will show up there too!"

Jerry exclaimed breathlessly, "You mean God will be there like that giant man who stood by your side on that day I met you?"

"Absolutely." Charley grinned.

"You guys about ready for that hayride out to the back forty? I have a place all set up for a campfire," Phillip announced.

"A hayride?"

"A campfire?"

"Yes!" Many voices blended together, some hushed, some electrified.

"Well, it's Pastor Paul's idea." Phillip laughed out loud.

"We have so much to be thankful for. Maybe we can express our thanks while sitting around the fire tonight." Under the full moon, Paul glowed.

"What is it about that man and John?" Abby half whispered. "There is something so inspiring about those men. There's a restful, peaceful, almost divine quality about them."

"Why"—Mable chuckled—"why, it's the very presence and anointing of the Spirit of God."

"I agree." Lexi nodded vigorously. "It is much more overpowering than the aura from the rulers of darkness, where, if you wait and watch long enough, you'll begin to feel an evil wind."

"Yes. Because in John and Paul, God's mark shines through. They reflect the love of God because they are carriers of His love." Mable's arms wrapped around Abby and Lexi. "These men deserve double honor. They are messengers of the Most High God."

Sherry packed the chocolate bars and marshmallows. "Okay, almost ready to leave. Oh, Phillip can you guys get that cooler of beverages on the wagon?"

"S'mores?" Blake asked, licking his tongue. "Love those things!"

Sherry turned to Jamie, who stood silently beside Jack in the background. "Honey, I forgot the napkins. Can you kids run back to the house quickly and get them?"

Jamie's words were as motionless and blank as the expression on her face. Jack was the one who said, "Sure. I'll get them."

"We're ready to roll!" Phillip yelled from across the yard. He jumped up on his John Deere tractor. The wagon was ready for passengers.

Jezra was driven. She could feel the force of the Spirit's energy pushing her on.

Jezra wore a long, black robe. Under that black attire was a flawless, dazzling white and flowing gown. This would be the great event where the ultimate sacrifice had to happen. She was to be honored by sacrificing her blood to please the high master.

The moon was full, and the renowned high priest, who would be hailed as "Baal's Voice," along with his bloodthirsty worshipers, was waiting. The forces within Jezra pushed her toward the twisted birch.

Even though her attire was black, the large moon reflected its light on Jezra's long, black tresses as she rushed toward the woods.

The light grew! It began exploding around the woman in black. She stood blinded by it. It continued to expand in every direction. It surrounded her. It stopped her.

Jezra shook her head, batting her eyes open and closed. Bad vibes were coursing through her body. She heard voices. She felt an overpowering presence happening in the light.

"Jezra." John spoke softly. "Don't listen to the lies of death. Your master has lied to you. He does not love you. He wants only to destroy you."

"Jesus!" Paul prayed. "Jesus, help this woman."

"The voices!" the woman screamed. "The authority in the voices! The Anointed One is near!" Jezra shrieked. "The Jesus in John and in Paul! The Anointed One speaks in them!"

Fear flashed like lightning from the crazed woman's eyes.

Jezra backed away and fled into the night.

What strength is this that I'm experiencing? Jerry wondered as he stood bravely behind the podium. *Is this a taste of what resurrection power might be?* Pastor Paul had preached about this resurrection power. He had told of how a Paul from the Bible had written, "That I might know Him and the power of His resurrection."

"Hi. My name is Jerry Bargains, and I have been invited here to tell you my story. I see many faces in these bleachers. I know that each of you has a story. And each of you has a definition of what life means. Many of you may have the wrong definition of life. To think you are living and to have the wrong definition of life is a tragedy waiting to happen.

"I thought life was about my survival and getting my needs met. I didn't care about anyone else. I had hate growing in me. This hate almost caused me to come to school this past spring with a gun. But God stopped me from bringing that gun.

"There are a lot of kids pretending to be alive. I can only say to you that things do not define life. I was hurting so badly inside, and I tried lots of things. I tried drugs and drinking and sex, and I was even willing to kill my brother, Charley here, because I only knew hate. That isn't life, man. I only knew death. You know you have only death when it hurts way down inside of you. It's when you try to prove to people that you are tough, but you know you're not. It's when there is an iron wall inside of you that keeps you from being honest.

"Like I said, hate was defining my life. Love was something I wanted desperately to feel. But what a lie I believed! I thought I could gain my father's love by killing Charley. I'm here to tell you that was hate talking. It was the wrong voice. Love doesn't come that way.

"But that very day, love did come my way. There was this big light around Charley. There was love there. I can tell you there is power in love. Everything began changing for me when I let Jesus take that cement wall down. I said to Jesus, 'I'm not tough at all. I'm scared. I'm lost.'

"There I was a loveless vagabond. But when I reached out to Jesus with that kind of honesty, I felt His arms around me. I wasn't lost any longer. I wasn't scared or even lonely anymore. I was home. I had finally come home.

"Death quit living in me. When my father asked me to bring a gun to school and shoot at other kids, I couldn't do it. I chose life. And love happens in that life. I began to care about other people."

Jerry sat down while the crowd cheered. Balloons were released into the building. People stood and clapped.

Silence happened again when Blake walked to the front of the building.

Sherry's hand covered her heart. Tears rolled down her face at the sight of her son behind the podium.

Jamie sat still beside her parents. Her eyes were heavy. Her head hung.

"This I find marvelous," Blake began. "When I was beyond help, when I thought it was all over, Jesus came. I don't really know how to explain it other then I faintly remember the day I was shot. Then there were flashing lights. The lights came to me. That's how it happened really. Jesus came with a mighty light. He came to me like the flashing ambulance in the night. He rescued me from death. He saved me. I'm so glad I didn't die that day. If I had died, I would never have known life. Jesus is the way, the truth, and the life. He is the miracle ride to life, just like that ambulance that came to me in the night."

The crowd was cheering, whistling, and applauding.

When Charley walked to the front of the auditorium, the merriment intensified. Teenagers were clapping and waving banners. Others were chanting, "Charley. Charley."

Charley took his place behind the podium. His face was aflame with what he felt so deeply in his heart.

"Thank you, everyone, for having us here tonight. Most of you have heard my testimony on television. Jesus is my testimony. One very cold night, like all of the nights I had ever known, I was all alone with hundreds of voices in my head. Jesus came to find me at the Wilderness Group Home. He came in a man named John. And that night Jesus Christ set me free from all of those voices. I'm here tonight to say that Jesus is the Miracle Maker. Blake met the Miracle Maker, who came like a great ambulance with flashing lights in the night. Jerry met the Miracle Maker, who came as a bright light from heaven. I met the Miracle Maker, who came as a light shining from a man of God. This man, John, was filled with the Spirit of God. The demons fled in the name of Jesus Christ.

"People didn't want to believe Jesus delivered me from all that suffering and from all those voices. Even preachers tried to explain it away. There I was, brand new, and people were angry about that. It's like what happened many years ago when Jesus physically walked this earth. He came to a poor, crazy, and demon-possessed man who lived miserably in a graveyard. Jesus commanded the demons to flee, and they caused a herd of pigs to rush to their drowning. The man was set free. Jesus did a wonderful miracle for this man. It made the people angry, and they wanted Jesus to leave.

"It is great to see all you kids excited here tonight about what Jesus can do. I guess what I'm trying to say is that I believe Jesus is very serious about wanting to give people real life and set them free."

Tears were strolling down his face. "Some of you have never known love. I know what it is like to feel unloved. My mom knew that feeling, too.

"I'd like to dedicate this moment to my mom. I know she is watching me right now from the bleachers in heaven. I have never met my mom in real life. But I've read about her. She had experienced a horrific life of abuse. I had been torn from her arms as a tiny baby. Her arms would have loved me. But I can say this. My mom found her miracle of love when she found Jesus. I know she prayed to find me, and she prayed that love would find me, too. And it did.

"I think He is calling out to this generation to take a stand now. He wants young people to be changed by His love and then to go back to their schools and their homes and everywhere and prove that the mark of God in someone's life is shown by love. He wants you kids to be His hands and His feet. Follow Him. Show other kids the real definition of life."

Cheers were soaring to the top of the building again. As Charley made his way back to the bleachers, kids pressed into him. Some thanked him. Others hugged him.

———⚬⚭⚬———

Abby fiddled with her pen. She had decided to start a journal of her own. But tonight there were hardly words to write what she was feeling. So many phenomenal things had happened. Words like *amazing, astonishing,* or *shocking* held no more meaning than chocolate chips being dumped into a cookie batter.

Once Abby had not believed in miracles. Even when she saw Charley transformed she had not been able to bring herself to believe in the Miracle Maker.

A lot of hate had happened after Charley's miracle. People didn't want to believe that Jesus was around any longer to do miracles of any kind. After watching the young people cheer Charley, Jerry, and Blake on, she wondered if something was changing.

Or maybe it was that something was changing deep within her.

The cold and damp cellar inside of her seemed to be unlocking.

A warm cleaning rag was wiping away the mold. A powerful hand was pouring healing over the cold of her past. She was ready to step out of the abuse of her past and into healing arms.

"Jesus, I'm a mess inside. Please forgive me for sinning against You. The Bible says You shed your blood to wash away my sins. Please let Your blood clean me up and make me new. Thank You for rising from the dead. Because You are alive, I know, through the power of Your Holy Spirit, You can help me live right. Please be my Savior. I am opening my heart and my life to You right now. Give me the eternal life You offer, and be the Miracle Maker in my life. Amen."

Abby put her pen to the paper. There was a peaceful surrender in her eyes.

> Julie, you would have been proud of Charley. Your prayers were answered. Charley and I are a family now. I started going to church with Charley. I've learned a lot at this church. And now I believe in the Miracle Maker. It is a miracle that He has come into my heart and has brought a hope and a reason to live into my life.
>
> Last Sunday Pastor Paul preached on a verse from the Bible. I wrote the verse down, and I intend to memorize it. This verse has changed the way I was thinking.
>
> Julie, you discovered that you were not a castaway. And in this verse, I learned a very important thing. It is that *I am not a misfit.* Instead, *Jesus has qualified me.* He has delivered me out of the kingdom of darkness and brought me into His kingdom of light.

This is truly a new beginning. That part seems settled in my mind.

Pastor Paul said in the kingdom of God we need to learn new protocols. It's all about a new way of living. He said it involves "a character change."

That scares me some. Still, I must admit, I think I need a lot of changing to happen.

I believe I'm ready to learn these things.

Yes, I am very hungry to know more about Jesus.

I'm writing it down now. I believe Jesus is the Miracle Maker. I'm willing to let Him prove that in my life.

Since He has now brought my heart into His kingdom, I'm setting my mind on the same purpose. I want to learn how to let Jesus be King in my life.

Julie, you really started something. You started a new journey and a new journal.

I was devastated when you left me the first time.

I was angry when you came back in a pine box. The box screamed out that you had left me forever.

Then your journals came to me. Your pain seemed to live on in much of what you wrote...

until your new journey started. Then your words changed.

Julie, I realize now that the old you was buried in that pine box. The new you could never be confined to its death.

Your new story won't end. I've found the same new beginning. Our stories will not end, but together they will live on.

Chapter Thirteen

Abby looked out her kitchen window. Stars lit up the night sky. Never could she remember any shining brighter than tonight.

Car lights were coming down her driveway. Maybe John was bringing Charley home. Abby breathed in a contented breath. It was wonderful sharing her home with Charley. She wasn't surprised her nephew had decided to be a preacher. She smiled, imagining what that would be like. "He is an inspiration," she mumbled.

Abby made her way to the door to welcome Charley home and to wave good-bye to John. She opened the door, still smiling.

"Hi, Abby."

"Caleb?" she asked, feeling her temperature rising. She grabbed her face, supposing it was flushed red. "I wasn't expecting you."

He chuckled. "Maybe I should have called you first?"

"No. I'm really glad you came. Care to come in?"

"Actually, it is such a beautiful night. Maybe we can sit out here on your porch." He gestured for her to sit first.

He sat there for a while, staring up at the stars. "Love them. They sparkle so brightly." He fidgeted in his chair for a moment before turning his gaze away from the stars and toward her. "Abby." He smiled.

"Yes?" she answered with a hint of impatience.

He was looking up at the stars again. She waited breathlessly for his next words.

"I came here for two reasons."

"Yes?" she repeated.

His smile spread larger while his eyes were still gathering in the stars. "You are about to become a star too."

"What?" She smiled with an amused expression.

"Yep. I was contacted by John Abbott from the Abbott and Towle Publishing Company. Know who they are?"

"Yes!" She shot off her chair. "They're only the number one traditional publisher!"

"That number one publisher was quite taken back with all the breaking news coverage in Edge Water." Their eyes locked. "He wants to write up a contract with you, Abby. He wants the story. And he thinks it will be made into a movie too."

"Caleb, this is so exciting!" She laughed, dancing in a circle. "God is good, isn't he? Me—a star? That is a miracle!" She danced over to him, and softly kissed him on the cheek. "And what is the second reason why you came to see me?" she asked with the stars twinkling in her eyes.

"Well, Abby, I want to be one of the main characters in your book, and especially in the movie," he laughed.

"I wouldn't have it any other way," she answered. And she meant it.